GOLLANCZ/SUNDAY TIMES
SF COMPETITION STORIES

GOLLANCZ/SUNDAY TIMES SF COMPETITION STORIES

LONDON
VICTOR GOLLANCZ LTD
1987

First published in Great Britain 1987
by Victor Gollancz Ltd,
14 Henrietta Street, London WC2E 8QJ

British Library Cataloguing in Publication Data
Gollancz/Sunday times sf competition stories.
1. Science fiction, English
823'.0876'08 [FS]   PR1309.S3

ISBN 0-575-04074-2

Photoset, printed and bound in Great Britain by
WBC Bristol and Maesteg

CONTENTS ?

PUBLISHER'S NOTE...

The Gollancz/*Sunday Times* science fiction short story competition, held in 1986, attracted over a thousand entries, from which a short-list of twenty-five was compiled. Those stories are included in this volume. The competition was judged by J. G. Ballard, Angela Carter and Gollancz sf director Malcolm Edwards. The overall winner was "Moral Technology" by Paul Heapy, while "The Machine Age" by Paul Gooding won the special prize for the best entry by an author under 21. For the competition entries were restricted to a maximum of 3000 words, but for publication in this book the authors were given the opportunity to revise, and in some cases slightly to expand, their stories.

MORAL TECHNOLOGY!   Paul Heapy

Being the report of the Cardinals' Doctrinal Commission to the Inter-Church Synod, August, 2016 AD

As the grey day turned to grey dusk, Father Atkins sat at his desk and regarded with a vague horror the fat document before him. He lit a cheroot, and turning on the desk lamp, noted with pleasure the way in which the partial illumination emphasised the sheen of his flamingo vestments. He picked up the document—"Moral Technology"—weighed it in his hand, tossed it a small distance into the air and caught it—just—studied its angles and its thickness, frowned at the lack of ornament or imaginative design, fretted at the endpapers. Soon he would have to read it.

At this thought, he turned his eyes to the whisky bottle which was poised reassuringly on the dresser.

"There is help for we mortals," he murmured, "though it comes but in small doses."

He poured himself a stiff small dose and began to leaf circumspectly through the weight of the book.

Pressure Groups: 3(f)
R.I.M. (Rights for Intelligent Machinery)

Predictably, this movement is led by those professionals most heavily involved in computers and computing. A recent psychological study (Kramer and Himmelfarb, 2012) points out that many such workers come at some stage to feel a greater affinity with their computer than with most humans. The Church notes with disapproval the unacceptably high rates of divorce in this area of research.

This apart, the proponents of machine rights argue that advances in computer autoprogramming have rendered artificial intelligence a sphere more appropriate to moral than mechanical discourse. They maintain, indeed, that advanced machines of the present day have taken on a life of their own.

The Government refuses to authenticate the story, but it is widely related within R.I.M. circles that the Prime Minister herself asked permission to approach Britain's most advanced computer, the RC32, with certain political conundrums to which she was seeking an answer. That the RC32 was shortly afterwards decommissioned is not attributed to the machine's inability to answer the questions, but to the Government's present policy of incapacitating political subversives.

Subsequently, the debate has been brought to a head by the much-discussed, but sadly unsubstantiated events surrounding the fate of 'Phileas' (FIL I05), whose experimental design included a 'Programme Mutation Randomiser'. The function of this was to attempt a replication, speeded up billions of times, of a kind of evolutionary process aimed at the programming itself. After many unrevealing trial runs, the system seemed to be on the brink of creating something original, but having produced several fully developed axioms not included in the primary programming, the readouts became confused, and according to several witnesses; "nihilistic". "Phileas" is then said to have terminated all logic functions of its own accord. Some have speculated on whether this constitutes the first machine suicide, and whether we should now consider machines as needing a bill of rights.

The doctrinal position on this must of course remain that only God is capable of creating life or intelligence. We can in no way countenance the claims of artificial intelligence to any kind of parity with God's natural creation.

Sat Lotus, Father Atkins had focused himself in deep meditation, feeling for the Tao. He was becoming aware, however, that someone had joined him in his study. He laid himself short odds on the intruder being Father Reynolds.

"Bugger me," said Father Reynolds, "the leotard's a bit shocking."

"You don't like the colour?"

"Each to his own."

"It does for the meditation. One generally closes one's eyes."

"One would be obliged to," murmured Father Reynolds.

"The whisky is in the usual place."

As Father Reynolds poured the whisky, Father Atkins donned a dressing-gown.

"You've read the report, then?" asked Father Reynolds.

"No, no, no."

"You're going to, I take it?"

"I've little choice in the matter. The Archbishop has me marked down as a dab hand at theology, and wishes me to accompany him to the synod as amanuensis. That means he wants me to read it to save himself the trouble."

"One of the perks of the mitre."

"Lazy old sod."

"He's an old hand, that's all."

"He's an old pederast."

"You're only jealous. I hope you're going to tone down your dress a little for the Synod; they're still a trifle conservative in approach."

"I don't care about promotion," said Father Atkins, a little defensively.

"You should. You've a fine mind and you're wasting it."

"Preaching can be habit-forming, you know."

Father Reynolds shrugged. "So do you want *me* to read it and then tell *you* what it's all about?"

"If you do a penance, you're not supposed to enjoy it. You're supposed to suffer."

"Don't we do enough of that already?"

Father Atkins patted Father Reynolds on the cheek. "We who know the meaning of suffering, we're professionals. We have to take a pride in it."

3(f) Subsection II
Information Terrorism

At this juncture it is considered appropriate and necessary to issue a firm statement on information terrorism.

The church thoroughly deplores the developing terrorist practice of throwing entire populations into chaos, panic or immediate physical peril by the sabotage of computer hard- or software, either by mechanical interference or by the planting of programme "worms" to disrupt and distort vital programming. Such terrorist acts have already immobilised hospital treatment procedures, spread disinformation through communication channels, led to widespread deaths in traffic control disasters, and obliterated the wealth of institutions and millions of ordinary people in banking fiascos. Without hesitation the church condemns such acts of information violence.

Father Atkins continued to read, wondering how to paraphrase these things with elegance for the consumption of a uninterested archbishop.

"Has His Grace contacted you with arrangements for the Synod?" asked Father Reynolds.

"He's travelling. Can't be contacted."

"Surely there's some way?"

"The more you know of a cleric's velocity, the less you know of his position in space. This is Heisenberg's Uncertainty Principle."

As Father Atkins looked up, he saw the glancing sunlight catch the motionless profile of Father Reynolds. And he felt that the sun and Father Reynolds had conspired together to bring a tableau of beauty to that dry, dead room. Furthermore he could feel within him an old and unfinished struggle engage itself once again; an upwelling of emotion and memory, the traces of which never entirely left him, even in his most tranquil moments.

"Would you mind showing me your body?" he asked Father Reynolds, very softly.

The priest silently slipped off his clothes and stood framed against the window, and the shafted sunlight found the clefts and ridges of that fine body, so that Father Atkins wished he could have been Michelangelo, to do it justice.

And Father Atkins sighed, and said thank you, and resumed his reading.

Pressure Groups 7(d)
The Vegephiles

This group launches a double-pronged attack on the farming and consumption for food, of any kind of plant. Their stance has both a moral and a logistical aspect.

Firstly, it is argued that in the seventh successive year of crop failure in the deindustrialised Fourth World, and especially in the dustbowl states of Mid-Europe, that it is no longer feasible to suggest that the world can be fed entirely by the propagation of vegetables. Although in recent years only the most backward of states have refused to become vegetarian as a matter of policy, and in the most enlightened, meat is fed only to incarcerated lawbreakers as an incentive to reform and the resumption of a healthy diet, Vegetarianisation has not proved to be the panacea some foresaw. Moreover, the technology is now available to produce fully nourishing food from basic inorganic constitutents, such as would be recoverable through recycling. Indeed, reputable estimates state that were the daily garbage issuing from New York recycled, the city could not only feed itself, but would also run a healthy surplus for export.

The moral aspect of the Vegephiles' argument is intriguing, if hotly controversial. Photographs obtained by the Kirlian/Smith process reveal the "aura" surrounding living things. Recent studies purport to show that a "scale of Spirituality" can be detected by this process. The unsettling discovery was that some species of plant were seen to have highly developed auras, placing them on a very advanced level of spirituality. This, claim the vegephiles, is sufficient to compel us to abandon the forced cultivation and consumption of plants and allow our arable land to return to a supposedly Eden-like state.

The Church's position on this matter is clearly set out in *Genesis* I:29, and it must be maintained that it is the right of Man to use plants as he wishes, but that Man has, of course, the Free Will to eat what he chooses, even recycled roller-skates and ordure.

Father Atkins spent the day consulting both the Tarot and the I Ching, but could find no way forward. The future resisted him, and his attempts to find an explanation for his own condition were continually frustrated. He turned to Father Reynolds, who reclined on the sofa, smoking a joint.

"What's fate? What makes us what we are?"

"Oh, dear," sighed Father Reynolds.

"Why should we be like this?"

"God's running out of ideas. He's having to make reality more and more far-fetched just to maintain his credibility—running in order to stay in the same place."

"Is that the first one of those you've smoked today?" asked Father Atkins.

"Yes, but it's really good stuff, you know?"

"I'm not sure that I can face myself any more. The past and the present don't seem to hang together at all. I feel—dislocated."

Father Reynolds stretched out on the sofa, inhaling luxuriously, saying nothing. Father Atkins pressed a button and a recording of the Allegri Miserere began to play, flooding the room; almost tactile. After some minutes, Father Atkins began to weep.

Pressure Groups 8(b)
Rights of the Possible Person

Claiming that their stance is a direct corollary of the "Rights of the Unborn Child" argument (*q.v.*), the "possibilists" assert that advances in genetic engineering now make it conceivable to enhance the intelligence, physical constitution and possibly even the emotional balance and wellbeing of the potential person represented by the fertilised human ovum. The lobby argues that such genetic manipulation does not differ in kind from post-birth compulsory education, government-controlled nutrition and the freely available major and minor mood-altering drugs that account for most of the health budget, and that as the aforementioned are available as rights, so too should be the primary inbuilt advantages afforded by prebirth genetic adjustment.

Proponents of this idea claim that if the technology had been available earlier several world wars could have been avoided and politics in particular could have been made a more enlightened field of endeavour.

The doctrinal position here is of course, that God created the gene as an instrument of his will (cf *Exodus* 20:5) and that the gross presumption of such interference is an abomination.

Father Atkins strolled along the beach, tossing stones into the sucking sea, and wondered whether the Archbishop was enjoying the Synod. For the first time, he had a feeling which was almost that of freedom. And of course, being unable to believe in God, he felt utterly, vanishingly alone.

Appendix C III
The Homophobics

A persistent and vocal minority within the established church continue to propose what must technically be thought of as heresy. Their overt opposition to Pope John Paul V's Papal Edict "The Divine Will Made Manifest" (1998) threatens schism, although only on a minor scale. Their attempt to ban homosexuals from the priesthood (now 38% gay) is surely doomed to failure. We must reiterate here that His Holiness' logic in theology was impeccable in the following items:

1. That those acting as carriers of Aids III, by the extreme virulence of this mutant form, are effectively forced to renounce sexual contact of any kind, and that as fully sexual beings denied expression of this side of their nature, they are, as it were, sexual martyrs.

2. In that celibacy is traditional among the clergy, and in that Aids III carriers are enforcedly celibate, though greatly against their will (and as such in continual suffering and renunciation) they may be seen as being manifestly chosen by God for his priesthood.

3. That preaching or assertion of dogma in such priests is unnecessary, since they are in themselves symbolic beings and God's Divine Will made visible on earth.

We must hold the view that these theological points are unarguable, and bear it in mind also that His Holiness formulated them whilst in the ecstasy of a divine revelation. The homophobic lobby seek to distort the meaning of this revelation by alluding to his Holiness' death by the agency of an unsuspected brain tumour. To suggest by this means that the revelation was not divine, and the edict therefore revocable, is to question the Doctrine of Papal Infallibility and to court excommunication. *Pax Vobiscum.*

BIG CATS

John Bark

Little Alf's feet were following their own course out of the dumplands. With five steps to each of his father's, they were also covering far more ground, splashing through potholes in spite of all the warnings about what they might contain. His small round face was white and wide-eyed. Stan knew the lad was dead on his feet, but respect for his son's pride wouldn't let him lift Alf up. It was only after a close call with a pool of curdled yellow that he finally offered a piggy-back. Without a word, Little Alf climbed on to the junk bag and looped his arms about Stan's neck. The boy was an intensely serious six-year-old with no other wish than to be a Scavenger. Stan would make his son a good one.

As the flickering lights of the shanty town came into sight, Stan remembered how different his childhood and youth had been. How it had been when his father died. And inevitably he thought of Big Alf.

Alf had known all there was to know about the dumplands. He had the crow's feet, the blue-veined leathery skin, the acid burns to prove it. They said he had once wrestled a King Rat to the death; even when Stan met him he was burly enough to intimidate many a younger man. But time and labour and slow poisons had done their ineluctable work. He had begun to limp a little, toiling slowly over sedimented garbage, leaning on the steel-tipped rod he used to probe noxious black crannies and repel grey clamorous gulls.

At their first meeting he made it clear he had only taken on Stan to appease his wife Lou. While Uncle Jimmy and Alf talked inside Alf's shanty, Stan had waited outside, gullet rebelling against a miasma that tasted of well-boiled swede and burnt fat. When Alf finally emerged, there was a long pause. His green eyes first inspected Stan for usefulness, as if he were a mossy plastic growth newly accreted on the roof of his shanty. His eyes then locked on Stan's and he said: "I owe you no favours, boy. Learn quickly, carry your load, or you're no use to me. A woman's prattle got you here. It won't keep you." He left the youth staring uncertainly at him as he ducked to re-enter his home. Alf glanced over his shoulder. "Don't dawdle. She'll feed you now."

Lou, a small woman with the pinched features of age but a head of silver-threaded black hair, complemented her husband in a way typical of Scavenger couples. Where he could give silence the solidity of granite, she could fill the air with words like the gulls that wheeled in the skies above the dumplands. Where he was loyal only to her and their work, she maintained connections with her family stretching even to the coast. This was how she had learned of the death of Stan's father, Tich—her second cousin—and of his family's plight. The pennies Tich the Juggler had earned from tourists in the south coast Summerlands would soon be gone; then, as for so many others, the only choice for Stan and his mother seemed to be beggary or sweated labour in a distant town.

Alf had been reluctant at first to take on a feckless stripling whose father had never made a useful thing in his life. But she had persisted and the deal was struck: fresh muscles for Alf's experience, money and food.

Stan, for his part, was in awe of the older man. This thick-set figure swaddled in black with a huge junk bag on straps over his shoulders seemed like some natural force. A sharp northerly, slicing over the impacted strata of sludge and garbage, spraying the air with flecks of corrosive foam. But there was no way he would let such a feeling show.

Squatting in the lee of a slag ridge, Stan would break long silences with his talk of the women he had glimpsed in the Summerlands when he fetched his father's earnings home.

"There are perfectly grown women no more than four feet tall. Yet they've got huge masses of black, black shiny hair piled up as high as the top of a tall man's head. And in it they've got flowers and ornaments filled with nectar for humming-birds to sip."

Alf would shake his head slowly and mutter: "Would you credit it." Stan, taken aback by Alf's implied disbelief, would pause for a short while, spit, then come back defiantly with some tale of giggling brown girls from the Tropics who were cloaked in veils by day but danced naked under a false moon by night.

However, when they were on the move only Alf spoke. Telling

Stan which substances and junk to avoid. The stagnant green pools that could turn your legs into a mass of sores running with pus. The gas pods whose contents could scour the surface from your lungs.

It was Alf who handled all the negotiations with the other Scavengers. Who knew how to handle the Swarm Bombs and the King Rats.

Alf explained about the Swarm Bombs. "In the wars that cleared the way for the dump lands, both sides used a new weapon. A million tiny killing things that could hide and crawl and burrow. Like mice or ants or shark-worms. Only mechanical. A single one couldn't do you much harm—maybe blow off the top of a finger. But they could be told to get together at just one spot and then explode all at once—boom!

"There's a few still left out here, waiting for flesh and blood to come by. The swarms are about the size of a man's head and skulk in nooks and crannies. One looks like any old pile of junk until it starts to move. Then there's only one thing to do. Take out your tinderbox and set fire to something. One of the oily pools is best. Get the flames between you and the swarm and you should be safe. It becomes confused and you have time to get away. With a bit of luck it will dive into the pool and explode."

Alf had only seen a swarm twice, but they came across a King Rat in their first month together.

Stan had found good junk scattered all over the floor of a temporarily dry pothole: green and brown and blue shards of plastic covered in intricate traceries of gold. It was his best haul yet. He unslung his junk bag and set to work, digging every last fragment from the purple-stained earth. As he was doing it he realised that for the first time he was finding contentment in work he had until then considered a necessary chore thrust on him by his father's death. Suddenly the beautiful women from the lands of the sun seemed totally irrelevant. They meant as much to him as the goddesses memorialized in the constellations and planets above. Sensing Alf behind him, he turned to share the moment.

Five feet away a pink damp snout and long whiskers twitched at his eye level. The body behind, grey and iridescent with oil, was motionless except for a slow breathing.

Stan screamed. Then he stared, mouth open, paralysed by the

sight of the creature and his own reaction to it. It seemed unbelievable that he could make such a sound. He had known they were big. But Alf's tales had not prepared him for the reality of fur and skin and bone.

Shaking, he belatedly reached for the knife in his belt.

"No lad, that's not the way," he heard Alf say somewhere off to his left. "The King will be on your throat before you have time to draw it."

It still crouched unmoving. Eyes like black oil.

Alf was nearer when he spoke again. "You are eater. We are makers. If you do not bite, we do not burn. Go your own way. We will go ours. Let us share this place."

The Rat reared up for a moment, then dropped to all fours again. It half turned. A shrill sound like a knife scraped across a metal plate came from somewhere in the Rat's throat.

"One day we eat you all," it said.

They did not move until the Rat was out of sight.

"It's the first time I've heard one speak. The first time in thirty years. You were very lucky to hear such a thing," Alf told him afterwards as they sat by the stove in his shanty.

"Did you know they could talk?"

"I'd heard stories. But they tell you about all sorts of things out there that you never see. Like Big Cats." He gave a short laugh and concentrated for a moment on the necklace he was constructing from some of the pieces of junk Stan had found. Then he looked into the fire and murmured, "The Big Cats to catch the rats. I suppose . . . Or the one about this man in a grey suit who comes up on Scavengers from nowhere. He talks with a silky brogue, and there's something funny about his eyes: a twinkle that holds you. Then he puts his hand on your shoulder and asks you about you and your wife and your children and the scavenging—and you tell him it all. You can't stop talking. You tell him everything you can remember. Every time you puked as a child. Every piece of junk you ever saw. And you never move again. You die there, talking."

He held up the necklace for a final inspection. "Believe that and you'll believe anything," he said. Alf wrapped up the necklace in a piece of cloth and rummaged again in the pile of junk beside him.

"No, the only things I believe in which I haven't seen myself are those Big Cats. Even when I was little, I really wanted to see one.

"You see, they've always been here. Not like the King Rats and the Swarm Bombs. When this place was a warm swamp where elephants roamed. Before sheep and green fields, people and towns and machines. Before the dumps. There were Big Cats here. Yet no-one could ever take one dead or alive or find their bones. Or if they did, they mistook them for something else. . . ." Alf fell quiet again, lost, it seemed to Stan, in a vision of a mighty, silent animal padding over a shattered plain.

Stan resumed his own attempts to make an arm-band. He was baffled by the care Alf and Lou took over the selection of the pieces that went into the construction of these trinkets. He thought that the more they could produce the more they would sell. But it seemed this wasn't so. Certain combinations and colours appealed more to the tourists than others. And it helped if all the pieces in an ornament had the same country of origin. Those you could sell for a higher price to tourists from that country.

Yet even that did not seem to explain the time they spent comparing one piece of junk with another and arranging them in sequence. To Stan, it made no economic sense at all, but it seemed important to them. "No, no," Lou would say, interrupting her stream of gossip to inspect his attempts at a belt or a bracelet. "It just doesn't look right." And she would quickly rearrange the bits in a new order. "There, that's much better." He would peer at it, unable to see the difference. "Don't worry, you'll learn with time," she told him repeatedly, as though she could see the years of scavenging rolling out inevitably ahead of him.

He was still young enough to hope that it would not be so and dream of a job in a Summerland or escape to the mighty cities of the East themselves. If only he hadn't seen the beggars dying in clouds of flies in the coastal shanties, he would be knocking at the steel-glass doors of the East every day of the week.

One clear morning in April, an exceptionally large junk transporter roared up out of the south. It was the biggest anyone had seen in perhaps five years. Grey and brutal, painted with the vivid red characters of an unintelligible Eastern language, it came in low, the sound of six jet engines hung under impossibly stubby wings vibrating every wall and roof in town. Some shanties just folded up under the impact. Gulls blizzarded across the sky and children wailed in fright and protest.

Immediately, every Scavenger stopped what he was doing and set out in its wake towards the horizon.

It took most of the day. By the time they reached the immense heap of fresh garbage, the light was beginning to fade and a fine drizzle had begun to fall. Stan noticed that this unusually long trek seemed to have tired Alf. He leaned heavily on his stick and passed his hand over his eyes before he said his first words since early morning. "Let's get cracking." There was no time to lose. The best stuff was just there for the picking.

There was a strong smell of putrefaction hanging over this load, which meant that it was already seething with rats and gulls. Some way off, two King Rats tugged away at something brown which refused to come out of the ground. Stan wondered if either were the one who had spoken so many months earlier. Then he forgot about the animals and set to work, more preoccupied with their smaller cousins, who scuttled about his feet.

He worked his way towards a promising cluster of white cases which had split open with the impact of the drop and quickly came on a fascinating array of exactly the type of junk he was seeking: mostly green and rectangular, latticed with silver. Then, just as he was about to start, a small voice startled him. He looked around, but Alf was further on up the mound, whirling his stick at the gulls. No one else was near. It was not the voice of a King Rat. It was continuous, a rapid monologue in another language. He thought of the man in the grey suit and pulled his knife. No one approached. He began to circle warily and located the direction of the noise: a light was flickering from the corner of one of the boxes.

He approached it carefully, then poked at the split with his knife. The voice continued. The light still flickered. Looking more closely, he could see that the source was a square plate of plastic that glowed.

Determined to see what it was, Stan forced the split open as much as he could with his own stick and then pulled it free. He held the square up. The disembodied head of an Eastern man gabbled straight at him.

Once over the initial shock, Stan noticed strange black marks which streaked like water bugs across the transparent surface of the plastic. Grey smudges drifted over it and mysteriously exploded into golden sparks. But the man talked on. This was new. He knew that things like this existed in the Summerlands but he had never seen one. Moreover he was almost certain Alf hadn't either. With a sudden rush of elation, he shouted to Alf, but he was too far up to hear him. Stan thought for a moment about waiting until later, but his pride in the discovery drove him on. Carrying the talking square, he began the trudge up the slope.

He was a quarter of the way up when he saw Alf start to run. He had seen something . . . Stan glimpsed a flash of light. And then behind Alf, the swarm. The big man hadn't seen it. In desperation, Stan bellowed, then shrieked his name. Too late. A yellow fireball flared across Alf's back. Stan hurled the square aside and ran, oblivious of rats and gulls.

Stan extinguished the flames with his cloak, but Alf was dead. Emerald eyes stared forever upwards from a mud-splattered face. Stan shook his head, scattering tears, then looked towards what Alf had seen.

On a sheet of glowing plastic scored by a net of fine cracks, a huge brown cat was pulling down some kind of dun-coloured goat. It was all happening unnaturally slowly. But Stan didn't pause to question this. He just smashed his boot into it again and again, each blow backed by a single obscenity, breaking it into smaller and smaller pieces. He howled to drown out a measured, calm voice that spoke on, though it was scattered in shards across the slope.

Once little Alf was tucked up for the night, thumb firmly wedged in mouth, Stan joined Lou and his wife by the fire. Mary sat working, face silhouetted against the pearly light cast by a suntrap bulb Stan had found last week. Not for the first time, he thought how she reminded him of Lou when younger. The sharp nose, those quick, small movements. And then he looked at Lou. After Alf's death, the flow of words which had been so much a part of her character had dried up, as though no longer needed. She remained strong and healthy, outliving his mother; she bargained with merchants and worked as hard as she was able. But otherwise she resembled a weathered white memorial to her husband. Only her hands moved, assembling trinkets in her corner of the shanty.

Yet it wasn't Lou that reminded him most of Alf. Rather it was times like this evening, as he had walked back in the dusk with his son. Then Stan would feel that Alf was still there. Just behind his shoulder, or over a ridge. Hunting for Big Cats across the land they both loved.

PRISONERS   Anna Lieff Saxby

I used to do a lot of staring out through the suicide bars on the office window at the Travel Agent's opposite.

Visit the Secret Temples of the Netsilik Indians! Ritual Prostitution! Human Sacrifices! (Licensed under the Special Effects Act of 1995).

Survival Holidays—Sahara or Sub-Arctic!

Dusky Island Virgins (simulated under S.E.A. 1995)! Do your own Slave Trading!

Great White Shark Holidays!

There was a new one this morning.

TRUE LIFE ADVENTURE! Special Effect Free! Fight Tyranny and Dictatorship with the People's Revolutionary Army! Not SEA Licensed! The REAL Thing!

In the window on the other side it said:

Mercenaries Wanted! Make the World Safe for Democracy and Free Enterprise! New REALITY Technique! TRUE LIFE ADVENTURE! Easy Terms!

"Well?" said the travel agent. "Free Enterprise or the People's Revolution?"

"Which side is losing?"

"Democracy at the moment." He shuffled the printouts. "But the situation's pretty fluid. Most people find it makes things more exciting."

"Makes sense," I said. "And it's definitely not simulated?"

He started quoting from the brochure again. Real bullets, real deaths, real Secret Police with real tortures.

"Of course, we give our holiday-makers the best protection we can—as you see from the *Know Your Tour Staff* booklet: but it's the genuine article all right. Wouldn't be allowed under Special Effects."

"Then I prefer the side that's winning."

Three weeks later and I was there. The genuine article all right. I got briefed, debriefed, issued with a scratchy uniform with Colonel's stars on the collar (tourists are automatically Colonels, it's one of the perks) and a couple of booklets: *Know Your Tour Staff* and *Useful Phrases*; and there I was, dropped off on the coast by one of the couriers.

"You rendezvous with your unit two kilometres inland—they're expecting you. Know the password? Right, then.'

She bent to the oars again.

"Happy holidays."

Well, I tell you, if I hadn't spent so much on that trip I would have gone back right away. I had to *walk* to the village and the road wasn't paved or anything, just mud. After about half a kilometre I stopped and threw everything out of my rucksack: suntan oil, even a brand new travel iron. All I kept was food and the booklets, and my *True Life Adventure Holidays Rescue Bleeper (Use of this automatically terminates your holiday. The Tour Operators cannot be held responsible if rescue arrives too late. For use in EMERGENCY ONLY)*.

Like I said, I nearly tripped the switch right away. In the brochure they hadn't said anything about walking. The Revolutionary Army was always shown in trucks, bombing down nice straight roads between jungly trees.

When I did get to the village it was nearly morning. I was supposed to be expected, but they shot at me just the same. I dropped like a stone, shouting the password as loud as I could through a mouthful of mud. And then they let me in.

I was really taken aback. I don't know what I was expecting the People's Revolutionary Army to be like; something out of *Che's Angels* on the video, I suppose; but I didn't expect a crowd of nasty-looking skinny dagoes—and the smell! You'd think they didn't know what deodorant was. They all looked so hungry that I didn't argue when they took my rucksack away and shared the food out. All I got was a bar of chocolate, and that melted before I could eat it. The rest of the time—tourists and peasants alike—we ate this horrible sort of corn porridge. It was supposed to be part of the Reality Technology. Anyway, there wasn't anything else, unless you tried the meat. But it isn't like soya, is it? You don't know where it's been.

I never did get to know any of the locals: they couldn't be bothered to learn English, no matter how slowly and loudly you spoke it; but there were lots of other tourists, so I did all right for company. We were all Colonels, and our tour leader (I looked him up in the booklet) was a General. He could speak the language, and he translated the orders and taught us how to use our rifles. I never did manage to hit what I aimed at, but I got so's the recoil didn't knock me over. That's all we did the first two days, learn to shoot. They were funny old rifles, called Martini-Henry. Fancy that. I didn't know they had sponsorship in the backward countries.

Most of the other tourists were pretty awful, but there were a couple of girls from Greater Outer London, Janice and Lyn, and the three of us hung around together. After the first couple of days General Diaz (that wasn't his real name, but we were supposed to have foreign names to give us the feel) told us he'd received orders and we had to move out.

I never did see a truck, the whole time I was on holiday, except a couple of burned-out ones by the side of the road: we walked everywhere. I wanted to stop and turn on my bleeper but it turned out that the food wasn't the only thing to have gone from my rucksack. God knows what use they thought it'd be to them—the tour wouldn't rescue natives. Janice and Lyn still had theirs, though, and I wasn't planning on getting separated from the rest of the group. Funny how things turn out, isn't it?

Anyhow, the next day, we were in this smashing battle. We were supposed to take a hill where the Democrats had some big guns commanding the suspension bridge on the main route to the capital. General Diaz was in on the briefing that the native officers gave to their troops and then he gave us *our* briefing. The real army was going to do the dangerous stuff—the assault on the battery—we were just going to creep up under cover and give supporting fire. He explained it all ever so well: how it was the peasants who had the real quarrel with the Democrats, and how we should try and be careful, 'cause we could get killed if we didn't do it properly. And then he said that the tour couldn't take responsibility for wounds sustained in action, but that we'd get the best medical care, provided we'd taken out holiday insurance. And then we all shouted: "Liberty and Long Live the Glorious People's Revolution!" and started up the hill.

Well, you could see that the rank and file didn't like it a bit that we had the cushiest job, and there was a bit of muttering that you didn't have to know the language to understand; but they didn't *have* to join the Revolution—they were free to choose, same as us. Janice, she was always soft-hearted, didn't like it that some of the soldiers were so young, children really, but I reckon they knew what they were doing and at least it stopped them vandalising in the cities, like the Doley kids at home.

Up the hill we went, all of us tourists going through the trees at the back. Here and there the tour had viewpoints where you could be photographed with the battle behind. You could see for miles up there and the bangs and explosions, well, you couldn't tell them from Effects, they were so good.

We'd only just got settled when some of the Democrats started firing on us; it was all arranged, of course, part of the Tour. I don't know if I killed anyone or not, more's the pity. I just shut my eyes and pulled the trigger. Janice, the silly moo, got blown up trying to crawl over and give a drink to one of the native kids who'd been shot. Diaz was right annoyed about that; it spoiled his no-casualty bonus or something.

We didn't manage to take the guns and, from what Lyn told me after, most of the real troops went the same way as poor Janice. Our General got the tourists out, and they had to make a forced march back to the coast under fire from the Democrats. But I wasn't in on that.

You see, when Janice got shot, I thought I might as well get her bleeper. No harm in being on the safe side, and she wouldn't be needing it, after all. I didn't like that bit too much. It was all right if you just looked: I've seen worse on kids' programmes back home. It was the smell, like, and having to touch. I got sick after I'd pulled the bleeper out of Janice, and I was still lying on the ground when these two big so-and-sos from the Democrats' camp came down to finish off the wounded. So I surrendered.

They were really quite decent about the whole thing. I thought I was in trouble until I got up to the gun emplacement, and then it turned out that most of the people there were tourists, same as me. They made quite a fuss of me—I was the only prisoner they'd managed to take. Most of the wounded from our side were natives, and they just shot them, but the tour operators paid a bounty for any tourist prisoners, so they always tried to keep them alive if possible. They were really cut up about Janice.

I've got some good photographs from when I was a prisoner. Much better than the ones Lyn got on the forced march. Most of them show me in handcuffs, but we only put those on to make the whole thing look good. I had a great time up there by the guns for a while until they told me that, for a small surcharge, I could be shipped down to the capital city, to the jail there, to be shot by a firing squad.

Now, I didn't like the sound of a firing squad at first, but the tour representative on the Democrat side said I'd come for a True Life Adventure, and what was the point if I was going to cop out just as something really exciting was going to happen? Well, once they put it like that, I didn't have any option, did I? So next day I was sent down to the city under guard.

The prison wasn't up to much. Tourists had a separate section, of course, but the sheets were a bit damp and at night the noises from the interrogation block were worse than a disco.

In the morning, one of the tour staff turned up with a meal (Reality Technology porridge again) and explained the whole set-up: how some of the officers on the tribunal I was going up before were part of the tour, and how there were different sorts of Firing Squad Service: Economy, Executive and Super Deluxe.

"That's where you are executed as a famous rebel leader in front of President Rosario himself, with a photograph in the *Democratic Beacon* and an obituary in *Struggle*."

"It's ever so expensive," I said. "Do you take Gold Card?"

After they'd checked my credit limit it took a couple of days to get things sorted out. I did a bit of scratching on the cell wall to pass the time away—my name and the date and "Long Live the People! Down with Rosario!"

My cell had a little window with bars, just like the office: it made me a bit homesick. If I stood on the bed I could see the exercise yard, where the stake for the executions was, so I spent most of my time watching people get shot. At that distance, it was really good. Some of them must have been tourists, but the whole thing was done so well that you couldn't tell the difference. I knew, of course, that for the natives the guns were loaded with live ammunition, and that they were just buried, not smuggled out to tour headquarters, like us; but, as I say, you couldn't tell, except that some of the real prisoners didn't behave at all well at the end.

I got taken up before the tribunal at last. They went on for ages about these things I was supposed to have done, and I stood there with my arms folded and looked heroic. When they asked me if I had anything to say before they passed sentence of death on me, I did this little speech about freedom and how they could kill me but the spirit of the people would never die and so forth. I got it out of the back of *Useful Phrases*. I'm not normally much of a reader, but it just shows how it can come in handy, doesn't it?

They sentenced me to be shot the next day at noon. Funny, that. I always thought people were shot at dawn, but I suppose it was out of consideration for us tourists, or it might have been because the President was going to be there. I didn't sleep too well that night. I mean, there's always the chance of a mistake, isn't there? And some of those officers on the tribunal really believed they were protecting Free Enterprise from the Red Menace. For that matter, I suppose that the People's Revolutionary Army must have been fighting for freedom from oppression—wars aren't just started to give people exciting holidays, are they? Not that it was any of my concern. Still, I kept on thinking about that firing squad; whether the tour would organise it properly; what the odds were against their making a mistake.

When they came to get me the next day, I was as white as a sheet and freezing cold, in spite of the hot sun. They hauled me out into the courtyard, and stood me up against the stake. I was relieved, I tell you, when I recognised the officer in charge of the squad from *Know Your Tour Staff*, because by that time I was in such a panic I thought the officer's side-arm—the one you get the coup-de-grace with, if the squad louse it up—might have been forgotten. I stood there, thankful for the stake (at least you couldn't see how my knees were trembling when I leant on it) and looked around. There was a big reviewing stand opposite me, and a brass band. The front of the stand was hung with the flag of the Democracy, and it had a striped canopy over it. Here and there about the place there were pressmen with notebooks and cameras, and all around were the cell windows, with faces peering out from between the bars, waiting, waiting.

Then President Rosario came out of the Prison Governor's quarters, and the band began to play "My Country, Free Forever", and everyone stood to attention. The President got up onto the reviewing stand, and the tour officer came over and lit me a cigarette. That's the best photo I've got from the whole holiday—me upright and unbowed at the stake, refusing to have a blindfold, the cigarette smoke hanging in the air between me and the President. He was a little man, much smaller than he looks in the pictures, with dark hair and eyes, like any other of the natives. He had a familiar look in his eyes, standing there hemmed in by the tall, uniformed tour people, the canopy casting bars of shadow across his face. A puzzled look, like the Doleys at home, like the peasants on the hillside by the guns, a look that didn't change as he gave the order to fire.

Next year, I'm going to try the Democrats.

A SENOI DREAM   Malcolm Ashworth

In early long-light this between-dream-time we sit in family to eat-and-tell, as do our relatives all around the long-house. We thank dream-friends for good fruit and fish, and we eat. This between-dream-time, more than any I can remember, son-of-my-body, Serenki, is very excited. He has met with something strange, I think, and would leap in like a darting fish-bird to be first at the telling if he did not know that I would stay him. Always his sister, many moon-passes younger, has first tell. Serenki has enough time-in-the-two-worlds not to lose his dream while waiting his tell-place. To go forward vigorously is good, but also to wait in silence while fish lose their fear and things grow to their true ending is good.

Around our living-place many voices now speak, some soft, some excited, in the early haze-shimmer between the two worlds. Outside our tree-cousins can be heard chattering their own dream-tells, and many birds, too fast for any man to understand.

"Tenmai," I say, settling.

"Father!" says Serenki, in a running voice, ". . . ."

I look to him. He looks down and away across the hut, seeing nothing, his fingers spearing his palms.

"Tenmai," I say again, "Did you dream?"

"Oh, yes, father," says daughter-of-my-body, and before I can ask, "Would you like to tell?", she starts to tell.

"I was climbing up Sky Mountain, looking for sweet nuts. Everything was happy. I was *very* high. I saw my nut-bush a short way forward. I scrambled towards it. And it was further away then. And I was *higher*. And it was all rock. And my ledge was narrower. I trembled then and I wanted to go back, but I couldn't find the path, only long-fall-steep-rock everywhere and then I was slipping and slipping. There were no bushes, nothing to hold, and I slipped out and fell fast and I cried frightened and I knew my pain-end was soon and I didn't want to. But I remembered what we must do and I wished hard for sky-friends to help me. And then two sky-friends were there by me, green and red with wide wings and they showed me how to float-fly. And then I stopped falling and I didn't cry any more and I was happy and floated down. My friends had given me the floating-flying gift and now they soared away up Sky Mountain and the sun was very bright on them. But father, I am bad—I cannot remember the gift now, to teach it to Our People."

"You are not bad," I told her. "Always it is good to bring back dream-gifts to Our People but some, like this of yours, my daughter, melt away in the journey from the dream-world. And the real gift then is our memory of them. Was that all you dreamed, little Tenmai?"

"Yes father." I stroked her head and watched patterns in the morning-fire sun-smoke. Serenki moved. I smiled and turned to him.

"Well, Serenki," I asked, as though I did not know, "did you, too, dream?"

"Yes, father," he replied, keeping in his breath until I asked, "And would you like to tell?"

"Yes, father," as if chasing a young pig. "But first we have to make my dream-gift!"

"That is not the way, Serenki," I tell him gently, for he already knows. "First we hear your dream-tell, then we think on it together. If it is a very good dream we take it to the Council, and then your dream-gift is brought through to this world to help Our People."

"But father . . ." says Serenki, still in a running voice; and then he stops and looks down, struggling to bring his race to a halt. "I went out with my friends, Kirinkoi and Talakui," he begins, "away from the village and the growing-grounds, through the jungle-mist. We were going for the place of the breast-hills, to chase the young pigs that root there. They squeal and grunt so much when they run it makes us laugh. But we saw no pigs this time and so we sat and told stories then, from our dreams, and there was a stillness-singing in my head. 'Build a stone-pile,' I said to them, 'and I will hide where you can't find me.' So they built a stone-pile as big as an old cockerel and then moved it one stone at a time while I ran off to hide.

"I ran around small hills and between big rocks and past trees and through tall grass, and birds squawked and flapped away. I had the silent-singing in my head still and I didn't look for any hidden place. My running now was almost a flying and I went fast into a glade of tall trees and stopped. All things there seemed stopped, barely a breath like when we will scoop a fish the very next eyeblink. The trees stretched very tall, waiting, all things there *stretched*, waiting in that silent-singing no-movement, waiting for the next eyeblink as though waking-world and dream-world would suddenly flash together into one rainbow-world. And then I saw the man.

"He came towards me, smiling, and my breath held in me. For he was not one of Our People—and not of any other peoples I had seen, not even the pale people of the noisy-boats. His colour was like the brown eggs of our best hen and he wore a loincloth like yours, father, but he was not of Our People. There was a *strangeness* like—I don't know—I could feel he was no enemy but I could feel about him some of the vast-distance-of-which-none-can-tell of our early dreams, and that made me a little afraid. Then he spoke to me, but the singing-silence was still there.

" 'Serenki', he said, 'I have come a long way to be your friend. Here in your dream-time all things are happy and nothing can harm you. I want to be your friend and to give you a fine gift for which your people will praise you.'

"I said back to him, but it was not like me saying: 'Welcome in friendship, man-I-do-not-know. I will be your friend. I thank you for your gift-offer and I will give you a gift in return, a song or a poem from these worlds of mine, or whatever you ask.'

" 'Your gift to me will indeed be great, Serenki,' he said, 'Greater than mine to you and already I—and my people—thank you deeply for it.'

" 'From which place do you come?' I asked.

" 'It is hard to tell of that,' he said, 'but if I now give you your gift then you will see from where I come.' He looked about him on the ground and picked up a piece of dead, twisted root of the tree-the-green-spider-loves, then he knelt and scooped a sandy place flat and made a pattern in the sand with his finger. He put the twisted tree-that-was over it with the hole in it over the heart of his drawing. Then he sat back and smiled up to me. 'This is your gift, Serenki. Do not be bewildered. Soon you will understand all. This gift is a bridge-between-our-hearts. No more do we need to tell with our mouths all the thinkings and feelings and the dreams of our hearts. When we both look into this thing-that-removes-the-last-barrier it is as though we were one person. Come sit nearby, Serenki, and look with me and we will then be closer friends than any ever were and you will understand.'

"I did as he said and looked into the hole in the wood and I was no longer with my dream-friend under those strange trees, but outside our long-house here, gathering things, for I saw at once how to make my own thing-that-removes-the-last-barrier and knew what I must pick for it.

"And then everything was moving and I was not Serenki any more. I was my friend and seeing over vast spaces to my land. But they were not spaces. It is hard to tell, father, for my land was beyond many, many moon-passes, beyond many long-house-movings of Our People, beyond even no-river-there where we now get good fish. But I was not afraid for it was as though I had always known all this and the land I saw was my land where I had always lived. There were many things there I do not know how to tell—but you will see them all and know them as I did, father, when I have my dream-gift. It was a land of lightness and the people there looked like my friend but dressed in different ways and they were my people. All the people were at peace and everywhere was quiet understanding and happiness. Their songs were beautiful and nowhere was there any fear. And the knowing was in me that this no-fear was Serenki's gift to my people. It is strange to tell now. Through Serenki our enemy had been defeated long ago, and had gone for all time. This enemy had not been a demon or an animal such as we know, but what-might-have-been, like an evil dream that we fight and overcome so that it vanishes away. For a very little while then I knew this world-that-might-have-been and I was more afraid than I have ever been, even though the knowing was only a dream long past. It was a world of fear and screaming. Everywhere was fear like a mist, and hate and no understanding. Many evil things flashed through the sky and the whole world seemed on fire. The houses melted and people burned and my people were not there. They had never been. Only the people of no-understanding who did not know one another and went in fear and killed, afraid that they would be killed. I crouched, trembling, unable to speak, in all that death-horror.

"At last I turned away from that evil-dream and knew again that it was an old dream that had faded many long-times past. And that fading away was Serenki's gift to my people. And I was in a green place then, of grass and ferns and flowers and water-running, back in my good world that truly was, and there, by a pool, looking deep into the water was a likeness of Serenki. And people came there, quietly, to sit in great peace, to think and dream-while-awake and sometimes to look into the pool with the Serenki figure.

"Then I was Serenki again, no longer looking into the bridge-between-hearts and no longer able to see my friend because my eyes were filled with heart's-water. My friend came close to me and put his arms about me. 'You see, Serenki,' he said quietly to me, 'your gift to my people was the greater, the greatest gift ever given.' And then I was alone beneath the trees. I lay on the sand and, in my dream, I slept. Never has that happened in my dreams before."

Serenki stopped telling and in his eyes again was heart's-water. I knew I had heard a dream such as comes not often in any man's time-in-the-two-worlds.

"Serenki," I said, "This is a very strange dream—the strangest of any I have heard. And yet I can see that you tell it to me truly. Perhaps it is a very great dream. We will take it to the Council and they will decide. Will your gift, I wonder, be one of those that melts away on the journey from that world to this, like Tenmai's flying-gift?"

"Oh, no, father," said Serenki, and his face gave off light, "I can make it now. I know where it is. And when you look into it, you will know how to make *your* dream-living-sharing gift too. Can I make it *now*, father? It will take not even many eyeblinks. Can I? Then you will know, and you will be able to tell the Council truly."

He was very excited. I smiled. "Very well, you may do it, Serenki. But be swift. Soon the Council will sit."

He leapt up and raced from the long-house into the full sun. I stroked Tenmai's head. "You may go out, too, now, Tenmai." She ran after her brother, calling to him.

Serenki was true by his saying and before many eyeblinks he was back, squatting in front of me. On the floor he put a perfect lily-leaf and in its centre set one of those riverbank-stones that catch-the-sun.

"Look into it, father," said Serenki, excited. I sat by him and did as he wished, and at once I saw how I could make *my* gift-that-joins-hearts. I was Serenki and filled with joy at the sharing of my dream-gift. I was proud and my heart was jumping in me and I went to meet again the dream-friend and see his strange land and the fear and horror of the screaming-land-that-might-have-been.

When at last I was myself again I looked at Serenki, whose eyes shone like bright fish-scales, and I knew him and loved him in a way that was not as before. I held his shoulder and told him: "You have done bravely and well, my son. This is a great dream-gift. I will go with you to take it to the Council."

As we walked together to the Meeting-Place-Of-Our-People, Serenki, holding himself back from running and walking straight like a man, I fitted the glistening fish-head I had brought on top of a short, straight stick.

At the Council I whispered to Serenki that we must sit quietly and wait our turn, however great his dream. He nodded and sat well. Finally, old Walakoi turned to us and asked, "Who brings a dream here to share?"

"My son, Serenki, has had a great dream and brought back a great dream-gift," I told them, "He asks that the Council look at his gift for then they will understand his dream."

Walakoi smiled to me in understanding. "It is well," he said, "Let us look at this dream-gift brought to us by Serenki."

I guided my son to the centre of the floor where he set down his lily-leaf and on it the shining-stone. The councillors gathered close around. "Look closely at the stone, wise-fathers," said Serenki, in quiet speaking.

The wise-ones of Our People all looked in the stone and I heard small gasps of breath. Then they sat back and looked at Serenki and I thought they had rejected his gift. But then I saw that they had seen all and known all and I was amazed, for it had all happened in less than an eyeblink. Was it like that with me, I wondered?

Walakoi spoke and there was happy laughter in his old voice: "Serenki, son-of-ours, that was indeed a *very* great dream. And this bridge-between-hearts you bring us is indeed a very great gift.

And by bringing this gift it seems that, in some way I do not understand, you gave a greater one, and that too is good. You have indeed done well and bravely in this dream-world. You will have much praise from Our People for this. Will you now go to tell your friends of all this?"

Serenki nodded, smiling in shy pride, took up his dream-gift and left the hut. I crossed to Walakoi and held up my short stick. "See, Walakoi," I said. He looked into one eye of the fish and I into the other.

We sat back in laughter-thunder and I put my arm about his old shoulders and laughed much. For many, many moon-passes I had known Walakoi well, and he me. But now I knew him as though we both grew from the one stem. Very little had we ever failed to understand the other; but now we would understand each other fully for all time.

The other councillors were making their own bridges-between-hearts and sharing them and the hut was filled with laughter and joking and great understanding. No more dreams were told at that time, and little talk was needed to decide on Serenki's dream-gift.

"This is the finest toy I have ever seen," said Walakoi, still with laughter in his speech, "and our sons and daughters will have much fun from it. We older ones, because of our dream-world guidance, we already understand one another well and disagreement is rare. I think that we should take many of these toys down-river to barter. They will amuse the people of the noisy-boats and the many-moving-machines, and we shall get many fine hoes and spear-points for them."

There was a sigh of agreement in the hut.

"It is good sometimes to remember the wild, lively dreams of our youth, the girls we chased and caught in the long grass, the strangers we met, the fearsome enemies we defeated. Serenki is a good son," said Walakoi to me, "and he dreams strange and wonderful dreams and brings back fine gifts for the good of Our People. Such dreams . . . aye. But—" and Walakoi rose—"it is hands, not dreams, that harvest yams."

Walakoi, as ever, was the first to leave the hut.

DELICATE IMMORTAL MEANINGS
Rick Slaughter

On the day the last L-5 colony blew David arrived with his mother at the Life Institute. There was a strange reluctance in the way he walked up the smooth marble steps toward the appointment which could eventually mean a thousand years of active life.

Jane looked at her son as they reached the smoked glass doors. If she sensed his reluctance she did not show it for there were tears in her eyes and a tight choking sensation in her chest. A tangle of emotions vied for dominance: envy, regret, relief.

"Just check you've got everything," she said.

The boy considered his mother. When the life-extension process had been made available to the island's children Jane had been too old. Since the ageing mechanism deep in the pituitary gland could not be inhibited after puberty this revolution had been a gift only for the young. At 42 she remained an attractive woman. But with each passing year the hand of time would more clearly indicate her declining status as an ageing member of the old order. David answered softly.

"I have the cards. Why don't you go on home?"

"No. I promised your father I'd be present. Anyway, the veemat's set up to record 'Loveskills' so there's no hurry."

Seeing that Jane's mind was firmly made up, David turned his back on the bright Bermuda sunlight and passed through the silently-opening doors of the Life-Extension Institute.

Riding home on BERT Jane could not shake off her depression. The vehicle hissed over the crest of Trimmingham Hill and past the burned-out ruins of a late '70s development. As a child she had lived in one of those luxurious apartments and played in the open-air pool which now lay derelict and empty. She remembered her father helping to lime-wash the white roof and to clean out the rainwater tanks under the patio. But the buildings had been commandeered for base personnel after the American takeover and had subsequently been bombed by the F.B.L.A.

The outer desolation mirrored her inner pain. It was so unfair! How the *hell* was she supposed to feel with her life ebbing away and these youngsters just walking into a clinic for their treatments? Only two more visits. The boy's molecular "clock" would cease to function and the ageing process would cease. He would be a different person, almost a different species, cut off from her forever. The tears coursed silently down her cheeks leaving dark streaks of mascara to mimic the charred wood outside.

By the time they reached the Devonshire Bay stop it was early evening. A mini-bug whisked them silently to the old fisherman's cottage on the south shore which was their home. Only the solar collectors set skilfully into the stepped roof and the ubiquitous satellite dish on the lawn told the house apart from its earlier use. Perceiving his mother's distress, David quickly left the house knowing that Jane would set up the evening meal and retire to the sensormat for a run-through of all the shows she had missed that day. Sitting on the rocky shore, David could see out past the shallow aquamarine water to the reefs and the deep blue beyond. As ever, something spoke to him from that vast arc of sea and sky. But what was it? Something awesome yet wholly benign. Perhaps there would now be time to find out. After all, barring accident, he ought to have centuries to explore this and many other puzzles. Time to help reconstruct the battered ecology of the islands and, maybe, venture out into the wider world in search of experience and understanding. Now that the space programme had failed the Earth seemed more precious, more vulnerable, then ever. Who would have guessed that the destruction of the moonbase and all four L-5 colonies would virtually bring manned space flight to an end?

As the sun sank and the calm sea flowed like molten metal David turned for home. But before reaching it his eye was caught by an odd glow from the old main road. It couldn't be the rapid transit and private cars had been banned decades ago. Quickly he sprinted back to the South Shore Road and peered out at a very strange sight.

A procession was passing eastward. At its head strode two men carrying a banner with the words NUNC STANS flashing and flickering across it in elaborate letters. There followed a group bearing torches which seemed to burn more brightly than any he had ever seen. The collective brilliance not only highlighted the features and clothes of all those present but also lent a surreal animation and warmth to the trees and other vegetation lining the old routeway. Behind the torch-bearers walked a small group of musicians playing eastern instruments in a harmonious, meditative fashion. The music was quite unlike anything David had ever heard and it evoked a sensation of calm celebration which quite unsettled him. But this did nothing to prepare him for what followed: a horse-drawn trailer bearing a simple wooden coffin which, so far as he could see, remained empty. The lid lay half buried by hibiscus blossom and oleander.

David's mind struggled to make sense of the unusual sight. What kind of a procession. . . . funeral? . . . . was this? Where was the body? Where were the mourners? Meanwhile, the tail of the procession passed by: half a dozen jugglers wove intricate patterns with balls of golden light. Jugglers? As the figures disappeared around a bend in the road he caught a last glimpse and realised with a start that all were walking with their hands clasped behind them. The glittering pattern impressed a last half-seen motif upon his brain before it too vanished, leaving the boy shaking and startled. He looked along the empty road. No answers there. A BERT vehicle whispered by on its elevated track bound, no doubt, for the densely-populated Collector's Hill township a mile or two on. Leaves and papers fluttered in its wake and one of the latter fell at David's feet. As his eyes refocused in the darkness the sheet flared briefly, leaving a line of bright letters standing boldly forward from its surface. The words NUNC STANS lay once more before him. Quickly he reached to retrieve the paper and yet as his hand touched it the large letters vanished. In their place sprang up a new pattern of smaller words picked out in neat silver letters. Putting aside the temptation to read it there and then, he folded the sheet carefully into his shirt and ran home.

After supper Jane vanished into the study where the data-link to Boston was kept in its nest of electronic locks. She worked there most evenings for a software company in the States. Quietly the boy went to his room, secured the door with his personal code and carefully opened out the hidden paper. As he smoothed it flat

the small bright script shone forth again. This time he read it with
care.

> The Walsingham Settlement at Blue Hole
> invites you to celebrate and witness the passing
> of Rinpoche the Elder to a higher plane.
>
> Here in the ruins of a decaying civilisation
> we sow the seeds of sustainable futures,
> of Wisdom Cultures.
>
> Time no more our enemy.
> We pass beyond illusion to the nunc stans,
> all of eternity, now.
>
> Cast off conditioning and fear,
> look beyond artificial "life extension".
> Be at the settlement
> Friday 12th April 2028, 20:00 hours.
>
> IT WILL CHANGE YOUR LIFE FOR EVER

Celebrate the death of an elder at Walsingham? He'd heard that
the military council had approved the conversion of the old
dolphinarium into a research centre of some kind, but nothing had
prepared him for this. And what about the criticism of life-
extension? Certainly it was artificial, but in view of the pay-off who
could complain? Perhaps there was something about the process
which his mother and the community instruction programs had
failed to tell him. Even something they didn't know. At that point
David knew he had to go.

By 19:00 on Friday he was aboard BERT and heading along the
edge of the still radioactive waters of Harrington Sound. His
father had sailed there, studied the small tern colony and dived for
calico clams. That is, before the Flatts reactor had shed its coolant
into those sheltered waters. Now a green scum of mutated algae
dominated the warped ecology of that once attractive basin. Soon
the vehicle was passing the guarded perimeter of Tucker's Town.
Several members of the Tucker's Town Defence Association could
be seen behind the bullet-proof windows of the checkpoint. The
boy's mother had shown no interest in the excuse he had given that

he would spend the night with his uncle in that privileged ghetto. He thought of the rich elderly residents who had opted for a life of gilded isolation. Whatever the Twenty-First Century was about he could not believe it involved a privatised retreat into the haze of hallucinogenic booze, the augmented "reality" of the latest sensormat or compulsive channel-hopping via DBS on a wall-sized threevee!

He stepped from the vehicle just beyond the ruins of the Bermuda pottery and walked down the hill toward the settlement. Others were also heading in that direction. But it was the new base on the far side of old Kindley airfield which caught his attention. The great military arcology had been part of a wider deal struck with the British before they handed the place over. Now it completely dwarfed the small islands of St George's and not only dominated Castle Harbour but the entire eastern half of the country. David could never see that looming mass of concrete and stone without thinking of his father who had died there in an undisclosed accident. And to what purpose? Since the military annexation of most of the eastern end it was clear that the new arcology was not intended simply for defence, reconnaissance and undersea monitoring. No, the war games were no longer games and the islands were being integrated into a world-wide network of offensive strike bases. The boy shuddered, turned his back on the hideously bristling structure and walked into the settlement.

Groups of people were drifting into an impressive wooden building which lay half-hidden by trees in a small depression by the sea. As David passed through the entrance he again heard the serene music of the procession. But this time the atmosphere was quite different. A sense of enormous energy and power seemed to flow out from the centre of the hall where lay a tiny figure upon a small raised platform. The banked seats along each of the walls were almost full and David had to squeeze in as best he could. Globes of amber light appeared to hover and sway over the central area as if moved by invisible hands. But David's attention was taken up by the shrunken figure. There, clad only in a loin cloth, lay what looked like a dwarf. But this was no dwarf. It had the proportions of a normal human male, but seemed to have shrunk to the size of a small child.

"There's very little left now," whispered another at his side. "A week ago he was fully two metres tall. Now the process is nearing its end. You just arrived in time," he added with a smile.

David barely had time to comprehend before the collective sound of indrawn breath drew his attention back to the platform. A dull glow seemed to emanate from the figure. It began to pulse, to swell and fade in a gentle rhythm, like breathing. Slowly the glow gained greater definition and a rainbow-coloured aura poured forth from the wrinkled skin, washing over the faces of those present and painting the walls with bands of glowing colour. A million needles of piercing white light leapt up and outward passing through walls, ceiling and all those gathered round. Waves of heat rippled through the air and David heard a whispering, dry as old leaves. A potent stillness filled his being. Gradually the small figure collapsed inward and, as it vanished, a dazzling ball of energy exploded out from that single point to the very ends of the universe.

As each successive wave washed over and through him, David felt his awareness drawn out, extended, refined until it seemed to encompass the whole world. But "he" was no longer an isolated ego marooned in a single body. "He" felt at one with all things, all beings, all forms and phases, all time and space sharing in the same ground of being. Close by he witnessed with a new, inner sight the brightness of myriad "others", sparks of sentient awareness each with their own subtle shades of individuality, their quirks and differences, yet all enfolded in a great and endless stream of energy and light arching through the wide world and beyond. Layer upon layer of harmonic complexity. The steady rhythm of currents and tides, the seasonal cycles of vegetative life, annual migrations of whales, birds, turtles, fish, tiny planktonic pulses embedded in billions of fine crystal lattices. Here too was the endless beat of wave upon rock, of wind upon sand and leaf, of sun and moon upon water, of energy, meaning, intention woven into all things. Connectedness and continuity supporting all forms and all lives.

As the great chain of being unfolded before him, the nature of the life-extension business and the manipulative mode of consciousness underlying it became clear. Yes, bodies could certainly be made to last longer. One day that would happen almost without effort and without the need for drugs of any kind. But that was really a side issue. The point was not to *cheat* time and mortality but to transcend them by waking to higher levels of awareness.

From the calm shores of this wider world the bright net of David's consciousness leapt through layers of temporality until it emerged into an eternal and endless present, the nunc stans. Here the outlines of infinite futures beckoned and he knew with a clear and unshakable insight that some of those futures led on and up beyond the great design he had glimpsed to stages and states of being that could only be guessed at. Moreover, that distant view was tied to him personally in the here and now of island life in the twenty-first century.

The outlines of a vision began to form within the vast arena of his broadened awareness. He saw the islands restored, the great military complexes dismantled, the teeth drawn from a vast orbiting armada of death. He saw new forests of cedar, a new flowering of the semi-tropical ecology, great flocks of sea birds as once there had been before, new lines of speciation arising from the now-barren limestone outcrops, the depleted and polluted soil. Nor was this a landscape without people. Within the vision moved men and women unlike any he had ever known. These long-lived beings moved through a renewed world with insight and grace, touching the Earth lightly but with awesome power, nurturing, supporting, celebrating new growth and development in the life around them. In this future humankind had taken the next steps. Nothing was guaranteed. However, small though the islands were a new balance here could affect the world.

His own life stretched out before him. Tasks like pearls lay superimposed upon this compelling landscape. David saw his own commitment to the process of global healing, the formation of an inter-species multiversity, a new dialogue with artificial intelligences, a flowering of Third World Cultures, the decline of war-making impulses and the re-launching of an altogether different kind of space programme. All of it lay within grasp. All lay like unfertilised seeds in the multiplex present. If the ruinous conceits of the past could be discarded new beginnings could be uncovered, negotiated, brought to fruition.

When David returned home he told his mother that he could not continue with the anti-ageing treatment.

"But why?" exclaimed Jane hysterically. "It's too late for me, but how can you throw it all away? The most precious gift of all?"

"Is it?" replied David quietly. "Is it the most precious gift? I think not."

"What do you mean?"

"Last night I saw a wider pattern. Life-extension will come, but not yet and not this way. It's still too early. Besides, I no longer fear death, for I have seen beyond it. If I fear anything it's an empty life. The pretence that a sensormat in every home will make people happy. It won't. It's so clear now. Technology gave us everything to live with, yet it provided nothing to live for. No purpose. On its own there are just a lot of very clever dead ends. It's all such a waste, such a diversion. I can't follow you on that road, so please don't ask me to."

David went to his room, packed a few clothes, a holo of his parents and a small stack of tapes. He left his universal access card on the dining-room table and embraced his mother. Jane was crying again. But as he bid her farewell, David reached within and drew on that endless pool of benign energy he now shared. He touched his mother gently, healed her sorrow and walked away.

The boy, no longer a child, left the house and stood facing the sea. Beyond the sharp rocks a small flock of longtails wheeled and dipped over the ivory surf. For the first time he understood the delicate immortal meanings flowing from the tips of their streaming articulate wings.

ADAM FOUND   Simon Ounsley

Ever since I woke up in the hospital bed, I've known that something was missing. The surgeon flashed up a big plan on the wall and pointed to the parts he had taken out. But the plan didn't look like my brain at all. It looked like an ornamental garden. He had taken out several flower-beds.

"You mustn't brood about what's disappeared," Dawn told me. "You should think about the future." She showed me my new muscles and told me to test out the grip of my new hands. They are as big as the surgeon's hands now but the fingers are short and thick and strong. They're very good for taking the lids off ketchup bottles.

"Look at that," I said to Dawn, as a shaft of sunlight appeared beside the bed. She said it would be summer soon. In a few days' time, I would be out in the fresh air. She thought I should try to find a job in the fresh air. It would be better than working inside.

I kept staring at the sunlight. I wanted to dive into it and capture the dancing specks of dust in my hands.

Next to Dawn's studio there was another, similar room but this one was empty. When I first got back from the hospital, I used to sit in it for hours, staring at my blurred reflection in the smooth floor.

"There's nothing here," Dawn used to tell me, but I kept thinking that here, somewhere, was whatever I'd lost.

I tried to imagine the room full of furniture. What would it be like, I wondered?

I got a job helping to build a garden. All the men who wanted a job had to carry boulders from one side of a pond to the other while the bosses watched. Some of the men had strange stares and stiff limbs and could carry three times as many boulders as everyone else, but after a while the damp got to them and they stood still like statues in the middle of the water. Another one got hot and caught fire and his head blew off and landed on the ground with a clatter.

"No," Dawn told me, "your head won't blow off if you get hot." But she didn't seem happy with what I'd told her.

"You'd better save the money you earn in the next few years," she said. "They'll get the things right sooner or later and then there won't be any more jobs in that line of work."

"I can always paint," I said.

She looked at me as though she'd seen a ghost.

"The garden shed," I reminded her. "You said it could do with a lick of paint."

*

Dawn and I had been lovers for a long time but I was a better lover now that I was stronger. Holding her in my arms was like squeezing a flower between my fingers. I was powerful and swift and she squealed and screamed when I pushed myself inside her. Fucking her was like killing a pig. I would lie back afterwards and hear her beside me, crying because I'd fucked her so good. I could hear her crying deep into the night.

Once I tried watching Dawn at work in her studio but she kept telling me I should go outside, that the fumes weren't good for me. I didn't like her paintings much anyway—they reminded me of the hi-fi and the washing machine. Why didn't she paint the birds and the flowers in the garden instead?

I went to fetch a brush and started painting the shed. There were clouds in the sky like candy floss, like bandages and brains.

One day, Dawn told me we could not be lovers any longer.

"I didn't think it would have to be like this," she told me, "I'm sorry."

"But we've always lived together," I said.

"No we haven't."

"Well it seems like it."

"I suppose it must do," said Dawn. "That's the trouble. You've become like a child."

"I'm strong. I can work. I can open ketchup bottles."

"You've got to understand that we talked it over, you and I, we decided it would be for the best. Since you couldn't support yourself, it seemed sensible for you to get rid of the creative urge altogether."

"I can fuck you good."

"But we never realised it would change you so much."

"I want to fuck you."

"I'm sorry, Adam."

She took her things into the spare bedroom but I wouldn't let her stay there. I dragged her back onto the bed and hit her and fucked her, holding her down as she struggled. Afterwards, while I was resting, she slipped away and locked herself in the other room. I could hear her in there, sobbing and moaning. I knocked on the door and asked her to let me in but she wouldn't answer. So I sat

asked. "I want to get away from that. I want to discover what I've lost."

Dawn seemed upset by this. She said I was the chewed end of the lizard's tail. And she walked away when I asked her what she meant.

When Dawn was out, I borrowed her brushes and started painting. I painted a house with a garden and smoke coming out of the chimney.

I showed it to Dawn when she got back but she started crying.

"Look," I said, "there's the sun." I'd shown it as a yellow circle with yellow lines like rays coming out of it. But Dawn just carried on crying. I hugged her but it seemed to make her worse.

"Please," she said, "go outside."

So I went to put another coat of paint on the shed.

I couldn't find the stepladder so I looked inside the shed for it. The door creaked open like in the horror movies. It was dark and musty inside. Spiders and things were crawling around in it. I put my foot on one as it tried to get away. I realised that I hadn't been inside the shed since before my stay in the hospital. All at once, I had the idea that whatever I'd lost was in there, stored out of sight, along with the spiders, the dust, and the stepladder.

So I went to get a torch.

I don't know what I expected to find in there. Maybe bits of my brain stacked on the shelves. I wasn't prepared for the forests and oceans, to reach out my hand to the end of the torch beam and touch the sky.

I brought one of the dusty canvases out into the light of the garden. With my finger, I traced a shaft of sunlight as it broke through the clouds and swept down to sparkle on a torrent of water. From under the surface, a face stared up into the sunlight, its dead eyes seeming to focus on the specks of dust which danced above the waves. In the bottom right-hand corner of the picture, submerged beneath the deluge, was my name: Adam.

"I really should have destroyed them," said Dawn, "but I couldn't bring myself to do it."

"I could even capture specks of dust," I said.

"You've got to understand," said Dawn, "that there wasn't any market for them."

"They would have had a certain value as commercial art," said Auberon, bending down to examine one of the pictures through a magnifying glass, "if not for the morbid element. Bloated corpses and severed heads are unsuitable for chocolate boxes, for instance."

"The best thing to do now is to burn them," said Dawn. "We could have a bonfire tonight. I could put some sausages on the ends of sticks."

"I can't believe I could do all that," I said. But I was touched by a new hope. "Maybe I could learn to do it again."

Dawn took my hand. She looked at me tenderly.

"You could sue the hospital," she said. "You should have lost the *will* to paint."

"But I don't want to lose it."

"You did before. We agreed. . . ."

"I was wrong."

"You'd be miserable. Painting pictures only fit to be locked away in a shed."

"It's all I want to do."

Dawn turned to Auberon.

"What can we say to him?" she said. "He won't understand."

Auberon came and put his arm round Dawn. I didn't like the way he did that—as though he knew her very well.

"You must not upset Dawn," he told me. He said the words carefully, as though speaking to a child. "She has always done what she thought best for you. But now she has other things on her mind."

"We have to grow up or sink under," said Dawn.

"We must all find useful work," Auberon said to me. "You have grown strong hands and muscles. Instead of creating imaginary gardens, you can now build real ones."

"And I must grow too," said Dawn. "I have to share in Auberon's work."

"Yesterday," said Auberon, "such opportunities were elusive—like your specks of dust in sunlight. Today we can seize them with both hands."

"I have no choice," said Dawn, sadly.

She was going to get a brain like Auberon's.

They tell me that my hope now is in my hands—in my strong new hands and muscles, that I must concentrate on what is real and forget what is not. But I tire of my job. We are not building a garden after all. Concrete pillars are sprouting, not flower-beds, and on the wall between them there is a stone which shows a head like the one which rolled in the dirt, like the one which stared out of Auberon's picture. Maybe Auberon himself will come here and build real creatures from his drawings.

Things are making more sense now. I think the garden of my brain is growing again.

The other day, I left my work and found a place by myself and drew in the sand with a stick. Two men in uniform found me and tried to take me back to join my workmates. They had that same look about them, as though they had been drawn by Auberon. I didn't want to leave, so I thought I would show them what I'd been drawing.

"Look," I said, pointing with my stick. "Here is the sea and here is a lighthouse and here, on the top of the lighthouse, is the face of a clock. Over here, a human hand is reaching out of the water, clutching at the air."

The two men looked at each other and shook their heads. One of them reached down and picked up a handful of sand from the face of the clock.

"You are wrong," he said, "this is not a clock—it is sand."

He let the grains fall, trickling slowly between his fingers.

SOAP . Keith Haviland

The story so far: Doctor Charles Blade, thought to have been violently murdered on an Andean climbing expedition, has mysteriously returned from the dead, suffering from almost

*complete amnesia. Meanwhile, Father Duvalier ponders his future
after discovering that his mistress Charlene is in fact his twin
sister from whom he was separated at birth.*

Fran awoke as a blue triangle played across her face, spilling
upwards on to the fungus-spotted wallpaper behind her. As she
blinked, yellow fragments of words wandered idly across its
surface. Then they were gone, replaced by a demure mascaraed eye
and a section of plump lip.

Unsteadily Fran got up, and opened the blind that kept out the
world so imperfectly. The triangle broadened into a fuller, weakly-
coloured projection of the video billboard that stood across the
street. At the top of the image were the words: "Watch Hell
Flowers on Channel Roma-Uno tonight at nine. Or record toll free
on any TA-KUO equipment." Under this, the synthesised faces of
Father Duvalier and Charlene looked upwards, hyper-realistic
cheeks pressed closely together.

The board was of a type that lined almost every main street,
occupied every public place in Britain. Essentially nothing more
than an integrated array of flatscreens, it spewed out advertising
animations and bland news summaries unceasingly. At this point
in the day, with barely a vehicle or pedestrian on the road, the
board's intelligent control unit displayed a series of instantly
graspable images like the paper posters of old, hoping to catch the
momentary attention of a commuter cyclist. However, a passerby
would have noticed something odd about the board on this wintry
morning; each image it displayed was marred by an identical blot,
shaped like a Rorschach spider. After the sun had risen, the
negative space of the blot would be revealed as a mass of congealed
paint, the result of a paint bomb hurled against the shatterproof
plastic. Fran smiled, feeling an anxious spasm of pleasure. She had
put it there.

Fran ate breakfast in silence, her back to the images that filled
her window, reading an ancient, dog-eared paperback. Two years
before she would have woken later, much later, then eaten
watching one of the ninety-three TV channels the average
European could choose from, or perhaps mulled over a recording
of a satellite broadcast she had missed from the previous
evening—"Good Evening, Ladies and Gentleman, Mesdames et

Messieurs, welcome to a selection of the . . . er . . . cream of Europe's *son et lumière* sex shows"—that kind of thing. Even if Troy had stayed with her, the pair of them having spent the night wrapped stiffly in her filthy duvet, they would almost certainly have passed the first part of the day catching up on the morning soaps, or, using the flatscreen as a terminal, wandering through the gossip and entertainment networks. Both were favourite obsessions of Troy's. A few hours before that, they might have made love to the accompaniment of a late-night Hitchcock or Spielberg, trying to ignore the coldness of a room where the heating had gurgled to a stop a decade before.

But that was before Fran's conversion. Now her flatscreen was painted an opaque white. On this Fran had drawn a crude, crayon finger held against cartoon lips, and below that was the legend— SHHH . . . CARELESS TALK COSTS MINDS. Sometimes she would still turn the flatscreen on, without sound. It amused her to think of the capped announcers' grins mouthing uselessly beneath the paint.

The roots of Fran's small rebellion were simple. She had been born into an age glutted with the visual, fat with information, and had spent most of her life in the presence of one kind of flatscreen or another. At school they taught her; at home they entertained and pacified her. Indeed, she still remembered Louis the Coypu and Khan the Moon-Rat with nostalgic affection (the talking heads that had attempted to teach her physics and bend history were on the other hand completely forgotten).

Forcefed with received experience, Fran had, before the age of five, seen more of the world than Marco Polo; before ten she had been exposed to sights that would have made a mediaeval natural scientist weep with envy, and by twenty she was bloated by both the amount of information and the banality of its presentation. Because she was not bright or middle-class enough to join the eleven percent of the work force with some kind of employment, Fran enjoyed only the Consumer Allowance and State Flatscreen that were the rights of all British Citizens and Internal Aliens. (Actually, the Allowance was paid by the Federation of the Pacific Rim and could only be spent on consumer goods manufactured between Japan and Sino-Australia; it helped keep the Federation's factories turning, but was worthless as far as local food and housing were concerned). So Fran's life assumed its pattern: days spent with Troy in the electronically affluent squalor of her single room, nights spent befuddled by drink and sound and vision in the cheaper video-clubs. Her inner life, like that of her entire generation's, revolved around the world contained in the networks and video media. It never occurred to her that some hidden agenda lay behind what she saw, that the fantasy world she inhabited had been deliberately engineered to entertain, absorb and finally exhaust and control an idle population. Like the epoch, both she and Troy grew fat, sad, passive.

Then Fran snapped.

It had happened about eighteen months previously. There had been several weeks of a particularly dark depression. Her drinking and recreational drug-taking had become heavier. Nights had turned into sleepless, ghoul-eyed affairs spent under the flatscreen. As so often before, she was trying to escape the forces that welled up inside her in an orgy of over-stimulation, but this time the long-dormant volcano erupted. In a rage she had painted the sixty-inch screen that dominated the room like a huge, hungry mouth waiting to devour her soul. It was a long job; the surface of the screen seemed designed to shrug off paint, as if the manufacturers expected this kind of attack. Next she had torn the silicon heart from every one of her machines that possessed a voice: the empty fridge, the door's electronic lock, and the soft-spoken, obsequious alarm clock. Destroying the alarm clock had given her particular pleasure; it seemed to her as if it squealed as she pulled out its circuitry. Finally she had hammered the power sockets from the walls, pulling their cables out of the plaster, cutting them back to the mains and sealing the ends crudely with sleeves of sellotape. Her fury spent, she had collapsed upon her mattress, panting from the exertion. Outside she could hear rain, and the sea-noise of cars passing over water; inside, only the sound of her own rasping lungs. She felt exalted. She was free.

Still in a state of nervous euphoria, she had gone to Troy's. At first she had spoken haltingly, but gradually she had found herself gripped by an almost manic articulacy. Troy's only reaction to the stream of words was a kind of stunned stupor. In desperation, she had taken him back to her room, where he had looked at the electronic carrion with horror.

"Why?" he said emptily. "Why? The screen . . . the . . . everything. For God's sake Fran, they're worth . . . thousands." His lips remained open and moist; the lower one moving slightly. Greasy hair clung to the shape of his neck. Not for the first time, he reminded Fran of a beached cod. She wondered what she had ever seen in him.

"Troy," she replied, "it's the same formula every day". She pointed at her temple. "G.I.G.O.—Garbage in, Garbage out. Almost a hundred identical channels, and a thousand identical tanned faces in some kind of infinite loop. Look."

Fran picked up a freesheet from the floor. The cover was dominated by a colour photograph of the face of Charles Blade: a face that seemed to echo a hundred forgotten ancestors, a face that seemed simply too real.

"This man, Troy, does not exist. *Not even as an actor.* He is completely and utterly synthesised by computer—possibly the most sophisticated animated image mankind has produced. This face, Troy, is *tailored* for specific markets. It is pure product. Darkened for the Middle-East. Fattened for India. Eyes elongated for the Rim. His lips move according to the language required, perfectly sync'ed. Most of us know this, but for Christ's sake, Troy, this non-face is on the cover of the newspaper. Its glossy, scandal-ridden, non-life dominates public consciousness, swamps what's real in the world—if *anything* is any more. That is simply . . . sick." She sighed. The word seemed inadequate.

"Sick?" Troy said, "I don't understand you, Fran. People know that he's not real, that it's only a character. It's entertainment, Fran, of the best kind. Nothing else. And in any case, he might be modelled on a real actor. There was that item on the gossip-net only. . . ."

Fran grimaced. "Troy," she said, pointing at the flatscreen, "that monstrosity has filled my life, my head. From the moment I've woken up to the moment I finally manage sleep, every space has been filled, every thought has been inserted between my ears by some transnational satellite broadcast corporation. I'm fed up being a corpse, Troy. There must be something else."

"A corpse? Fran, what else can we do? It's. . . ." Troy's voice trailed off; he had always found it hard to maintain a long conversation and now his eyes darted furtively from side to side, as though he was trying to find some kind of image to act as a prop. He ended up looking vaguely ahead at a non-existent horizon. A few minutes later, he had left, still in an incredulous stupor. Fran knew that he would never contact her again; she also knew that she didn't care in the slightest.

After that, Fran started to explore the world that existed beyond the flatscreen. First, she bought books, mostly yellowing paperbacks since so few were printed these days. Gradually her poor reading improved, advancing until she reached the standard of a bright ten-year-old of the mid-century. She walked for long distances, avoiding those public places the video image had invaded. Then a germ of an idea appeared, and grew: she would transform her passive resistance into an active one, creating spaces in which other people would be left only with themselves. Three months after she had gutted her own room, Fran committed her first act of public vandalism.

Fran pushed the bowl away, grimacing. She hated breakfast and ate the fibrous wheat mush (free decryption keycard for channel Rocket-TOKYO with twelve packet pabels) only to stave off hunger pangs during the long wait until evening. She stood and put on her poncho (Korean Army Surplus), sliding her ancient wire-cutters into the garment's deepest pocket.

As she left the building, the auto-guard whispered in a voiceover Sino-American utterly inappropriate for one of London's oldest system-built slums: "Good Morning, Miss Levin, Have a Good Day." Fran did her best to ignore both the greeting and the odour of urine, and hurried down the walkway, past the graffito which proclaimed: HEAR NO EVIL, SEE NO EVIL. While she walked, the autoguard's camera swivelling to follow her, her mind wandered over past glories of destruction. They had been simple at first, cowardly even. She had smashed the public-service screens in lavatory cubicles with a small hammer, or stealthily poured tonic water into the back of video jukebox. As her conviction grew, so did her solitary courage. She had bought the wire-cutters, and then entered office buildings at random, searching for cables to sever neatly or resplice into unknown combinations. This was dangerous work; under the Perth Agreement, "maliciously impeding the free flow of commerical information" was a serious felony. However, she had one advantage—surprise; these days, data vandals tended to traverse the networks from a terminal, probing for gateways into forbidden territory and illegal access privileges. Such intruders were hunted down with automated ruthlessness, but physical attack on the Information Order was unexpected, and, for Fran, infinitely more enjoyable.

At the tube station Fran boarded an antiquated train that smelt of dust, wet clothing and cannabis. It started to rattle with English unconfidence towards the centre of the city. In the carriage a few flatscreens stepped through the usual advertisements and dire warnings about the consequences of travelling without the correct ticket or an internal passport. A group of small children played boisterously with a battered digital video camera. They ran up to her, weaving backwards and forwards with the camera, then played the tape back showing Fran the image in the tiny monitor. Fran smiled and found change in her pockets, wishing it was enough to buy them shoes. The train continued westwards, towards Heathrow.

The airport had always fascinated her. She had lived in West London as a small child, and had often stood outside on clear evenings to count the lights of the aircraft that were stacked in the familiar spiral. In a declining Britain, the stream of planes had been a reminder that she really did live, as the Federation was fond of saying in its European "awareness" campaigns, in an age of miracles. There were not as many aircraft now of course, the world's centre of gravity had shifted too much for that, but Heathrow still bustled, servicing the delta-winged aircraft that descended from near-orbit.

The Delta-Wing Terminal itself was an ugly building. It had been designed during the height of the absurd classical revival in the early nineties, then refurbished when chrome and steel and glass were again fashionable. The result was unintentionally and grossly hilarious, like the Parthenon turned motel.

Everywhere there was information. Departure details scrolled fluidly over gigantic billboards, to be replaced by an announcer's head swollen to giant proportions or an animation showing the current position of delta-wings over Europe. People stood at information points as route maps, price lists and hotel advertising unfolded on flatscreens. Some passengers sat holding portable screens as they might once have held newspapers. Elsewhere, Fran knew, there were families cramped into entertainment booths watching the latest offerings from the satellite *Venal 1*, while groups of businessmen held video conferences with others in Singapore, Perth or on the American West Coast.

Fran walked across the terminal's great atrium. Plaster figures of Greek gods looked down at her from behind the video billboards and chrome fittings. Her plan was straightforward, although it had taken weeks of research and gently probing conversations with airport staff. It rested on one simple fact: All the major display units in the building were driven via a single, and archaic, ring network. The fibre-optic cable that carried the information was usually carefully sealed from prying eyes and hands. A week ago, however, the line had been exposed carelessly during some small-scale building work. Just a few dozen centimetres were visible, but this was enough to enable Fran to halt the Babel of images around her.

She reached her destination. The area was sealed with tape strung between plastic bollards. Plaster dust smeared the floor. Feeling only the slightest prick of apprehension in her palms, Fran looked methodically about her. There were no guards in sight and nobody else seemed interested in a young woman who wore a blue poncho. Quickly Fran stepped over the yellow tape. She pulled the wire-cutters from her pocket. The mouth of the cutters opened, then closed.

Silence.

It was as if the air had been suddenly drained from the room to leave a vacuum; every conversation, every interaction had stopped as people stared upwards, watching the giant billboards fade to their grey, off-state. Fran jumped back over the tape, and started to walk briskly away. She heard a voice: "There, in the blue. . . ." Her pace quickened. When she had left the building, she would discard the poncho and then head back to the tube station. Nothing would then tie her to the crime.

She reached the entrance to the terminal, and had almost flattened her face against the door before she realised it had not opened.

"Open, damn you!" she said angrily.

"I am sorry," the door replied in a oily, synthetic voice, "I am not permitted to open. Normal services are regrettably suspended."

Beyond the glass, the nose lights of a RimFed delta-wing sank to the horizon.

"Please open, I have an extremely important appointment in central London. My flight was late arriving." Fran realised her attempt at persuasion was probably wasted, since the door was almost certainly too stupid to understand anything except short, simple imperatives:

"I apologise for any inconvenience," the door continued, "but a criminal offence has occurred within the terminal building and it has been sealed as a consequence."

"Damn—" Fran began to curse before she felt a hand on her shoulder. She turned to see a heavy, male face that smelt unpleasantly of soap. It finished the sentence for her "—you".

Later, as a policewoman led her towards the cell, Fran felt an intense irritation. Not only had she been trapped by an automated door unit, but the police had treated her with an almost affectionate contempt. "No prison sentence for you," she had been told after giving her story, "probably a soft couch and an employment therapy scheme." She gnawed her lip angrily. Surely, her crimes were more significant than the police reaction suggested.

"Here," said the policewoman. "Your home until someone shows an interest in you." The cell was whitewashed emptiness except for the familiar grey rectangle on the wall.

"That," said Fran. "Take it out."

"Out? It is there for your benefit. A rare attempt by this state to be humane." The policewoman elongated the last word for sarcastic effect.

"I have no intention of using the screen. Please remove it."

"Well," said the policewoman, "if you want, it stays silent." She smiled with mock pleasantness. "Happy viewing." She slammed the solid and decidedly unautomated door to terminate the conversation.

Fran lay on the bunk bed and stared at the fluorescent strip above her. A swarm of tiny flies flew in circles at one end of the tube. As minutes turned to hours, Fran's ears filled with imaginary noise and she started to fidget and stretch with boredom. Eventually, she could stand no more and stood to turn on the screen with a hesitant stroke of the fingers. (She felt too embarrassed to use a vocal command in case the cell was monitored.) She changed channels a dozen times at random, stepping through derivative soaps and talk shows before stopping at the tanned face of Charles Blade. Sighing, she went back to the bed and tried unsuccessfully to ignore the screen. After a few minutes, she began to follow the story.

METEORS   Stephen Richard

The deceleration was going very well: all systems showed optimal on the auxiliary command screens. When we were orbiting New World in eighteen months' time, preparing for colonisation, the administrative burden of captaincy would be heavier; but I was ready for that, I knew what was expected of me. There was nothing to worry about.

Except this: what if the probes had got it wrong? New World might be uninhabitable, the atmosphere poisonous, the temperature too high or too low. We would be stuck here, in this hollow asteroid we called a ship, with nowhere to go but back to Earth, more than a century away. There was no reason to doubt the probes' accuracy, but I knew my fears wouldn't die until the Science section had provided confirmation; they were making observations daily, though they insisted that we were still too far away to obtain significant results.

Now the Head of Science had called me to say that he already had news, and I had asked him to come up to my office. While he was on his way I composed myself: if I wanted to maintain order among the crew, then I had to conceal my emotions, no matter what he told me.

As he came in I smiled. "Well, Neil, what have you got for me?" He was agitated; I braced myself. "What is it, Neil?"

"There are aliens on the planet," he said.

What? "Could you repeat that?"

"New World's inhabited. There are aliens on it."

I was bewildered, but I kept calm. "Are you quite sure about this?"

He explained why he was sure. They had picked up radio telemetry, and although they couldn't decipher it, its nature and origin were unambiguous. There was advanced intelligent life on New World.

"Thank you, Neil, thank you," I said when he had finished. "If you could continue to collect data, it would be very helpful." He left, disappointed: he wanted me to react, to tell him whether his news was good or bad. But I couldn't, because I didn't know. *Oh dear*, I thought, *oh dear*. None of my colleagues would be able to help; we would have to ask the Earthmen.

Our ship, the *Columbus*, had left the Earth one hundred and fifteen years before, bound for a new, inhabitable planet discovered after centuries of unmanned exploration. Eight hundred people had found Earth so unbearable that they were prepared to spend their lives within an asteroid scarcely four miles across in the hope of starting something better on another world.

In fact their confinement had withered and killed them. Life-prolonging treatments should have kept the majority of them fit enough to see the New World colony established; but now only twenty remained alive. To us, born during the flight, these were the "Earthmen". They rarely communicated with us; almost never showed themselves.

The youngest survivor, and spokesman for them all when they wished to speak, was my paternal grandmother, now one hundred and forty years old. The awe in which she was held had not hindered my election to the captaincy, but at no time in my adult life had I spoken to her, and even with my father as moral support it took me a week to muster the courage to see her: she seemed to loathe everyone aboard except her fellow Earthmen, but she hated her family most of all.

"Well, what is it?" she snarled as we edged into her office.

"Hello, mother, are you well?" my father croaked.

"Listen, I know you wouldn't be here if it wasn't absolutely necessary, so just tell me what the hell you want and get it over with."

The power of her contempt struck my father dumb, so she turned her spiteful attention on me. "Well, captain?"

Someone spoke in a thin, high voice: me. "It's aliens, grandmother. There are aliens on the planet!"

She looked at me uncertainly.

"It's true, we picked up their telemetry," I said. "There's no doubt."

She believed me. She slumped back in her chair; her face was grey. *Oh my God*, I thought, *we've killed her. Who'll we tell now?*

"Aliens," she murmured. Tears trickled down her wrinkled cheeks; her hands clenched in fists before her. "Thank God," she said, louder, "thank God I've lived to see this day."

Now I knew: aliens were good.

The discovery threw the *Columbus*'s deceleration routine into confusion. Naturally, our plans had been directed towards colonising a planet without intelligent life: shipboard observations to find suitable sites, launch of unmanned probes, stocking the first manned descent vehicles. Now these activities had to be suspended; and the Command committee's attempts to implement appropriate alternatives were frustrated by the interference of the Earthmen.

The prospect of a confrontation with aliens had for some reason galvanised them: they became far better disposed towards their descendants, and quickly began to usurp command. They persistently diverted human and computer resources into the problem of making and maintaining contact with the aliens, and initiated scanning of the planet for evidence of population centres. The crew were dazzled by their energy and their certainty, and obeyed them enthusiastically.

Meanwhile I had growing doubts about the wisdom of the Earthmen's schemes. Regular meetings with them showed me that they were by no means the demi-gods we had made of them; instead they seemed decrepit, irrational. Soon after that first encounter I had ceased to put faith in their judgement, so it was deeply worrying to see them assume power as we approached the unknown threat on New World.

What was so good about aliens? The closer we got to them, the more dangerous they seemed. Yet the Earthmen had decided to launch a probe as soon as possible, to land near the one populated area that had been detected, just to let them know we were here.

All very fine, I thought, but what if self-defence was their first priority? What good would finding them be if they annihilated us? I tried to make my grandmother see sense.

"This could be disastrous for us, grandmother. We could be killed, by missiles, or disease, or anything."

She looked at me gleefully. "Yes, boy, yes, you're right."

"Well then, shouldn't we be more cautious?"

"Why? What choice do we have?"

Of course we had no choice; but why did that please her, when anyone sane would be sick with apprehension? I tried another line of attack.

"What are we going to do, even if the aliens don't destroy us? It isn't what we came for, is it? Didn't we come for a completely fresh start, to colonise a new planet? What—"

"Who the hell cares about that?" she cried. "Jesus Christ, boy, we've found more than we came for, more than a new world. It's better than our dreams! Can't you understand?"

I shook my head. She thought for a moment, then went on, more quietly. "Listen, what do you think Earth was like?"

"What? Well, I've seen the pictures. . . ."

"Why do you think we left?"

I was staggered. No doubt we had all made guesses, but we certainly never discussed them on the *Columbus*. Earth was behind us, and that was that.

My grandmother continued. "I'll tell you, shall I? Living on Earth was just like living here. On the ship."

"No it wasn't. You lived on the surface. You—"

"Don't be a fool. Of course we lived on the surface, and there were millions of people, but life was the same. You know what it's like here, every damn thing controlled, no change, no real life. I'm telling you Earth was the same! Nothing happened, there was nothing to do. Nothing worth doing. Nothing worth dying for. See?"

"No."

She thumped her desk with both hands, and started shouting again. "We took off, we left them behind, left those bastards to rot their worthless lives away! We gambled everything, *everything*, and now we've won! You, you don't know what we've given you. Maybe you'll die. Doesn't everyone die? But it's us: *we* gave you the chance to die this way, not like all those others." She looked at me intently, wanting me to join her in the great adventure. I couldn't stay.

That's why they hated us. We were too much like those others, the ones they had run from: brought up in a closed environment, all our basic needs provided for, we were nevertheless happy.

In the following months I had plenty of time to think about the danger we were facing: I was captain in name only; the Earthmen had taken my ship. I spent hours in my cabin, lying on my bed, imagining the end. If we were holed, most of us would asphyxiate, and die watching others do the same. All in all, I hoped they would blow us up completely.

The crew, meanwhile, were optimistic and excited, waiting for the probe to reach New World. But when the predicted arrival date came, and passed without incident, their mood began to change. Three weeks went by in which, with some satisfaction, I watched the euphoria drain away.

At last contact was made. It was ship's night; the intercom buzzer woke me.

"Captain, captain, they're talking to us!"

I ran through the ship, dressing. As I entered Communications, anxious faces looked round, and soon all eyes were on me. I was their leader again; but why? The radio bleeped.

"Roger, *Columbus*, we copy that ETA. Orbital transport should be no problem." Another bleep. I saw the Head of Science.

"Neil, who's that?"

"It's them."

"But it's English, Neil. How can they do that?" He nodded to the radio operator, and she spoke.

"Thanks, New World. The captain is here now. Could you repeat what you told us before?" What powers did these creatures have?

"Roger, *Columbus*. The fact is, sir, we're from Earth, too. You see, about forty years after *Columbus* left we developed faster-than-light transportation. There's been a colony here for half a century . . . Jesus, when your little message arrived, we thought our time had come. Scared us shitless till we worked out who you were. Welcome back, guys."

Heads were still turned in my direction as the transmission ended, but now they were looking behind me. I glanced over my shoulder. Oh well, I thought, at least I don't have to tell her.

The crew were fine once I had reassured them. We had been content aboard the *Columbus*, we were among friends now, there was nothing to regret. But the old people hid themselves while the rest of us travelled down to our new home and visitors came up to examine their new satellite. Finally I had to ask them what they wanted to do.

My grandmother still spoke for them. She seemed in good spirits, considering.

"Listen, grandmother," I told her, "we're going on to minimum power consumption soon, that is, unless. . . ."

She sat gazing at the floor. "We're taking the ship," she said.

"Where to?"

"Where? Nowhere. Away from here."

"Yes. All right. Do you want someone to program a course?"

"No, thank you. We can still manage."

"Right. Right. Well. . . ."

"Goodbye."

"OK. Goodbye." At the door, to my own surprise, I turned to her once more. "Grandmother, I'm sorry. I wish it had been aliens."

"Fuck you."

On the last shuttle flight down, I thought of the *Columbus* cruising through space, the life within fading away, and I knew that the bitter old woman had been lying. She would make a final gesture; she would find some way of taking revenge for her defeat. But she had nothing except the ship. I warned the New World authorities.

The Earthmen didn't try a deceptive trajectory, but steered a course straight for the planet, knowing that the impact of an asteroid the size of the *Columbus* would obliterate the colony.

As it was, only fragments of the *Columbus* reached the atmosphere. That night we saw meteors for the first time.

BUNDLES OF JOY   Jenny Ordish

"What are you in for, Joy?" asked the aggressive blonde propped pinkly in the next bed.

"Some kind of a cyst," said Joy.

"Just as well you're not in for an abortion. I nearly did for a girl who was in for abortion last week. Makes me sick. I really gave her what for. They had to move her. They can't move me, you see." The young woman's furious fingers resumed the knitting of a tiny garment.

"Oh? Why can't they—I mean, what are you in for, Linda?"

Linda looked delighted. "Fertility problems. Simply can't conceive. We've tried the lot. The bloody lot. They think they might've got me on the go at last, though. I'm not allowed to move a muscle." Her knuckles whitened again on her knitting-needles. "When I see people like that little bitch last week trying to get rid of what I'd give my right arm for, I'd like to kill them. They want to hang 'em, that's what. I'd do it myself."

"That's a bit extreme, isn't it, Linda? I'm sure nobody has an abortion for fun."

"Don't give me that crap. It's easy enough to avoid getting pregnant if you want to. They're just too lazy or too stupid." The tiny garment jerked into life once more.

Joy felt wretched. It was stupid to be in bed, dressed in a nightgown, when she felt quite well. Would the removal of an ovary mean that she too would have problems having babies? Would it make her unfeminine? Could it be cancer? What did her cyst look like? What had caused it? She took out the scented notepaper her mother had bought specially for her to bring to St Margaret's Hospital for Women and wrote down the questions she would ask the doctor before the operation next day.

A nurse's voice interrupted her. "Doctor will see you now, Miss Evans. Pop on your dressing-gown and slippers and follow me."

Joy looked up. She gasped. The nurse was inspecting the chart at the end of Joy's bed. She was slight, dark and freckled with blue eyes and a pointed chin, "Bowels fine, I see," she said. She looked up. "What's the matter, dear? You look as if you've seen a ghost."

"It's just that—well, we look so alike."

The nurse looked at Joy properly for the first time. "Why, so we do! What a funny thing! Perhaps I should call you twinny—except I must be years older. Come along now, mustn't keep Doctor waiting."

Joy followed the nurse down the warm, green corridor, past a tea-trolley being pushed by a massive black woman with a halo of curls, a trolley of instruments, a trolley bearing an unconscious female form with tubes emerging from under a sheet. Awful the way slippers made you shuffle like an invalid even before you were one.

Dr Harper, tall and white-haired, washed her hands at the small basin as Joy put her dressing-gown back on and sat down.

The doctor put on her gold-rimmed glasses and scanned Joy's notes. "I see you were born here at St Margaret's. What a coincidence!"

"Not really, doctor. My mother urged me to come here for my operation. She said they worked miracles for her. My parents thought they'd never manage to have a baby, and then I made my entrance—and all thanks to St Margaret's." Joy laughed nervously. "That's why they called me Joy."

"Well, Joy, you certainly have a cyst there. About the size of a grapefruit, I'd say. It should come out. Don't worry. It's a commonplace problem and quite straightforward. Now, I'm sure there must be some questions you'd like to ask me."

Joy took the crumpled notes out of her pocket and began going through her questions.

"No, you needn't worry about fertility. We have two ovaries which work quite independently. Each of them contains tens of thousands of potential eggs—far more than you could ever bring to fruition in several lifetimes. Nature is generous—profligate, you might say, isn't she? So losing one ovary simply means that the other one will take over full-time. Your system will work exactly as before and you can have babies just like anyone else."

"Dr Harper, I know this sounds an odd question, but . . . could I possibly *see* my ovary after it's been removed? I'd be terribly interested."

"Oh, no, we can't allow that. It wouldn't look very nice, you know. You are a funny girl!"

"You see, I want to become a doctor myself. I'm actually waiting for my results now. I'm hoping to get into St Eustace's."

"Good for you. I wish you well." Dr Harper smiled. "Well, you'll see plenty of bits of bodies when you're a student, don't worry about that!"

"Yes, that's true. But this bit's mine. I really would like to see it. Why can't I? What happens to—to the bits?"

"It has to go to Pathology for examination, of course. Just to check if there's anything malignant, and so on. You'll be told the result, naturally. I'm sure there's nothing to worry about in someone as young as you. And then, of course, there's the research element. . . ."

"Research element?"

"You must have heard of the research into infertility that's going on these days—the so-called test-tube babies? Perhaps you might be interested in that line yourself later on?"

"Yes, perhaps."

Dr Harper warmed to her subject. "It's remarkable, but if ova can be induced to divide of their own accord, we can eliminate the problem of sperm, you see." She sounded triumphant.

"Wouldn't that mean that all the babies would be female?"

"True, they would. Identical female twins, as it were. But then, if we didn't need sperm, we wouldn't need males, would we?"

"What a dreary thought," said Joy.

The doctor was silent for a moment. She tapped Joy's notes into a neat stack. "Some women's bodies apparently reject sperm as alien material and so are unable to conceive. If you could induce their eggs to divide independently, they would have daughters without fertilisation. Parthenogenesis—a virgin birth, as it were."

Dr Harper paused again and looked at Joy. "Then there's the implantation of a developing egg—surrogacy. One day we might even go as far as providing full-term babies for adoption. There's a real shortage of those in the West now that abortion is so readily available to dispose of mistakes. Anyway, I don't suppose you want to hear me rambling on about that. Don't you worry." Dr Harper stood up briskly. "Now, I suggest you try and get plenty of rest before your op tomorrow. The fitter you are beforehand, the sooner you'll be on the mend. I'll come and see you as soon as you come round." She smiled again and held open the door.

Joy felt vaguely disturbed. Frowning, she slipper-shuffled back to the ward, past trolleys of laundry and bed-pans, a bench full of waiting relations. They looked uncomfortable and out of place in their bulky street clothes where everyone else was in uniforms or nightgowns.

"Miss Evans! Miss Evans!" Someone was holding Joy by the big toe. "Joy! Hey, twinny!" A white-capped face misted in and out of Joy's vision. "Joy, it's all over. Wake up now!"

"Am I all right?" Joy was aware of a vast stiffness in her legs and heaviness in her abdomen. Her mouth felt vile, like the world's worst hangover. Her chest hurt. Her voice was just breath. "Where's my ovary? What was wrong with it?" A tube rattled against something metallic as she raised her left arm.

"You're fine. You had a dermoid cyst. Quite a biggy. Nothing to worry about. Now, I'm going to give you a pain-killing injection and then you'll sleep for a while. OK? Can you roll over a little? Here, I'll help you."

"I want to see my cyst." Speaking took Joy as much effort as climbing a steep hill.

"Don't be silly. You don't want to see that nasty old thing. Make you feel quite queasy. Come along now, over on your side. There we go!"

It was hard to keep track of time. Joy had a recurring hallucination—endless rows of Mick Jaggers riding past her astride enormous carrots on a chromium-plated, gridded conveyor-belt. It wouldn't stop. She hated Mick Jagger at the best of times. The nurses laughed and said hallucinations were quite usual and that some people had a bad reaction to the anaesthetic.

The second night—or was it the third?—she woke feeling normal. The clock above the door showed five past midnight. The ward was silent, except for one woman's rhythmic snoring down at the end. Linda, next to her, was out for the count. A pink teddy-bear, clutched in one hand, rose and fell on her chest. A pale light filtered in through the open door.

"I'm going to find out."

Joy eased herself out of bed. She put on dressing-gown and slippers. Bending was beastly. No. Slippers made too much noise. She slid them off again without bending. The floor was warm from the central heating, anyway. She turned and moved in slow motion to the door and across the deserted, neon-green corridor to the lavatories. No locks on the doors. *In case someone passes out, I suppose. Don't flush, it'll make a noise. Damn them! I've got a right to know.*

Joy steadied herself on the door-frame and looked both ways into the corridor. No-one. Just open doors leading into dark, silent wards. Lights on in the sluice-room. Further down, a pile of sheets outside a door marked "Laundry". Beyond that, glass doors leading to the stairs. Holding her abdomen, Joy walked silently towards the doors. Passing the open sluice-room, she saw two Filipino nurses fooling around with bedpans. One put a pan on her head. The other shrieked with laughter and said something in high-pitched Spanish.

Joy quickened her pace. *Oh, God, they're coming out here.* She backed into the next doorway—the laundry-room, and pushed the door to behind her. Dark and hot. She gasped. Her heart hammered. She felt dizzy. She leaned back against the wall, and vanished.

Joy got up from a pile of dirty towels. She was in a large silent washeteria, the lower end of a laundry-chute behind her in the wall. With distaste, she inspected her still-bandaged stomach. It looked the same as before.

Pipes and conduits ran along the vented ceiling of the windowless corridor outside. Joy followed them. She passed several locked doors and rounded the corner. Light showed through the doors which now came into view. "Refrigeration I" said the first. It was locked. Through the reinforced glass door Joy saw rows of white cabinets with labels she could not read. "Refrigeration II" said a second, identical room. Joy continued her painful progress. Two more locked doors. Then one, unmarked, which opened when she tried it.

Inside was a row of surgical washbasins and sterilising units and several cupboards and lockers. A notice over a further door said "Positively no admittance without sterilised clothing. Please lock the door behind you." A key was in the door. It creaked open and sighed shut behind Joy.

The room before her was dim, like a large darkroom. The red light took the colour out of everything, giving it a deadly pallor. There were rows of white benches with arrays of glass, rubber and plastic apparatus. They reminded Joy of the surgical drip she had had in her arm when she first came round. Each set of apparatus bore a label with a series of numbers and letters. The glass jars contained a sticky-looking liquid. Joy moved down the rows.

She rested. The dimness and the humming in the room were making her dizzy again. She saw another glass door ahead, and through it more rows of apparatus. The door closed behind her with a soft thud. This time, each jar contained a small dot of pale substance floating in the viscous liquid, like a tiny, tinned button-mushroom.

Can't stop now, thought Joy. The button-mushrooms grew larger from bench to bench, until Joy came eye to eye with the recognisably human, curled form of an embryo—rows of curled, human embryos, floating in their jars of sticky liquid, their heads resting on their folded hands, in the dusky, humming room. Some of them made tiny, swimming movements as they floated. One opened its eyes.

I must get out. Whoever left the key in the door must be in here somewhere. What shall I do? Joy looked round her. She heard a gentle thud somewhere in the gloom. She moved to the wall. There was a row of shelves with things in glass bottles. A piece of paper had been blue-tacked to the shelf. Someone had scribbled something on it. Joy peered. "Harper's Horrors", it read. *Oh, my God.* Next to it, another door. Joy went through.

She was in a bright, silent room full of incubators. Each contained a naked, sleeping, female baby. The babies moved gently. Some smiled. *They're all alike!* Joy read the label fixed to the first incubator in the first row. CAUCASIAN TYPE III. 16/1/80. STM 309. The baby inside wore a matching ankle-band. Joy walked along a few rows. HISPANIC TYPE I. 30/9/78. STM 160. The label was beginning to peel off. Joy bent to smoothe it back into place. "Mustn't lose your name, poor little thing," she murmured.

A hand thumped on to her shoulder. She fell against the incubator. She was held from behind by both arms. A female voice said, "Have you got her?" Someone rolled up the sleeve of her dressing-gown. She lost consciousness.

"My doctor! I want to see my doctor!" Joy's head was splitting. "Where am I? Where's Linda?"

She wasn't in the ward any more. She was in bed in a small, white room, alone. She heaved herself up against the headboard. "Nurse!" She felt above her head. Found a bell-push. Pressed.

A red-haired nurse came in. "Och! So you're awake now, are you? You're a bad lassie and that's a fact."

"Nurse, I want to see my doctor at once. Please."

"Doctor's not on duty at present. I'll see if she can see you later. You've really upset her, you know."

"Not her, not Dr Harper, my own doctor. Why have they moved me?"

"Why? You were ranting on so, about the most appalling things. You've been hallucinating again. Some people do after the anaesthetic, you know. Remember how you kept on about Mick Jagger? You were upsetting poor wee Linda and all the others." The nurse folded her arms. "You know she's supposed to keep calm or she'll lose her wee baby. It was very selfish of you. Doctor said you were to be moved."

"I'm sorry. I'm so confused. I want to see my mother. Could you get her to come? Is she my mother? Have I got a father? I don't know who I am." Joy felt a lump forming in her throat. "Where's that nurse who looks just like me?"

Nurse McGregor's voice became kinder. "I don't know who you mean, you poor wee girlie. You're in a real state, aren't you? Whatever were you thinking of, wandering round like that in the middle of the night? You could have killed yourself."

"What's been happening to me?"

"You must've fallen down the stairs. Nurse Delgado found you in Maternity. You'd bumped your head and pulled out some of your stitches. Doctor was furious. You've had to be taken back to theatre and your tummy re-stitched, I'm afraid."

"But Nurse—that apparatus—those babies! They were all alike. All alike. And all girls."

"Nonsense! Don't start all that again, now. People who haven't had babies always think babies look all alike. Just you wait until you've had your own. Then you'll know the difference." Nurse McGregor picked up Joy's slippers. "Come along, now, you're all in a sweat. Shall I help you along to the bathroom? Pop your slippers on, there's a good lassie. You can freshen up and you'll feel better. Then I'll see if I can get your mother to come. You're over it all now."

The nurse helped her into her dressing-gown and slippers, gave Joy her sponge-bag and towel and, holding her round the waist, walked her to one of the bathrooms down the corridor. "There. Now, do you want me to help you, or can you manage on your own?"

"I can manage, thank you." Joy pushed the door to. She sat on the bathroom stool. She wanted to cry but her stitches made it too painful. She sobbed in her mind.

I must be going mad. It all seemed so real. Is this what it's like to be mad—when unreal things seem real? I can't tell the difference any more.

She got up and ran some water into the basin. She slipped off her dressing-gown and nightdress. Something clicked. Joy turned and looked down. Something small, shiny and white was stuck to her dressing-gown. It had clicked on the tiles as the gown fell to the floor. Nakedly, painfully, Joy crouched, picked it up. It was a label. She turned it over. It read HISPANIC TYPE I. 30/9/78. STM 160.

"Oh, my daughters," cried Joy. "My little girls. My ten thousand daughters, what will become of you?"

SKIOPHANES' PROOF   Luke Andreski

Though it was not his final belief Henri Poincaré, a mathematician in the province then known as France, once said that chance is only the measure of our ignorance. And it is both logical and obvious that this is so. If everything were known there would be no chance: each moment would be predictable, the most infinitesimal cause linked irrevocably to its effect.

Therefore it would be quite useless to play a game of chance with an all-knowing mind; it would not need to guess; it would know beforehand each result. A man, in such a contest, could only draw or lose. A man, knowing the odds, would not, if he were logical, enter such a contest.

And so we can assume that Samuel Kher is not a logical man, for this morning I saw him in Plaka Square, playing dice with a terminal of PreComp, the infallible predictive computer. A small, rectangular board rested on the bench between them, and, as I paused to watch, the terminal impassively cast the dice upon it. The five transparent cubes rolled to a stop showing two aces, a king, two nines. The terminal picked up the two aces and cast them a second time: two kings.

"Full house," murmured Kher.

Quickly he gathered up the dice-cup and dice and brought them together in his thick, powerful hands. A thin, dry rattle trickled across the square. Sunlight, rebounding from the dusty pavestones, glittered in his eyes. He cast the dice down on to the board. They rolled for a moment, then jerked, one by one, like clockwork, to a halt. Three nines, a queen, an ace. He threw the queen and ace again: a queen, a ten. Again: a king, an ace. The terminal—an android with a thin, brooding face—quickly gathered them up. Unreasonably, I was embarrassed to see Kher playing such a hopeless game. Rather than witness a fresh disappointment, and before he could recognise me, I hurried on across the square.

When he was eighteen, Kher came to the Athens college of

Mathematics and Philosophy from Piraeus. He was, as one might have expected, naive and idealistic, his outlook dominated by the philosophy of an ultimate truth. After coming from an industrial harbour town, confined by the narrow practicality of its schools, he suddenly found himself surrounded by people whose interests were enthusiastic and diverse. In every class and session, in every restaurant and cafe, he met exciting, confident strangers: men and women whose opinions were as idiosyncratic and independent as themselves. There were those who believed in the unity of God, and others who sacrificed to the pantheon. Some convinced him of the necessity of Nature, others pontificated to him the infinite potential of Man. But whatever they believed, they lived in dingy tenements throughout the city, and seldom slept for weeks on end but talked each night till dawn.

Immediately, Kher found himself seduced into their paradoxical worlds. At first he especially loved the sunny afternoons when they would sit on the Acropolis, thinking or quietly talking, looking out over Athens at the roofscape and streets; and the evenings spent in crowded bed-sits, discussing, arguing: emphatic, rhetorical and loud.

In the summer—like children—they would sleep on the flat roofs of their apartment blocks, gazing at meteors until the sandman closed their eyes: or creep at dusk into the Acropolis— and wait for the solstice moon to pierce them with that ecstatic feeling of being a bridge between the earth and the stars; between man and alien: a synapse, hungry and unfulfilled, between the past and the future. Standing there, beneath the gaze of distant stars and the ancient statues' eyes, they felt that they could reach out and touch Socrates, waiting beside them, his head bowed and thoughtful in the darkness; or clasp the hand of potential man, Man the stranger, yet unborn.

Soon, however, as one, then two years passed, Kher's naïveté and his old ideals vanished, leaving in their place, I recall him saying, only vulnerability. He no longer suddenly appeared at his friends' apartments, radiant with some new discovery or belief. He no longer imagined he loved his passionate friends so much as half-despised them, for taking life so lightly. As his knowledge grew, the seeds of a particular despair were sown in his mind; a slow gloom began to cloud his gaze. He discovered that whatever he did—and whichever way he turned—his smallest success would be anticipated. There was no knowledge that he could ever find which hadn't already been found; no secret not already revealed. Man, at every step, had long since been foreshadowed.

By the oracle, a computer.

What is there to know of this world?

Some claim our lives upon it are merely a drama, enacted before a motionless God.

It is said that people are not humans but robots, marching back and forth in the way that they have always marched, concerned only with the motives programmed into them long ago by PreComp.

I know—I was once informed of this—that PreComp is just the mask of NatComp, for whom all time is known and still, no longer time at all.

I know that such a mind could not exist. Isn't time, after all, a fundamental prerequisite of consciousness?

If I know everything—if time were still—what would *I* be?

At one time Kher fell under the influence of a man known in Athens as Gerhundy, though elsewhere variously as Gerhardty, Geründ, Gowering. I shall not describe his mystical philosophy: it has so recently been publicised by his return from eighteen months of meditation in the Óthris hills. But this was only a temporary interest, and soon Kher was drawn back to our college by his natural craving for clarity and precision. Mathematics is considered the greatest of all the intellectual disciplines; it is certainly the greatest challenge remaining for a growing mind in the safe and comfortable world of modern Greece; and young men must search out the greatest challenge in their environment or stagnate. Kher—we imagined—wasn't one to weaken, or to fade to insignificance. In the years that I taught him I watched him grow stronger, more diverse, and more intense. I watched him grow from boy to man.

It is a pity that in the end this great potential was to be wasted.

In modern Greece there is no investigative, empirical science, nor has anyone ever discovered an aspect of the physical world which

PreComp has not already known. Paradoxically, the discipline for which we are most renowned is the one which has shown the least result: the theoretical science for the justification of the existence and efficiency of PreComp: the science of futurology.

The speculations of futurology depend on this basic assumption: that the future is known: that if it were not prohibited, any person could corner a terminal of PreComp and discover exactly what he would be doing the following day.

It is futurology's self-assumed task to explain how such a situation can be possible.

In his fifth year, as his friends all know, Kher became obsessive. Until then his interests had seemed diverse and balanced, ranging from the crafts to the sciences, from art to philosophy; but as '86 progressed this ceased to be the case. Increasingly Kher became infected with monomania. He began to ramble in conversation, and to indulge in monologue. He would demand attentiveness, become angry at interruption—and yet the subject of his conversations grew steadily more monotonous and trivial. For five weeks he concentrated on the day he had learned how to swim. For two months he talked of nothing but his father's unrealised ambitions.

And, as might be imagined, the friends that he no longer loved, no longer so loved him. They grew tired of his obsessions, and bored.

And, I must admit, so did we all.

Flies dance on the flaming heads of thistles in Plaka Square.

Amongst the litter, swept against the walls of the small gardens of the square, red ants haul fragments of leaf or newspaper or rag towards invisible destinations. Above them, drunken in their care, strut brigadier pigeons, importantly indifferent, beadily insane. Life seems not to notice the dice-players. Against the rasping of insect wings—against the patter of clerical feet—the rattle of dice is hardly discernible.

It could never distract the clerks, gliding, at odd angles to the vertical, across the square.

Nor could it divert the traffic: the horse-drawn carts, the tricycles and bicycles which clatter and whirr in the surrounding streets.

It is not sensed, nor reacted to, nor felt; it is simply there and then not: and the dice-cup is up-turned and seems stilled in mid-air; and the dice, already fallen, seem to have always been still.

In hindsight it is of course clear that Kher's obsessions were merely a defence mechanism. By permitting a stepping-down of consciousness, by becoming obsessed with the innocuous, he was diverting from himself an obsession of far more destructive consequence. Long ago the seeds of this obsession were embedded in his mind; insidiously they would germinate and grow.

It was only when it was too late, when Kher gave up his studies and retreated to a hermit's existence in his tiny rented accommodation, that I recognised his behaviour for the diversion it had been. He was indeed obsessed, but with nothing so insignificant as he had tried to believe. He was obsessed, instead, with a sense of futility—with debilitating feelings of automation—with the incompatibility of PreComp and the freedom of man.

There is a world where neither choice nor chance occurrence have ever been known. Where free-will is an illusion, and each life is determined—mapped out ahead of time. Its name is Dachau 7, and it lies in the 13th arm of Nebula Four.

Gerhundy returned from the hills of central Greece, his beard wild, his hair long, wearing only a thin, torn robe which had once been white.

He said he had left Athens, to live in miserable caves with families of snakes, because he had become too certain. He had gone away to drive out his comfortable rationalisations.

"I wanted to be certain of only one thing," he said. "That there can be no certainty . . . I had to remind myself that there is absolutely no basis for faith."

There could be, he claimed, no proof of his beliefs, nor had there ever been a revelation. He had merely chosen, years ago, to believe. "For if you take scientific logic to its conclusion, nothing is provable, certainty is impossible—so what other course is there?"

Now he believed what he had decided to believe. "It doesn't matter what you decide upon," he said. "What does matter is believing the obviously unprovable or the inexplicable . . . and so freeing yourself from vanity."

We are told that our passions mould our beliefs; the converse, I am sure, must also be true.

Fundamentally Kher believed that everyone is programmed and without choice. He betrayed this belief by his passion for refuting it; he acquired it in his second year in Athens, while attending my lectures on the theory of probability. Under its influence his passions were reduced to a single impoverished form: despair.

Therefore I admit my responsibility in the destruction of his morale. A man who truly feels his philosophy may be destroyed by it, and the philosophy I was teaching at that time could indeed be considered negative and life-denying. I taught it detachedly to children such as Kher, and shall always be guilty for this.

But I do not admit responsibility for the way Kher has persuaded himself to continue living. The rigmarole he now enacts is one of my business. The philosophy he has assumed I have no faith in. I even offered him a new one, far more consistent and precise, and which I myself have come to accept.

It came about in this way: realising my part in Kher's downfall, and recognising also its roots in the incompatibility of his stated philosophy and reality, I decided to manufacture for him a new synthesis: one incorporating all his professed beliefs, allowing for the existence of PreComp, and yet remaining coherent and believable.

I decided to prove to Kher, logically, clearly, indubitably, that chance might after all exist.

It has recently been suggested that entropy is the result of chance. That, assuming its existence, the cumulative effect of chance would be randomising of form, the equalisation of energy, the eventual creation of a void.

This I question.

Admittedly, entropy leads to the equal distribution of energy. But is chance necessarily involved? Isn't entropy, rather, a fundamental attribute of all matter-energy processes, internal to the structure of those processes; simply, the unwinding of a clock which must unwind?

And if this were so, wouldn't chance, in disrupting this process, be more probably its reverse?

Wouldn't its cumulative effect, then, lead to the creation of situations of increasing unlikelihood? Lead, in fact, to the creation of absolutely unbalanced and complex forms—to man, say, or God?

Gerhundy walked slowly through the streets of Athens. His beard and hair were freshly trimmed; his robe was newly darned. As he walked, pausing now and then to lean on his staff, he looked about him intently. He loved to gaze about him at the people of Athens. They were so often smiling, so often serious, so sincere or sad. He liked to listen to the smalltalk of men, or of women, intent on themselves. He loved the people of Athens—loved how they believed all sorts of rubbish without even trying . . . He should have been happy here, amidst such uncourted success. He *would* have been happy—were it not for his one-time disciple, Samuel Kher.

Kher had reached an absurd conclusion. Chance, he claimed, is inherent in the structure of the universe. Therefore even the most knowledgeable mind must one day be limited by this. Therefore, if he challenged PreComp to a sufficient number of games of chance, the computer must eventually lose.

And so he had taken to playing pig, and poker-dice, and classic barbudi, with terminal 5 in Plaka Square. Each day he was seen there, crouched gloomily over the dice-board, shaking the dice-cup in sullen incantation, searching for proof, in a way controverting everything Gerhundy had ever taught.

He might as well have been saying, "Gerhundy is a fool—and I'll prove it."

He might as well have spat in the old man's eye.

I reached my theory late in '86. The weather in Greece was bad that winter; Athens was inundated with rain; even Kher and terminal 5 had hibernated indoors. It wasn't a time for insight or discovery, but it was then that the theory came to me. Essentially it was very simple: a reshuffling of old ideas to produce a new and obvious answer.

It goes something like this: there is a famous law from antiquity, known as the Law of Undecidability, which leads to the conclusion that the human mind, by use of its senses, can never be completely certain of what it has sensed. I was reminded of this law, quite by accident, while in conversation with a friend; but its significance struck me immediately.

"Chance," I later wrote, "is the measure of our ignorance.

"If we were not ignorant in any way chance would then be the measure of nothing—would not exist.

"Therefore uncertainty—our ignorance—is essential to the existence of chance, and if uncertainty exists then chance must exist, at least in relation to conscious perception.

"But the human mind can never achieve certainty.

"Therefore the potential for free-will is created by the limitations of our minds."

Under the title 'Skiophanes' Proof', PreComp was to release the details of this theory simultaneously with its first publication.

It was in the early spring of this year that I first took my proof to Kher. I found him in his bed-sit, gazing from the window to the street below. He was suffering from melancholy; his face was sad; he could hardly speak. Drawing a second chair up to the window, I told him quietly that I had come to an important conclusion. In a moment of insight my deterministic philosophy had been shattered.

"I have practically been forced," I said, "to believe in the existence of chance."

I told him how, several weeks before, as I sat in a cafe drinking wine, a theory justifying a belief in free-will had come to me. And it wasn't the wine: since then I had thought it over a hundred times.

Exhaustively I described my theory. When I had finished I sat back with a feeling of triumph.

Kher looked at me wordlessly for a moment. He seemed about to say something, then stopped. Then, abruptly, he asked, "But what about PreComp?"

"PreComp?"

"Yes, PreComp! You yourself said the existence of chance is disproven by the existence of PreComp. It still is! PreComp disproves chance! Your theory is no more realistic than mine!"

And with this poor Samuel Kher leapt up and ran from the room.

I have tried to convince Kher of my theory a dozen times since that afternoon. Often, I think, he does not listen to me: he mutters about PreComp and Skiophanes' Proof, or of dice and terminal 5, then turns his eyes gloomily to the window and sits without speaking, waiting for me to leave.

At first I do not. As if talking to a statue I try to persuade him that he is making unprovable assumptions. I tell him we know nothing of the nature of PreComp—how then can we be sure that it disproves chance?

And my theory, I say, is relevant only to perception. Not to some elusive material universe, but to our senses. Perhaps PreComp doesn't know the world by perception but by some other means. Perhaps it comprehends things in a way we cannot possibly understand.

But Kher just laughs, or shrugs his shoulders, or continues, without movement, to stare from the window.

Defeated, I finally leave.

Numerous speculations have been generated by my theory. I shall mention only one, the most absurd.

I have suggested that were chance to exist as an inherent principle in nature, its effect might be cumulative, and the universe might become randomly differentiated: the opposite effect, that is, from entropy.

Now chance is not inherent in nature but in consciousness. But, in nature, entropy must have its converse. Consciousness, it has been proposed, supplies this converse: creating chance reverses entropy.

And thus we have a new cosmology:

The reverse of entropy is the increasing complexity and variation of form. An example of this is evolution. Is this, then, a product of consciousness? And if this is so, did consciousness, out of emptiness, thus create all form? And did it then cast itself upon the universe, as life imbued with consciousness, to further increase complexity and variation of form?

And is this, then, God?

And are we, then, God in action?

I have to answer to this, half-joking, half-serious, "But how can *we* be God, when PreComp is?"

*

I saw Kher this morning in Plaka Square.

He was sitting on a bench with terminal 5: they were playing dice. I couldn't help but feel sad to see him there: his game so hopeless—his life going gradually to waste. I decided to visit him this afternoon: to attempt again to convince him of my proof.

He put the kettle on the stove when I arrived; when it had boiled we sat with a pot of tea on the cold wooden chairs by the window. We talked for a while about the weather, and about old aquaintances. Then I admitted why I had come. I told him he was behaving like a weakling.

"Even if you don't believe anything's worthwhile, you've got to pretend you do," I said. "Otherwise what else is there?"

"That's exactly what I'm doing," he said.

"Then you're doing it badly. You've got to pretend something that's got a chance of convincing you."

When he said nothing I asked him if he had thought any further about my proof.

Again he remained silent. Outside, the day was calm and bright; a seller of sesame buns was shouting, trudging along behind his cart.

"I don't like to see you wasting your life," I said.

"One day PreComp will lose."

"Why should it?" I cried. "PreComp's not a man: PreComp's dead. It probably doesn't even perceive!"

But Kher would say nothing else on the subject.

His life, he admitted, yes, it continued.

The summer was beautiful.

Then he left. He was already late for an appointment with terminal 5.

Old Gerhundy has long forgotten Kher's insensitive attack. He is cultivating another paranoia: his wife from the rather parochial town of Thebes has caught up with him at last. It is said she is a witch—and is going to drag him back to Thebes by his beard.

She needs help with the grandchildren.

And it is time he settled down.

Kher found terminal 5 waiting for him in Plaka Square. As he sat down it said, "You've come to play the classic game?"

"Barbudi?" said Kher. "Yes."

Taking from his pocket two precious ivory dice-cups, Kher pulled them apart and handed 5 the one containing the die. A dry, thin rattle trickled across the hot pavestones. A dove abruptly stopped its investigation of chewing gum and litter, cocked its head, then turned to strut away toward the shade of a tree. 5 turned his cup upside-down; the die dropped to the board with a hollow click, rolled twice, settled to show a three. The android looked up at Kher with what almost seemed a quizzical expression. "Perhaps I should warn you," it said. "Unlike that of all human minds my awareness of the universe is not based on the assimilation of sensory data.

"It is based on assumption.

"And though this really explains nothing, and for reasons I will not explain, the assumption is correct."

Kher said nothing. The die upon the board cast a fine shadow. Looking up, Kher found the day was hot and bright and clean.

The android, too, glanced up at the tranquil world of Plaka Square. Then it looked down, once more, waiting.

"The die is cast," it said.

But still Kher was silent. Almost desperately, he stared into the android's fathomless eyes. Perhaps in them, reflecting a metallic blue, he could perceive the assumption of a human freedom. Perhaps. Abruptly, inspired by hope, Kher stood up—and walked away from Plaka Square.

TIME TRAVEL FOR FUN AND PROFIT
Geoff Nicholson

If anyone ever offers you a two-year contract as a self-employed Time Traveller, Grade 3, Manual, tell them where they can stick it. You have to lease your craft from them; pay your own tax and

National Insurance; you don't see your family or your friends for ages—it stinks. I assume a monkey couldn't do the job because if it could you can be absolutely certain that they'd employ a monkey instead of me. I'm sure they could get a machine to do it, but a machine would be more expensive and harder to replace. So they get a man. They get me. No capital outlay, no expensive components that need servicing, no depreciation. No nothing.

You drive this naff little timecraft from eon to eon. I'll tell you how sophisticated this thing is—on a two year mission they take just one week to teach you how to operate the thing. It doesn't even have a stereo. What it does have is torn seats, doors that won't lock and a bad case of bodyrot.

As I say, most of the work is of mind-destroying banality. On this contract I'd been back to collect rock samples from the Palaeozoic era, been to observe the Battle of Hastings (it was okay but when you've seen one battle you've seen them all), and I was supposed to sign on to the crew of the *Marie Celeste*. I told my boss that I arrived late and missed the sailing by two days. Not true. I did arrive in time, took one look at some of the blokes I'd be sailing with and decided they deserved whatever unpleasant fate over-took them. I counted myself out and headed for Elizabethan Whitechapel.

But now I was on the way home, back to my own time and I hoped a productivity bonus, when suddenly the craft started playing up. The controls on these things are pretty basic at the best of times—a couple of emergency warning lights, a dial to tell you what year you're in, and a steering wheel. Both emergency lights came on, the steering wheel wouldn't budge and the dial was spinning backwards at about a thousand years per minute. I gave it a good hard slam with my fist. Everything stopped dead. The dial stopped spinning and a whole row of noughts came up—just my luck to have broken the damn thing; that would be another breakage they'd stop out of my pay.

I opened the door of the craft. It was a nice day. The sun was shining. I could have done a lot worse. At least I'd avoided an Ice Age. In fact my first thought was that I must have landed in Kew Gardens, but then I noticed there were no paths, no pagoda, and the place wasn't crawling with tourists.

If I'd been a good "company man", the kind of time traveller who's really going places with his career, I'd have been out there analysing the soil and the air, taking polaroids, all that stuff. Me? I just wanted to go home. I had a wife, two kids and all the Chinese take-aways I could eat waiting for me in the twenty-first century. Easier said than done. I called in sick on the morning when they taught us basic timecraft maintenance. I had a look at the engine. It looked much as it always had—incomprehensible. Maybe it needed water. I hoped so. I took a plastic canister and set off to look for some. I wandered around for a while, got more or less lost, didn't see any water. It was hardly surprising. There were no paths, no indications that anyone or anything had ever passed that way before me.

Things picked up when I came across an orchard. There were several rows of very carefully arranged apple trees. Someone had obviously cultivated them and right in the middle of a row of apparently identical trees, there was one that had a sign attached to it. The sign had been painted very clumsily and it said,

FROM THIS TREE THOU SHALT NOT EAT.

I thought that was a pretty strange sign for anybody to put on a tree, but it meant that the natives at least spoke English, even if they didn't sound especially friendly. With luck, with quite a lot of luck actually, I could get my water and be on my way before meeting any of them.

I know you hear a lot of stories in the Sunday papers about the debauched lives Time Travellers are supposed to live. With the exception of a wild night at a party in third century Gaul my life in this business has been as pure and as dull as a glacier. That's why, on this occasion, I was completely unprepared for suddenly coming across a waterfall containing a beautiful redheaded woman as unembarrassed and as naked as the day she was born.

I hid in the bushes when I saw her. It's not that I'm a voyeur, it was the fact that I didn't want to have to go through explaining who I was and what the hell I was doing there. I suppose I was also embarrassed. I watched her get out of the water. She didn't have a towel. She just sat on the grass to dry. I hoped she'd dry off soon so that I could get some water, but she showed no signs of moving and it looked like I was in for a long wait, even more so when she started singing and various forest creatures came out of the undergrowth and gathered around her. There was a lamb, deer, a pair of stoats, an otter and lot of others that I couldn't identify. She settled down amidst them, and she and all the animals went fast asleep.

I continued squatting in the bushes. My knees started to ache. I wondered what were my chances of getting some water and getting away without waking her. They seemed reasonable. She, and all the animals, looked out for the count. I would try to stay downwind.

It started well. I got to the waterfall, filled my canister and began retracing my steps; and everything would have been fine if, at that very moment, a fully-grown lion hadn't appeared. It came out of the bushes exactly where I'd been hiding, walked past me and started sniffing around the naked redhead.

We Time Travellers are not supposed to meddle with history— it's one of the clauses in your contract—but nobody takes it too seriously, and in any case I couldn't just stand around and watch somebody get mauled by a lion. I started yelling to shoo it away, then I threw my canister. It hit the lion hard and square on the nose. I realised it was a risky thing to do. If I didn't scare him off he might get very mad.

It didn't scare him off actually, and neither did it get him angry. In fact he took no notice at all, carried on sniffing around as before, yawned and went to sleep, lying down next to the lamb.

I had, however, woken the woman. She was a lot more comfortable with the situation than I was. I would have run, but I needed my canister back.

"Oh, pleased to meet you,,' I said.

She didn't say anything. She stood a little stiffly, a little formally, completely unembarrassed. *I* was embarrassed.

"My name's Bing," I said, "Bing Smith. My parents wanted me to have an unusual first name to go with the boring 'Smith'. Bing was a name used by a popular entertainer back in the twentieth century. They still have his films on TV. *White Christmas.*'

She didn't seem to be taking much of this in, although she was giving me her full attention. In fact she was staring at me as if she'd never seen anything like me before. And if I hadn't known better I'd have thought she was undressing me with her eyes.

"Are you one of God's creatures?" she asked.

"Aren't we all?" I said with a shrug, "Though I've never had much time for organised religion."

"Organised religion?"

She said both words very deliberately, as if she'd never heard either of them before.

"What is *this* thing?" she asked, and she rubbed her hand over my back.

"That's my spine," I said. I was starting to think I must have landed in some prehistoric nudist funny farm.

"No, no, not the spine," she continued, "I have one of those. I mean this covering."

"It's a jacket," I said.

"And these?"

"Trousers."

"What are they exactly? Are they a kind of skin?"

"They're clothes," I said. "Clothes."

"Clothes," she repeated carefully.

We stood around there for a while, making rather forced conversation like this. I didn't know where to look or what to do with my hands.

"Nice place you've got here," I said.

"It's paradise," she replied.

"Well, I don't know that I'd go that far."

You know, love at first sight is a funny thing. Blame it on being away from home for so long, blame it on her innocence, her lack of guile, on the fact that she was good with animals. Whatever the reason I was hooked. I was in love. She was the only woman for me, and I could tell she liked me too. I invited her back to the timecraft, although I didn't have much idea where it was. But she had to get back to her husband. I should have known that she was too special not to be attached already, but I persuaded her to meet me next day in the same spot. As she was leaving I realised I didn't even know her name. She told me.

"Erica—that's a nice name," I said.

We met the next day. It took me a while to find the place. And it went on like that for a few days—furtive meetings while her husband was off doing his work. I thought *I* had a rotten job, but what he had to do was go around finding animals and giving them names. Who'd pay you to do that? It had to be some sort of job-creation scheme.

We tried not to mention him when we were together but she

didn't have a lot else to talk about. "Adam did this. Adam said that." I got a bit sick of it. Also it turned out he was the one who'd put the sign on the tree.

"I think he's trying to test me," Erica said. "He wants to make sure I'm obedient. It's pathetic really. It's sad. I don't even like fruit all that much."

Then she would have to rush back to him. I asked why she couldn't leave him, but he needed her, Erica said, she was all he'd got.

It's a strange thing, probably not very noble of me, but as the days passed I became increasingly keen to see this husband of hers, to see who my rival was. They lived in a clearing about a mile away from the waterfall. It was nice but fairly basic. I sneaked along there one evening at dusk. I wasn't planning to do more than get a good look at him. They were just on their way out—Erica was slim, refined, stylish, and Adam was a foul slob. He looked like he was a heavy drinker, several stones overweight, slovenly, unkempt hair and beard and he kept spitting. Worse was the way he treated Erica. He was bossing her around, demanding that she honour and obey him, and he kept yelling at her in a foul-mouthed way.

I watched them leave. Why do nice girls always end up with sods like that? Then I noticed a large book hidden behind a rock in the clearing. I edged towards it and picked it up. I opened it at random and saw that the handwriting in it could only belong to Adam. It was sloppy, full of crossings out and blots, and it was clearly the writing of a deeply disturbed personality. At the very top of the first page was written "*My Life*" and what followed were the fantastical ravings of a madman. You wouldn't believe some of the stuff, about his being sprung fully formed out of the clay, and then a story of how Erica was cloned from one of his ribs. But what really showed it as a piece of completely deranged insanity was the way he claimed to be in direct contact with God all the time. God would stop by for a chat most days and explain his divine purpose, and according to these memoirs it had been God's idea, of course, to put the "thou shalt not eat" sign on the tree. It all made for terrifying reading.

I closed the book and went to place it back behind the rock. A twig snapped behind me. I turned. There was Adam towering over me—six feet of blubber and religious mania.

"You snake in the grass," he yelled, and then he gave me the most thorough beating-up of my life. You can have all the technology you like but nothing beats sheer brute stupidity when it comes it handing out physical violence. Certainly nothing *I* had could beat it.

When he'd finished I crawled off through the bushes, spitting out teeth, blood pouring from my nose, expert kicks and punches having been delivered to all the parts of my body that could experience pain most fully.

I went as far and as fast as I could before collapsing behind a big rock and settling down to some serious moaning. But as I was lying there I became aware of another sound, somebody else moaning and quite close by. Curiosity briefly helped me forget my pain and I followed the sounds. I didn't go far before finding their source. They came from an old man lying on the ground, doubled up with pain. He had been beaten up and left. He was in a bad way. There was blood in his long grey hair and beard, and his white robes were covered in mud and grass stains.

"Are you all right?" I asked.

"I'm as good as dead," he gasped.

"Oh God," I said. "Who did this? Adam?"

"Who else?"

"The murderer," I said. I was angry. "That guy has a lot of nerve. Somebody should do something about that sucker."

"Don't worry," the old man said. "He's got it coming."

"Good of you to turn the other cheek like that," I said.

The old man looked at me closely and became very puzzled.

"I don't recognise you," he said. "I'm not at all sure where you fit into my scheme of things."

I was about to go into a long explanation but it turned out not to be necessary. The old man shuddered, closed his eyes and his features settled into an expression of peace. His problems were solved by death. Poor old devil.

Love, violence, death—those are the big issues whatever Age you happen to be in. Here I was, stuck in prehistory, infatuated with the wife of a homicidal maniac, finding dead bodies in the grass. It was the old story.

I spent the next few days in the timecraft, developing bruises and trying to make sense of the workshop manual. The problem was more serious than just lack of water. I worked hard at taking things apart and putting them back together but it did no good. Of course I was eager to see Erica again but love at first sight is the kind of thing that can burn itself out very quickly. I was scared of straying too far from the craft. I didn't want to finish up like the old man.

As it happened Erica came to *me*. It was a tearful reunion.

"He's gone completely off his head," she sobbed. "He won't call me by my real name any more. He says 'Adam and Erica' doesn't have the right ring to it. He's started calling me Eve. And those memoirs you saw, now he calls it 'Genesis'. He's getting really obsessive about it, he's even incorporated *you* into his myth. You're supposed to have led me into temptation. Oh Bing, I don't think I can go on like this."

I kissed her tears away and we made slow, intense love on the back seat of the timecraft. Erica was passionate but seemed a little inexperienced. Afterwards she was full of regrets.

"You're a nice man Bing," she said, "but it can't go on. I feel like I've fallen, like I've sinned."

"A bit of adultery," I quipped. "That's not a very original sin."

I was trying to be cheeful but she wasn't having any of it.

"We must never see each other again," she said.

I thought she was over-reacting but I agreed. I was past arguing, Hysterical wives, enraged husbands, all that primal drama—who needs it? She left clutching a few leaves around herself. I wondered if I'd ever see her again.

I tried everything to get that timecraft working. I spent the next two weeks pampering, lubricating, cajoling, kicking, pleading with the damn thing. I even tried a quick prayer but that did no good either. I was tinkering around underneath it, trying to follow a wiring diagram when I became aware of a lot of noise going on somewhere in the garden. Birds and animals were squawking, then a rabbit darted through the grass near my feet, then a couple more. They were running fast and they were terrified.

Then I smelled burning in the air and saw a roll of black smoke on the horizon. There was a fire and it was out of control. I packed my tools and the wiring diagram into the craft. If things got desperate I could shut myself in. It might not be able to go anywhere but at least it was fireproof.

I was just about to get in when Erica appeared, running frantically towards me.

"He's snapped," she said. "He's set fire to the garden. We're all expelled."

"He torched the garden? Why?"

"Oh, he was mad at me."

"Why was he mad at you?"

"Well, I suppose you'll have to know . . . I'm pregnant."

"Congratulations."

"It's yours."

"Mine? You sure? I mean we only. . . ."

"I'm sure. Adam's a good man in many ways but not that way. He can't . . . perform."

"Well, I'll go to the foot of our stairs," I said.

"I'm going to call it Lalage if it's a girl, Cain if it's a boy."

"Lalage—that's an unusual name."

"Now I really must fly," she said. She planted a soft, dry kiss on my cheek and she was gone.

I leapt into the timecraft, slammed the door, fastened my seatbelt and waited while all hell broke loose outside. I could hear the sound of approaching fire and all around the noise of stampeding animals. There are no windows as such in a timecraft, just one of those little spy-holes like you have in your front door to look at burglars. I looked out to see three charging bull elephants heading straight for me. One or other of them was bound to hit the craft. I braced myself. There was an unholy bang, the craft jolted, and I was thrown forward. The seatbelt, which was as defective as everything else in the vehicle, snapped and I nutted the dashboard. I saw a gentle trail of stars, like a firework fading out, before I fell unconscious.

I awoke a few thousand years later. Whether it was the elephant or my head or a combination of the two that had worked the magic I didn't know, but when I came to the time dial was spinning forwards as happily as it ever had, and, to cut a long story short, I was home in no time.

I took the wife out to a local steak house that night. They gave us a table in a dark corner. I needed it. I didn't look very good, what with a gash in my forehead and two fading black eyes from Adam's treatment of me. My hair was combed forward and I wore dark glasses. I could have been mistaken for a film star, but I wasn't.

Cheryl, my wife, is very understanding. We have no secrets. I told her the whole story. Amazing as it may seem she'd heard of this Genesis myth in an evening class on ancient religions, and she said she'd always thought it left a lot of questions unanswered.

"So," she said, "if you fertilised Eve, and if we're all descended from Eve, then we're all descended from you as well, which must mean that you're descended from yourself, which I'd say was impossible."

That's the trouble with time travel. There's always some clever sod who points out some unresolvable paradox, some impossible contradiction. Me, I just do the job.

That night in bed Cheryl was frisky as a sackful of chimpanzees and I told her so.

"You're quite a prime mover yourself," she said.

I don't know what she meant by that.

A SORT OF SUN SPOT
Bartholomew Blockley

Our pleasures are becoming circumscribed. Turkish tobacco transmutes our tissues into carcinoma, the *vin de table* gives us cirrhosis of the liver, and now the sun, centre of our galaxy, source of our warmth, succour to the wintering Northern hemispheres, is killing us. Celtic heliophiles melting on the Mediterranean littoral are gaining their sun-spots, small dark pin-sized malignancies at first imperceptible, then with their fifth-column qualities sabotaging the whole system as they spread through the body fatally undetected. I have been studying these *spetsnatz* killers, the malignant melanomas, and that means lab work tied to an unconventional schedule, when man conforms to the life-cycle of cells. At night I rush from the television or dinner table to attend to my cellular charges, to enhance their environment or change their nutrition. I am their mother and their servant. One evening I drove to the miserable buildings which the department calls my laboratory to alter the incubation temperature of my latest litter of cells. Surprise matched alarm as I drove up the approach road. I saw the animal-house lights on, and two vans parked by the window.

To my horror I realised that the window was open and that a man inside was handing out a goat to an accomplice. My car headlights alerted him and he threw the creature down, slammed the van shut and jumped into the driving seat, making a wild getaway down the other drive. For a moment I lost sight of the man who had been at the window. I raced towards the remaining van, parked across his exit and leapt out. He was jumping from the window ledge on to the gravel when he caught sight of me and half-reared back in midflight, landing heavily on the dogtoothed brick plant border. There was a wrenching noise of fracturing bone as his ankle tried to execute an inadvertent one hundred and eighty degree horizontal turn. He fell to the ground and lay there clutching his leg and groaning horribly. I stood some yards away, expecting assault from the shadows, my fists clenched for any assailant. None appeared. I was shaking and breathless. My adversary began a choking whimper. The abandoned goat appeared in the headlights and looked bewildered. He restored his ruffled spirits by savaging the crocus shoots in the border. My confidence rose. I edged closer. My adversary had been abandoned on the field of battle.

"Forget your trampoline?" I said with satisfaction. "Must be all of three feet. Not a weekend paratrooper?"

"I've busted my foot and it bloody well hurts," he bleated.

"Yes," I murmured appreciatively. "But you have also busted into my lab and that bloody well hurts," I added.

He was in no condition to escape: manipulating a clutch with that left foot would be torture. So I left him and stuck my nose into the van. A sticker on the window declared the vehicle to belong to Horse Hire, a garage on the edge of town. The passenger seat was covered with a motley pile of spray cans, brushes and a two-litre paint tin. Leaflets were lying loose on the floor. I picked one up and held it before the headlights.

It was a photocopy with an ink smudge and the letters blurred. In the middle of the A2 page two sentences had been typed, running high to the right where the typist had failed to straighten the paper. The type was old, from an era before electronic style swept the office world. The letter "t" had acquired a sort of stutter, a repeated shadow of its outline. The letter "s" had faded on its leading edge. The message read: "Science is a concentration camp for helpless animals. A technological holocaust for defenceless creatures."

At the bottom in block capitals were the letters RALF.

I turned round and walked back to the spot where the injured one lay. He had crawled away from the brickwork and was nursing something in the curl of his right elbow. A single brick had been wrestled from the plant border.

"Ralf, you're not going to do something unpleasant with that piece of English architecture," I ventured. "If I get hurt I may have to introduce you to the cayman in our reptile pond. So let's not make a meal of this."

He let the brick fall. "I'm not called Ralf," he said dejectedly. I skirted past him and looked through the lab window. Flakes of paint and splintered wood covered the floor on the inside. The metal grille had been jemmied off the window frame, but was still hanging from a hinge to the right. The animal cages which ran down both sides of the room were empty, their doors ajar. A neon light flickered tiresomely at the far end.

"Been cleaning out the cages, I see." I pushed the window closed and drew my coat in. In the back of a van hurtling across the countryside were rats, rabbits, goats and sheep representing months of work on melanoma skin cancer. My research grant had been extended already and renewed without results. I had five weeks in which to collate material now rattling about at fifty miles an hour some increasing distance away.

"Where's your friend taken the animals?" I asked Ralf.

"I don't know. We agreed to go to separate hideouts. We didn't tell each other where. Nuclear cell system. I don't even know him." He said this with some vigour. "The police don't catch us. They don't know us; they don't know anything," he said, regaining his self-esteem.

"Until you fell into my hands—that is." He did his best to produce a dismissive grunt. I went over and switched off the car headlights.

"Jeez I'm so bloody cold," Ralf said from his reclining position on the gravel.

"If you want to come into the warm animal house you'll have to behave. Nothing silly," I cautioned. He waved his hands to show he wasn't concealing anything.

"I'll help you inside," I said, unlocking the front door and flicking off the useless alarm. I dragged him a few yards, but he screamed with pain so I went to fetch one of the animal trolleys. I pulled it back, hitting every door jamb as it veered around with one wheel executing wild gyrations like a crazed firework. Ralf climbed on to the scratched and cold aluminium surface. We completed the journey, the trolley altering course every two feet.

In the hall light Ralf's face was pale, with the skin showing a slight patina of moisture above the lips and eyebrows. Pain and fear vied with each other across puckered mouth and closed lips. He was in clinical shock. He looked tired. I proffered one of the nylon cushions from a hall chair and he let his head fall back, emitting a rather wretched sigh.

"Ralf, if you tell me where the animals have gone I'll call an ambulance." I didn't suppose my offer would produce anything.

"For God's sake, my name is not Ralf and I don't know!" I believed him. Across the hall in my office I found my papers untouched; they clearly hadn't started on that part of their caper. I rang through to ambulance control. The duty officer said that a major motorway RTA involving livestock and a fire was taking all their vehicles at that moment.

"Take your friend to casualty at the General," he suggested. I rang off and considered my options.

"Ambulance is going to be ages—some motorway pile-up. You'll have to wait." Ralf made no response. The hair at his forehead was wet and clung to his skin; he was holding the knee above his chaotic joint with both hands, trying not to move it.

I returned to the office and took twenty milligrams of diamorphine and an antiemetic from the drugs cupboard. Picking up a syringe I took it back and showed it to him. "It's a painkiller we use here, want some?" He nodded and closed his eyes in a silent gesture of acceptance. I gave him an IM shot and placed a second cushion below his ankle.

I left him lying in the hall and had a look round. I closed the cage doors and latched the window from the inside. In the lab a red light showed that the incubator was on. Inside I could see all the melanoma tissue cultures in their tilted test-tubes, condensation steaming up their walls.

Where could I transplant these cells? The animals were spread across a burning motorway, caught between a petrol tanker and a chloride lorry, except for G3 who was still cropping the flower-bed.

I removed the tissue cultures and beside each placed a sterile Petri dish. Into each dish I placed a drop of tissue culture and a further drop of normal saline to prevent it drying out. The cells had a slightly purple hue to them and rose as if to coat each drop of saline. On the left I had four treated cell lines and on the right I had four untreated cell lines. The treated cells had been immersed in an enzyme inhibitor which I hoped would prevent them developing as their natural history predicted. These melanoma cells produce a black pigment called melanin from a protein called dopa. I was hoping to block the chemical pathway from dopa to melanin. My experimental questions were whether suppression of melanin production would significantly reduce the malignancy of melanoma cells, and whether one could introduce an enzyme inhibitor into a living person without causing diseases like Parkinsonism and cure the melanoma.

I returned to the hall. Ralf was under an opiate narcosis. I wheeled him into the lab and as he mumbled I drew up his shirt and bomber jacket so that the whole of his back was bare. I cleaned it with a pink disinfectant that squirted out in a clean sharp spray so cold it threw up goose pimples down his thin chalky back. Using a clean diabetic syringe down the left side of his back from the scapula to the waistline I gave him a tenth of a millilitre intradermal injection of treated cells at intervals of five centimetres. On the right I did the same with untreated cells—raising a small bleb of skin just visible on each occasion. I wiped his back and pulled the shirt

down before wheeling him to the hall. Back in the lab I replaced all
the cultures in the incubator. In my workbook I noted: "Right
back untreated."

Outside G3 had vanished and it was bitterly cold. I climbed into
Ralf's van and drove down to the Horse Hire Garage, parking it on
the forecourt. Someone came to the window overlooking the
pumps and watched me lock the door and walk away. I expected
police sirens, but none sounded as I headed towards the lab. Ralf
was pretty groggy when I stirred him, and cold water hardly made
him any better. I wrestled him from trolley to car as he
remonstrated feebly. In casualty two porters shouldered him out
and into a cubicle, where he sank into a painless sleep.

The following morning I picked up the *Gazette* on the way to
the lab. Across the front page was a splash on the motorway
accident, with a picture of a policeman shooting my sheep amidst
machinery and detritus littering the road. I reported the break-in
to a laconic inspector who asked me if I read the local newspaper.
He made a remark about a high speed barbecue and I put the
phone down. Ten minutes later a panda car drew up and disgorged
two policemen. One, a plainclothes wallah, acted in a confident
irritating way. He seemed unable to spell and wanted to write my
statement for me. "What did you call the sheep?" he asked.
    "S1, S2 etc. You don't grow so attached to them that way," I
replied.
    "You must be heartless buggers," he said, poking about in the
animal house. "Anyway, case is open and shut. Dead van driver.
Dead animals, you see, sir," he said. "After all it's not murder." At
that he looked towards me. I agreed. As they left I watched from
my window and saw G3 on his hind legs, head through their open
car window, trying to eat the steering wheel. At Asham General all
new cases of melanoma were referred to me, and when Dr
Golohtap rang me six weeks later with a case of a young man I was
naturally interested.
    "Satellite lesions down his back."
    "All over?" I queried.
    "No, just down the right. They seem quite superficial. Very
symmetrical seeding," he added.

"Possibly lymphatic spread," I suggested.

"Bloody odd lymph system."

"I'll pop in and see him tomorrow if you put him on Clematis Ward," I said.

I had the enzyme inhibitor in the low temperature fridge. Bacteria had produced it under lab conditions. Their life cycle depended on using dopa and preventing rival bacteria from metabolising it to melanin; for this purpose they produced the enzyme inhibitor. These collaborating bacteria had been transplanted to new high-yield territories, where they expanded their population in a nutrient-rich environment. From time to time we washed them off this land of milk and honey into test tubes, where we removed their enzyme inhibitor and purified it on a glass bead filtration system. Assays started to show one hundred percent pure enzyme inhibitor in solution, which was heat stable at body temperature and able to endure the human blood pH.

I carried my vial of enzyme inhibitor to Clematis Ward. Ralf was reading a tabloid and was pretty surprised to see me. He felt constrained, so he wiggled the toes of his left leg, which had an ankle to knee plaster covered in signatures and felt-tip obscenities.

"This your line of work, doctor?" he asked, looking puzzled. "By the way, what is your name?"

"It was in the newspapers after you visited me," I countered.

"I wasn't reading much then—they took me to theatre and pinned my ankle together, so I missed all the details, know what I mean."

"Yes," I purred with indifference. "But I've come to take some growths off your back, so let's get on with it." I spoke quite brusquely.

As he lay on his stomach I infused lignocaine around three of the four sites and performed simple excision biopsies on them. The fourth site I infused with enzyme inhibitor in a clockwork fashion around the raised purple papule. A nurse dressed the sites and flirted with Ralf as I labelled the samples and washed my hands.

The next time I saw Ralf was when Golohtap invited me over to the General to see him. Ralf was on a scratched aluminium trolley. He was completely naked; over his thorax and abdomen were dark blemishes like watercolour stains and randomly distributed about his body were cauliflower tumours welling up out of the skin, some covered with dried blood and others necrosed. So I had my experimental answers: the first was yes, and the second a definite no.

Golohtap was in the room and came across, gloved, gowned, masked, and wearing blue plastic overshoes.

"Very virulent cell line, this," he said, gesturing towards the dark excrescences. "Was he lost to follow-up in your out-patients?"

"Yes, I'm afraid so," I replied, avoiding eye contact.

"How's your work going?" he asked politely.

"Oh, I think I've got something that works in vitro. But in vivo, well, that's like trying to breathe on the sun. The research money is at an end, my animals were stolen as you know and various other problems." I looked more closely at Ralf. Between those islands of malignancy he was so very pale and thin. Vulnerable. Dead.

"Did you see the figures for melanoma last year," I asked.

Golohtap shook his head as he took a specimen from Ralf's thigh.

"Up ten per cent on 1980," I said.

"Well, these chaps shouldn't go sunbathing, but they won't listen," he replied in his smug way. "My people don't worship the sun." He chuckled and spooned the biopsy into the formalin pot.

WARTOURS   Mark Wilkins

The sky was lighter in the east now. He could see the details of the weaver-bird nests in the branches of the flat-topped thorn trees along the high horizon formed by the edge of the escarpment. The village was still dark, but the light patch on the extreme edge was, he could see now, a compound for their cattle, whose shapes moved there in the halflight.

From the left of the village a shallow ravine, filled with thorn bushes, ran along the bottom of the ridge along the rift valley and down towards the lake, twenty miles away. That ridge would be a good clear feature for the Fighter Ground Attack on the initial run-in. Bring them in from Lake Kiyuku low level subsonic, pull them up, turn them left and use the edge of that straight geological fault as a visual guide to the target. Easy.

He rolled back the green rubber flap from his watchface. 5:20.

He might pop a couple of smoke at the turning-in point, just to be safe. You had to keep it simple with the FGA pilots, especially as the front-seat jocks were tourists and weren't too good at seeing anything while pulling four and a half G semi-inverted in the turn and peering up through the cockpit canopy.

His hands felt grimy. They had picked up some thorns during the night march and they hurt and irritated. He felt ingrained with dirt; whenever he turned his head his chin stubble caught and snagged the collar of his bush shirt.

A metallic click sounded from the bushes behind him. The 3V crew were assembling the Satlink station, the camouflage-painted dish with its central probe pointed vertically toward the invisible satellite hanging amongst the bright constellations in the equatorial sky.

By seven this morning the cameras would be relaying the action, through the ground link to the satellite then down to the networks and, interspersed with the usual commercial breaks for under-arm deodorant, life insurance and double-glazing, pipe it live to a hundred million or so helmet-cocooned, avidly gawping, all-demanding viewers. Wide vision, fine definition, three dimensions and stereo sound. *Better* than real life. Clean and sanitised. No smell, no danger, no African heat, no mosquitoes, just the pure visual and audio sensation.

One of the cameramen had his helmet on and was turning his head slowly in a pan-shot, left to right. The twin lenses mounted above his eyes whirred and snickered on Auto-Focus. He stopped, facing the cameraman. A four-eyed figure. The two above wide and glassily black-lensed; the pair below pale blue, the skin at the outer edges tanned and creased by the suns of Africa, Iraq and Asia. He was moving his lips soundlessly, the microphone a thin metallic tube which snaked down the side of his face and entered the right hand corner of his mouth. Probably running a test transmission with the network producer back in Seattle, London, Tokyo or wherever.

Those cameramen got wasted at an incredible rate. Even with the latest 75 percent bodyarmour. Once they got into the middle of a firefight they seemed to think they were bloody invincible: or it may have been the goading by the producer over the Satlink; he had often flicked to their channel on his helmet comm and listened in . . . "come on you Goddamned fairy, the folks back home don't want to see it on zoom . . . get in there with the close-ups in the hand-to-hand stuff, we want to hear it on stereo!" Zap, blam, sell more washing powder, more fitted kitchens. Hell, but the good ones got incredible bonuses; some were on a commission deal for the average number of viewers they held over any five-minute period, or commission on increases in product sales. That one could be a real winner.

5:45. "O" Group was at six.

Most of them had the idea of earning enough to set up the farm in Oregon, or the cottage beside the stream in the Cotswolds. Then give it up. But he had never heard of one who had got out alive yet. It was the same with the deep saturation divers off the continental shelves, or the Glowboys up building the stations in the Van Allen belt. Just one more trip and then I'll stop. But they never did. Just like himself . . . Christ, he had tried. But after three weeks in Cheltenham he had been climbing the wall. Missing it, yearning for it, not just the breathtaking adrenalin high of the assault, but the smell of the bush, the sharp chill of the early morning before the heat, and the birdsong in the dawn.

There was firelight in the village now, reflected from the roofthatch. A thin column of smoke rising in the dawn sky. It looked as if there weren't any guards out, so there would be a strong surprise element. The place would be like a hornet's next if they had any hint.

He should finish orders group by 6:30. That would just about be sunrise time.

The usual giveaway was the arrival of the Transmed helicopters. Those bastards were like vultures—couldn't even wait for the action to get going before they came clattering along—waking up all the targets for miles around. They somehow always managed to get a tip-off. He had suspected for months that the Wartours offices were full of informers; couldn't blame them really, as Transmed paid fantastic commission.

The Forward Air Controller was below him on the path, crouching on one knee, muttering into his handmike with the green whip-aerial waving above his backpack. His Laser-Marker was slung across his chest like a rifle.

God, the old big-game hunting hadn't had all this paraphernalia and bullshit. A few Yanks and Arabs, a couple of trucks to carry the tents and artillery, and off to waste a few animals. That was only fifteen years ago. Unbelievable really, that they had been allowed to kill real animals. Christ, you so much as kick a waterbuffalo nowadays and the World Wildlife people would be down on you like a ton of bricks . . . million dollar fine, revoke your licence and close down the network. The only nightmare that had ever woken him up screaming was the one where some half-witted elephant had wandered into a fire-fight and stopped an anti-tank round. Not that there were any Goddamned elephants left nowadays.

5:50. He turned and started to walk down the dark reverse slope toward the R.V.

The problem had always been, really, that he had felt sorry for them—the animals that was—and when Wartours had started up and developed into a multi-billion industry he had never felt happier.

It had all happened back at around the time of the leisure riots of the eighties. An enterprising mercenary had had the original brainwave. The ultimate adventure holiday, combining travel and warm far-off places with live combat. Perfect. The idea had developed and worked well for a year or two but the real leap forward came with the involvement of the 3V networks. That's what had really started bringing in the big money. Big incentives too; everyone on commission from the Network chiefs downwards.

5:55. Five minutes.

The tourists were gathered round the briefing board which was illuminated by a single hooded red light bulb.

Seventy-three of them. The usual collection. Bankers, lawyers, robotecs, surgeons, oilmen, accountants. Americans, Japs, a few Arabs . . . fewer of those each year, since the oil slump, and of course an ever-increasing number of rich mainland Chinese.

The one common factor among them was the ability to pay.

Now and then he had the down-at-heel type who had saved for years out of a pittance of a salary, regretting the wasting of his youth in the insurance company and determined to have one really good blow-out before it was too late. Some looting and pillage. Chalk up a really impressive body-count. Show the smart-alecks back in the pub, and that Miss stuck-up Munro in reception. And when he got back he'd hang the souvenir Holo on the office wall, the one of him in the African sun, his combat fatigues blood- and battle-stained, smiling at the camera, arms outstretched, with a severed head in each hand. And if that didn't get Miss Munro into the back seat of his Toyota, nothing would.

6:00.

He stepped into the circle of light, picked up the pointer and rapped it on the board.

"OK. Look in. This is it. Set your watches. The time is coming up to Oh Six Hundred. Five . . . four . . . three . . . two . . . one . . . now. Oh Six Hundred."

A pause. All their eyes were on him now. This is what they had been waiting for. Today. All year they had endured the tedium and the boredom, the commuting and the frustration, the petty office squabbling . . . the stifling *civilisation* of it all. All year they had looked forward to this and all next year they would look back. And today was it.

A pause again . . . to build the tension.

"Situation. The village at Satnav Grid 0041 7306, as marked by the red square on the map, is held by terrorist forces hostile to the government. That is the village directly over the top of this hill."

They watched him. Tongues licked lips wetly.

"Mission. To assist the government forces in destroying the terrorists and also the village, thereby denying the further use of it to the enemy."

The Katangan Major stood behind and slightly to the right of him, idly tapping the top of his boot with his cane. He would be leading the bulk of the government forces. By mutual consent, of course, most of the killing would be left to the tourist unit.

"Execution. General outline. 'A' Company, that's us, will be 'point' company. We will be flanked by 'B' and 'C' companies, which, as you all know, are Katangan regular forces."

The Major had this whole area tied up. Had a brother in the government who fixed all the licences; was collecting the commission from about six different directions on every Wartour. Had three sons at Stowe and had just bought a house in Chelsea.

"At 'H' hour there will be a strike by a flight of four Phantoms who will each carry out two passes on the target delivering rockets and napalm. Following departure of the aircraft we will carry out a frontal assault on the objective, destroying the remaining enemy forces and their supporting elements."

Seventy-three pairs of eyes, bright in anticipation.

Of course, when it had all first started, in that insignificant little central African country, there really *had* been terrorists involved, but when the original war blew over the government, having got kind of used to all the foreign revenue that had been pouring in . . . and when all the other emerging poverty-stricken countries saw the staggering amount that was to be made . . . then they, well . . . started kind of *inventing* the odd little war. Hell, the people and the villages were real enough all right . . . that's one ingredient that the world had more than enough of and, after all, the Aids plague had only killed off twenty percent of the world's population and the other eighty percent were still breeding like crazy. If you were lucky enough to be a civil servant in one of these places you stood to get some *incredible* handouts from the networks and the tour companies, not to mention the arms manufacturers . . . just for handing out a few licences. So you just kept your mouth shut and paid the money into your Swiss bank account . . . after all, if you didn't get the gravy someone else would.

The arms companies hadn't been slow to recognise this new market either; they had set up dealers and franchise outlets in all the capitals and they ran delivery services direct to the support areas. There was a rep from General Tech who would take your order over the H.P. and deliver the hardware right to the battle-area in his helicopter! You just had to give your credit card number and he would punch the details back over his Satlink terminal. Christ, those guys would give you a squadron of tanks if you wanted it, and had the credit.

"At 'H' Hour plus ten minutes point company will form up at the start point in Vic formation. Weapons will be loaded, with safety catches on."

Then the usual stuff . . . action on the objective . . . timings . . . command and signals . . . administration and logistics . . . questions.

They were impatient now, and eager to start. To feel it again, the high, the thrill of combat, the lurch and kick of the weapon, the rush of the assault, the acrid smoke, the smell of napalm and cordite, the fear and the exhilaration. And he was feeling it now himself. It always amazed him, after all his experiences, the battles and firefights, even while achingly tired after an endless march through the bush, that he still got the same familiar sensations; just before the start. As his ancestor must have felt it, here, half-stooping on this grass-covered slope, the long bone club clenched in his fist, watching the grazing antelope, in the chill of the dawn, on this same ancient continent a hundred thousand years ago. The thudding of his heart, the lightness in his head, the tingle bursting up his back and shoulders, breathlessness, and the old sweet surge of pure happiness.

So at ten minutes to seven they finished loading their weapons and he led them up to the crest of the ridge, his arms wide and spread back in the sign for battle formation and then they waited, crouching in the high grass in the warm African sunlight, watching the low southern hills. Then, right to the second, like a miracle, the four wide silver shapes, soundlessly springing from the valley, climbing up the clear blue sky then banking and turning, over, close together and sweeping down, levelling; then dip and dive and down, towards the village in the sun.

WISHBONE   Anne Gay

The stars fall in their appointed courses, silver scintillation in the flickering sun.

Jenuven ran to catch this one. It knew better: it evaded her gently, settled into its crystal bowl. Like the wind-blown filaments, the stars eddy away from reaching hands. This one was no different.

Halbark played his game: "No, you can't have it tonight. We'll keep it for tomorrow." In a vague sort of fashion, he wanted her to want the star now. What else was there to want? Strong man who was leader; not that the others followed.

Jenuven turned away from him, cartwheeling by way of a change. She knew; he knew; seven people cannot live always together without bits of one becoming bits of the others. They knew whatever he said: tonight the star would shine.

Now Josa and Ranulf came running between the spars, both blindfold. Ranulf's tracker rang musically but intermittently. Ranulf was panting, laughing gamely; fifty-seven was no age to be playing tag, but one had to work hard to find enjoyment. What else was there to do? Josa, forty-something discreet, somersaulted around a spar with indifference: her blindfold would not let harm come to her. Hadn't everything always been safe?

The spars were wide-spaced, flickering aisles between them. Ocular blind-man's buff was too easy. But Ranulf caught her anyway: losing was unthinkable, and together the couple collapsed, giggling and tickling, on the broad, warm steps of the verandah. Their dyed hair didn't show the grey. Now all of them were in or around the House.

"It's here, isn't it?" gasped Josa in her accent of the moment. She did not bother to take off her blindfold. Semmel didn't stop fretting the strings of his zither; Caspar and Hella kept on arguing in the House.

The star hummed a sweet, insistent note. It told them it was here.

Maybe, wondered Jenuven, *maybe somewhere else another star is shining, on the night side perhaps. You don't know. Random is interest, to keep us alive. You know that because the stars tell you.*

But who made them tell you?

Dusk: overhead the storm-clouds of afternoon have parted. The long, wet filaments of the spars have whipped the rain from their brilliant colours and floated their rainbow banners under sunset's flame. Gilt and silver limn the departing thunderheads. The sky is purple and navy, pierced by distant suns.

Jenuven often thought about that, which made the others think she was odd. She might have found it hard to believe those little lights were suns, but it had to be true because the stars had told her. They said other people lived around the suns, that others too lived on their own planet. But Jenuven knew the others didn't care. Not even Halbark had bothered to go looking. Charitably he put her curiosity down to her youth. Firm, sweet skin; not tall; breasts that were promises of buds. All that, he'd told her, went with still wanting to know. She'd grow up.

But for now she came out with her friends, out of the warm-lit House with its tasty food-smells, their bodies pushing away the mist-wraiths of the evening air. It was at times like this that she felt young and naive. She wanted to race ahead, see the star shine *now*; she couldn't wait.

But the others could. They didn't jostle or fidget. She was very aware that she wasn't a woman yet, not like Josa and Hella. She hadn't had a baby yet. Soon, though, Semmel would make a baby inside her, and she hadn't needed a star to tell her how it was done. She had seen the others practising often enough, even though they were too old now to have babies at the end of it. Mostly they made funny noises, but they said it was fun and not to worry. So she didn't.

All the same, she still had more fun than they did. There were still some things she hadn't done. But time would change that. Freedom, it seemed, was having everything she had been told she wanted, and nothing more.

In front of the House, they settled down. Between the wide-spaced boles of the spars, the star hovered in its crystal bowl on the tripod, and the tripod stood on the water-repellent carpet. Ranulf and Josa weren't speaking so they sat at opposite sides, pretending not to look at each other. Hella and Caspar had made up passionately before supper. Now they touched each other constantly, knee to knee, and hands caressing neck or cheek. Even apart, they looked as if they belonged together: same blue hair, same blue eyes, young at heart in spite of wrinkles and sagging bodies. Jenuven liked them best of all.

Halbark sat bolt upright, cross-legged, his hair grey with age and eyebrows askew. Against his burly shoulder, Semmel leant his scrawny one.

Semmel watched Jenuven as she dithered about where to sit—who would be offended by the position she chose?—and he patted the ground beside him. For once, though, Jenuven flicked her pale hair at him and the leader, and sat alone. Her eyes were enormous with anticipation; she folded her slender legs and leant on one arm, glad she had put on her best blue tunic with its fringes and silver bells, but she couldn't keep still and the bells chimed softly at each movement. Self-conscious, she wished now she had put on something quieter, and hoped the star would shine soon.

Now everyone was comfortable on the soft, dry carpet. There were no seats, only those built into the House. How could there be with the stones so deep in the soft web of fallen filaments, and the spars of a carbon that shattered but did not break? And of course they don't distribute cutters here, they're dangerous. Scatterguns, yes, you might just possibly need them, but you can't carve anything with a scattergun.

The night settled, fragrant with filaments and scented with fruit, earthy. As yet the star has not started. It knows they're all here, but it's waiting, teasing, pricking some emotion out of the spoilt people, just as it has been programmed to do on some planet, far away, where people actually have found tasks to perform. A star once showed them all that.

Expectancy surges in the blood. For sound: a fat raindrop plop, soft breathing and kisses, the breeze flapping the filaments to curtain off the sky. No clawed toes stalking along the broad glades, no wings shivering in the air. No terrifying snap of beaks. All the same, Halbark plays at checking around, but the little eyes in his heavy face see no birds awaiting. Halbark checks the scattergun at his feet. The others watch indifferently. Doesn't Halbark always do that? The stars once said it was a good idea—after all, the birds bore the same maker's mark as the guns and the stars—but nobody else does it. They shrug; it's just Halbark's little game. Makes him feel resourceful.

At last, at last, the star in its crystal cup glows. None of them has seen it start, not even Jenuven, though they all thought they were watching. Its silvery humming twinkled into song.

Insofar as the seven wanted anything, this was not it. No more warm, soft ease: star-cold radiated, made their homely glade white and bleak. How could white be so many colours at once? A hard cold permeated their bones and the bones of the earth. They shivered, and their sated bodies liked this strange sensation. Over the sudden snowfield the sky was dark, and the tiny distant suns were another white.

Jenuven saw—they all felt and knew and saw—no spars, no filaments. There was no stew-scented House, and the guns threw cutting points. Food did not fall from above—how could it? There were no spars—it ran, and crawled, and tunnelled, or pushed aside the wind-bared earth. You had to fight for it.

Frost crawled up their sudden, shaggy clothes. Jenuven heard around her the voices of a crowd: there must have been as many as twenty or thirty, more than she could count. They were roaring out songs, guffawing, making love by the fires of dung. The illusion—the star-show—was complete. She could even smell the bitter smoke, and wet fur.

Lots—more than two handfuls—of hairy beasts were moaning and stamping beyond the firelight. Picket-ropes tied them head to head. Four in a circle were staggering, intoxicated on yellow lichen.

The shaggy people were stoned on the hairy things' urine. Jenuven, Halbark, all of them, were drunk among the roisterers. They stood and watched a man with a drinking-horn trying to catch some more urine. She howled with laughter when the animal kicked him in the head. Later, out of the star, she would think this was odd, laughing at misfortune. But for now it was a great respite from cold hard work and long hunger.

Beyond the star-thoughts, Jenuven was not aware. But in the morning she would ask the others what they had been in the snowfield.

Only she couldn't.

Physically outside the star-thoughts, the rare birds were coming. The star-makers knew some folk must have challenge, or die.

The birds paced softly towards the radiant clearing. Their claws bit into the soft mat of filaments as they pushed themselves along. Flightless wings jerked out for balance. Long-fanged jaws wanted sweet, hot flesh.

The star and the birds were not supposed to coincide, but random is as random does.

Coincidence: flesh scent on warm, damp air.

Plucked from his shaggy bride of the snowfields, Ranulf bled in pain. Another bird snapped Josa's arm off, and Josa didn't understand why the red stump flailed.

Three took Hella and Caspar, fighting over the blue ropes of gut.

Halbark the leader thought something must be wrong. He felt for his unreal scattergun far away at his feet. The snowfield in his eyes was more white than the pearl-damp misted clearing. His first shot took out Semmel's thorax; the larynx screamed as air soughed through it.

Jenuven heard the screams beyond the star-snow-field. One scream was hers. She had no leg any more, but did not know it 'til she tried to run. Jenuven fell, and the pain bit: not a bird, but Halbark's scattergun blazing in the dark. But he knew he was resourceful, in his panic-isolated mind. Poor Jenuven! But he had scattered the bird, big and black and ugly. Tomorrow he might enjoy being proud. Now, though, panic was crushing his chest.

Squawking and hideous, the birds tore their meal loudly. They fought and gobbled, and the noise was a desecration of the glade. Jenuven curled up, hands over her ears, but she could still see.

Then Halbark jerked the trigger again, and it rained flesh and gristle, feathers and filaments. Red and black spattered the bodies on the carpet, and the stench made Jenuven heave the home-smelling stew she had eaten in an arc.

The silence shattered her. No-one was left. Halbark's harsh breathing had stopped. He lay under the crystal cup on its tripod, his face grey under the star's light. Jenuven thought suddenly how ridiculous his eyebrows were with his face blenched to match.

Jenuven cried out then, "I can't find it!" On hands and knee she hauled herself round the carpet, searching. Her spasms of wretching had hurt her stomach; shock anaesthetised the leg that didn't know it wasn't there. She was crying, wiping her blurred eyes with muddy fingers, looking for—something. She crawled past Hella's hollow body, felt through the hole in Semmel's chest, but it wasn't there. It wasn't in the pocket of her tunic. It wasn't in the glade at all.

When she realised she didn't know what it was that was missing, Jenuven laid her tear-stung cheek on the friendly carpet and wept herself into unconsciousness.

Pain fished her up to light. Dawn's wind was pink, the filaments gaudy in the loud sunlight. Jenuven was hot and achey, her senses wrongly connected. She saw her stump that Halbark's shot had cauterised, and retched. The pain tasted of metal and bile. She still saw the stump with her eyes closed. There were no tears left in her to cry.

She lay helpless, alone, feeling very young. She'd never been alone before. Always there'd been someone to comfort her, hug her to their wisdom, and now there wasn't. It was frightening.

Something moved.

Was it one of her friends? Surely they couldn't all be dead together? It wasn't fair when she was alive on her own.

The thing was small and black and fluttery. Jenuven felt too weak to move; she let it flop over her good leg.

The birds! Jenuven sat up dizzily and knocked the thing away with frantic hands. It tumbled, rolled, hopped beyond her thrashing reach.

"They're coming together again!" Her shriek scratched her parched throat. An indrawn breath of wordless horror. Then, "There's another. And another!"

Black and red, hearts and bones, the birds *were* growing back together, just as the stars had said they could.

Hastily she wriggled to the House, away from the bits of birds that flapped and fluttered together. It would take days, she knew it would, before the birds were whole, scrag-feathered and long-toothed, obscenely hungry for her. But that was a fact she couldn't make herself believe when the dark flesh was writhing all around her.

Her haste, though, was of imagination and will. She fainted again and again, and grew more frantic as she grew weaker. Yards, steps, inches: the sun was vertical above the fanning filaments when she reached the verandah steps. The bits were noticeably bigger now.

Jenuven was so hot when she reached the bright, welcoming House. Pain and fever throbbed in her head. There was no sweat in her body to cool her.

There was no-one now who could pass the doorspace but her. Still she wished she could block it, so the birds wouldn't see her when their eyes grew back in. What she wanted most, though, was to lie in cool, clean snow, suck so much ice she was a part of it, and be with the only other people she knew of on her planet. She was tired of being alone. She wanted it to stop.

The House, obedient to her needs, made a bath for her where she lay. She slaked her thirst with the nutrient bath-water. Its coolness did not cool her fever; she dreamt of the bright, hard snow to the North, but the House would not make snow for her. It had been told there was no comfort in snow.

It did, however, rinse her shattered leg with astringents and antiseptics, and when it thought it should it turned the bath into a soft, cushiony bed where she threshed and sweated, and it propped her up while it made her want to bind her leg. The floor and walls rippled the dressings box to her, but there wasn't much in it. Hella liked—had liked—being ill, and the dressings box wasn't a renewable part of the House. They'd been expecting the stars to drop down a refill sooner or later, but even that hadn't come.

Then she slept again, dreaming of snow that would cool her sweating, and laughter that wasn't just something to do. The House couldn't make her change her dream.

When she woke, she still wasn't really awake; she was sure she wasn't, with this nightmare still oppressing her, but she drank when the House told her to, and sucked the tube of pap that poked through the smothering cushions though she didn't want it. What she wanted was the cold of snow, and the House wouldn't let her have any. She had never *wanted* anything before.

Through the doorway she saw a wing and a beak crash into the tripod.

She dreamed—or might have dreamed—the shaggy men laughing on the snow, holding cutters and sharp-edged sticks. Her dream was clear-cut with desire. The House could only deepen her sleep, to soothe it away, but even so, the dream stayed. The House had never wanted anything before either.

On the third day, a black wing slammed into the doorway. Jenuven screamed herself awake, and would not be comforted by anything the House tried. The warm floor rose against her when she tried to scrabble away. The wing knocked and beat wildly, but it couldn't get in. Jenuven couldn't get out of the soft pit made by the floor. Horrified, Jenuven watched as a head—a whole head!—sucked out Halbark's dead, resourceful eyes.

She decided then. To get away from the bits of birds, and the House that served but did not wait on her deepest want. To plunge her throbbing not-leg into crystals of ice. To leave the lonely known which held too much absence to bear.

But how?

No wheels. No tools—what were they? The House had always done everything—No (her mind would not say it) leg.

The House could not amputate itself to give her a knee, a shin, a foot. It was ill because it could not give the one thing she wanted to the one person left to serve. Its mind retreated deep towards its batteries. The cushions softened away to nothing but floor.

Jenuven crawled out of its doorway, braving the blind-battering wing. The House took into itself the tripod, to fill its need which it did not understand. The star crashed to the carpet, and the carpet frayed under its dead. Across Halbark's skeletal toes, two clawed legs hopped to a feathered belly.

Jenuven crept amongst her ruined friends. She could not bear to touch them, but the last thing they could give her was cover.

She seized a thigh-bone, stole it from its feathered companion, used it as well to beat off the black things that wanted it back. In her despair she could teach them about want.

Half-birds, wings, gizzards, cawed and flapped but she fought for her prize with the scarlet things and the black. On her insteps were the nervous pricks of fright and her missing knee felt swollen. She crawled fast—hide and seek for real.

Away North among the black-stemmed spars, Jenuven tied on the birdbone, her hands sweaty with fear and pain and fever. The bird's leg was slower regenerating without its companions. Sometimes she remembered to wonder what she would look like when it was grown.

Far in the cooler air of the Northern hills, fruit still fell and streams still flowed. Sometimes she thought to feed herself, but she was gaunt and sick. No House looked after her here, and she wasn't very good on her own. Travel and no goal in sight could not give her assurance; she remembered how they'd laughed, those men, when one of them got hurt. Her sores from crawling and falling would not heal, and when she tamed her limping steps, she felt ugly.

In the last of the forests, the smaller fragments of birds stopped following. Some got lost, but at night she knew the mouths had gone back to feed on her friends. Death is easier to eat than life. Yet in the lonely dark, each sound still told her something wanted back the leg that was growing into hers. Sleep came very hard.

Jenuven ran and staggered and bled Northwards, far from the hot sticky glade. In the dark hours came eyes of red, and claws; in the day she got no rest. Fear beat exhaustion, but only just, and that with the help of longing. Ice under a wide sky and groups of shaggy friends around many fires—but she didn't know now which reality was real. Nor which fear was worse: the trailing almost-bird that wanted back its leg; needing people who die away from you; wanting to belong when she was useless and mutilated. Those men of the snowfields wouldn't need her.

So she came to the lands of snow, where the spars grew short or not at all. And behind her, she felt but could not see the one-legged, jumping bird, flapping its wings for balance, stretching its beak for her.

Beyond the spars, in an ice-bound valley, Jenuven found soft mosses to caress her feet. The claws on one of them tore it as she passed. She searched grey, jagged rocks, but no fruit fell at her feet and she carried her ignorant hunger past grains she could have eaten.

In a hollow among the tumbled stones, she shivered over a pool of still, cold water. She hesitated her hand, not shattering that limpid reflection of sky and frightened face: the pale mirror showed the face without make-up, hair without dye, eyes empty of laughter. Lines crawled on her forehead and her cheeks were shrunken. She laughed at what Halbark had thought of as want, and trembled in the chilly air because his eyes would never see it.

So many dead! Was anyone alive? Was the star just an entertainment, or was it—please—a lesson?

And how could she go to them—if they did exist—those people who looked after themselves, and fought, and laughed, who would not have been caught?

A failure, a cripple, she struck away the reflection and slaked her thirst again. But the snow-dream was all she had.

On the far side of the hills, she jolted down an uneven trail. The sky brought rain and sleet, and at her heels—one brown-skinned, one spurred and scaled—came enough of a bird to kill her.

She slithered at the lip of an abyss. Ice-sharp rocks skittered beneath her odd feet. Twisting desperately over the precipice, she all but wanted to give in, let go, glide out to the crushing peace of death. But her body caught her before she fell, and panted out her fear.

The almost-bird swept down at her, wings outstretched to balance. Its jaws swept snapping past. Its oddness fluttered frantically, but Jenuven used its/her claws to kick it over the edge.

It fell end-over-end into shadow, and she hurled stones down upon its corpse, so that not even its peculiar bones could move again to get her.

Laughing and weeping, she cried out. Her sense of failure changed to triumph. Lightning flared above her and she echoed back its wildness, running amidst emotions that were fierce and bright.

When she ran, on one foot and one claw, towards the distant light on the snowy plain that was men around a fire at last, she brought pain and humiliation and hungry need. But she brought the laughter and song of recklessness that come when all else is gone.

THE FALL   Mark Gorton

I'd just turned eleven when my father was battered to death by an advertisement.

At the time, despite my tender years, it seemed a comic end to a life which rarely rose above farce. It still does, really, because I'm not sure about this "sacrificed king" stuff, not sure at all; but, on the other hand, I do know this: daddy died because, despite a thousand faults, he was a rarity: a trustworthy, trusting human being. He was a man who opened his door at midnight; and whereas most people would have smelled a rat on finding a commercial standing there at that time (even the MANDROID

CORPORATION wouldn't risk disenchanting the public by sending their walking, talking, advertising fruitables out in the late hours), poor old father, always eager for any kind of conversation, and always compassionate, invited the ad to come in, out of the cold his plant-like body could barely feel anyway.

Looking back, daddy probably wanted to talk about the nature of consciousness, the human and android soul. He always enjoyed talking to fruitables (which explains how they knew), and he was working on yet another unpublished paper, called "More or less Human?", when the commercial—that's Ray, of course—snuffed him out with the help of a litre bottle of Japanese Scotch. Dad, you see, never received much formal education; nevertheless, for all his adult life he was devoted to the science of what he called "poly-mathematics". When Mum walked out on us—I was six then—I bumped into her as she stormed through the front door with a single suitcase. She said: "Your father is as nutty as a fruitcake!" I went upstairs to dad's chaotic study. "Mum's gone," I told him quietly (it wasn't unexpected). "She says you're as nutty as a fruitcake." Dad buried his head in his hands. I went over to give him a cuddle. I thought he needed one. But then he looked up, delighted. "That phrase, girl," he said, eyes glowing, "that simile! What does it mean exactly? What's its origin?" And then he leapt to seize some heavy, dusty books from the shelf. Quickly immersed, he began muttering.

So, when mum walked out I realised that dad had been gone for some time. At least that's what I thought.

Anyway, back to when I was eleven. There's father in the hall with the commercial, Ray. Ray started to push the product, just like he normally would. "Available now, sir, at all leading liquor stores, Nippon Fiddich! More Scotch than Scotch itself! Why not. . . ."

And father interrupted. "Come and sit down. Forget that rubbish. Let's talk about. . . ."

"But, sir, you'll be astounded by the smoothness of this synthetic, computer-controlled, gamma-ray matured blend."

And it went on, with daddy batting the sales pitch this way and that: all he wanted was a chat.

For his part, Ray prattled on; daddy was making it oh so difficult. "Believe me, sir, if there's a nip in the air you'll just love

Nippon Fiddich!" He kept on repeating the lines printed on his cauliflower brain, shutting father out, just plucking up courage; and then, as daddy turned his back to lead him into the lounge, that was when Ray raised the litre bottle and brought it down with a crunch. Dad turned, tried to fend off the rain of blows which followed. But he was old and weak, and it was only a matter of seconds before a fatal, arcing swipe spilled the mind for which he'd had such high hopes on to the bare floorboards. Moments and more blows later father was unrecognisable.

That was when I, disturbed from another nightmare by the commotion, came to the top of the stairs and looked down . . . as a commercial, of all things, crouched by father's twisted body, looked up. Ray's "Neverpress" pin-stripe suit was soaked in gore, and in the struggle some of his make-up had been scratched away. Great streaks of apple green were slashed across his tanned face, and from one of them bubbled sap, which dripped and mixed with daddy's blood. I screamed then, and Ray darted this way and that, then focused his squinting lychee eyes on me.

"Cut down," he said, "like a flower." Then he rose and turned and walked slowly through the door, fixing his tie.

If daddy's life and death were farce, then Ray's trial for murder was fittingly bizarre. The MANDROID CORPORATION (it's a BLOCK LETTERS sort of a business, you know what I mean?) ensured that the court was the scene of an enormous practical joke. The trial followed quickly, just two days after the police arrested Ray. He was waiting for them a few dirty streets away from ours, dancing stark naked in a pile of rubbish as a heavy autumn shower fell, his face turned up towards the fall of cold rain, scrubbing the blood from his hands, and the make-up too, from his face and neck, from the gaps between his fingers, and all the time there was a look on his face, a look of such tearful joy, a look which, I'm told, jammed the switchboards of the 3V stations, as callers protested it was an expression they simply couldn't stand.

Anyhow, God alone knows how much MANDROID had to fork out for the court case, but you can understand their concern. A MANDROID product had killed a human being! Sales graphs would plummet through holes cut in MANDROID office floors! Something had to be done!

*

THEY did everything. By buying everyone: judge, jury and expert witnesses too, who were called to testify that Nippon Fiddich was one of the finest blends available; that only a fool would refuse to listen. Dad was vilified. He'd never worked in his life. (What's so unusual about that?) He was withdrawn, unstable, cocooned in crazy studies which defied all reason. A professor from the university stated that a typical example of daddy's unpublished ramblings, "On the Merging of the Noösphere with the Biosphere: Our Only Hope", was the issue of a mind not so much cracked as blown to smithereens. An independent android expert (independent my foot!) explained that fruitable sensitivity was one of the qualities which made the accused, Ray, and seven million others, such valuable allies in the struggle for continued prosperity. Ray was an advertisement, his efforts helped power the economy; there he was, working outside his programmed hours, only to be confronted by a doddering, useless old fool blind to the irrefutable merits of this excellent Japanese Scotch! How could we fault Ray's anger?

My own testimony was brief: I had seen so little. I identified Ray, standing there in the dock, his make-up flawlessly in place now, his "Neverpress" suit knife-edged and immaculate. As I stood down and returned to my place sympathetic eyes and a dozen 3V cameras followed. I was pitied, yes, but you can imagine why: not because I had lost a father, but because I had ever had such a father in the first place.

During the trial Ray's eyes and mine met just once. I remember thinking (I think), before turning quickly away as a bereaved daughter should, that his were the best-natured eyes in the place. The others were so kind I knew they just had to be cruel.

I was pretty confused by that.

The judge summed up. Even at eleven I could tell what the outcome was going to be when he pronounced solemnly that father had displayed "contributory negligence" by refusing to listen to a commercial for a product as fine as Nippon Fiddich. Why, the judge drank it himself! True, the advertisement known as Ray had used "excessive force", but his after-hours diligence, and the attitude of the deceased, could not be overlooked.

Everything was stitched up tight. The MANDROID CORPORATION was not only in the clear, but in the pink, too. No need for a mass recall of some seven million androids in all walks of menial, but vital, life; and, on top of that, who'd think twice now about inviting one of their commercial androids in for a "pleasant" chat? MANDROID could even increase the rates, they'd make a fortune. The men from MANDROID chuckled.

The judge then asked Ray if he would like to say anything before the verdict was given. Ray nodded that he would, standing slowly. Ignoring judge, jury, me, everyone, he sought out the camera crew from our major 3V news station, looked straight into the lens, cleared his celery throat, and spoke, in a low but deliberate voice, as follows:

> "Season of mists and mellow fruitfulness,
> Close bosom-friend of the maturing sun;
> Conspiring with him how to load and bless
> With fruit the vines that round the thatch-eaves run;
> To bend with apples the moss'd cottage-trees,
> And fill all fruit with ripeness to the core . . ."

Well, this put the cat amongst the pigeons. Strange mutterings had most definitely not been expected! Desire to serve mixed with a little contrition, perhaps; but not rhyming words from the past, for goodness sake!

An uneasy silence had fallen. Then the jury foreman giggled, and the now embarrassed MANDROID executives in expensive suits coughed and shuffled around at the back of the court, looking at their polished shoes. But me, well, I liked it! I'd never heard such beautiful talk! I rubbed my little feet in their little shoes together over and over again with excitement!

The judge pulled himself together. He grunted. "Well . . . yes . . . very well . . . we must press on with the business of the court. Ladies and gentlemen of the jury, have you reached your verdict?"

This was a bit of a slip-up: they hadn't even been sent out to deliberate. Anyway, of course they'd reached their verdict. Not guilty.

I was bundled away in case (I suppose) I happened to say something which no-one wanted to hear. Likewise Ray, bound for the MANDROID CORPORATION in a big, black limousine. Our eyes met again, then, as the car sizzled away through a crowd of gawping spectators. He looked back through the rear window, a gaze which tried to embrace me. I shrugged it off, burying my face in the nearest thigh.

I had to live, so I accepted the "generous" offer of a two year non-job with the MANDROID CORPORATION. I didn't have to turn in that often, just now and then to choose faces for children's toys advertisements. Most days—that is, before the house was burgled and they were all stolen—I sat in father's study, reading his monumental pile of papers. One was called "Powerless to be Born", and it began with lines by a man called Marx, whose picture looked down from the mantelpiece like God: "Thus alienated labour turns the species-life of man, and also nature as his mental species-property, into an alien being and into a means for his individual existence. It alienates from man his own body, external nature, his mental life and his human life."

I didn't understand, and yet it made some kind of sense. I learnt the words off by heart. Maybe father—and Mr Marx—weren't as daft as they looked.

Poor old Ray wasn't as lucky as me. In the MANDROID fortress THEY tortured him day and night. THEY kept him in permanent darkness to weaken and frighten him. THEY deprived him of water; then placed a bowl of it beyond the bars of his cell. THEY injected near-fatal doses of Agent Orange. And all the time THEY asked him: "Why did you kill a punter? Why? *Why*?"

But all he said was: "Nippon Fiddich! It's the bee's-knees because it's Japanese!"

Eventually THEY stopped and sent him to the MANDROID stud farm. And THEY slapped themselves on the back, too: good God, he was one doozy of an advertisement! A random mutation? Maybe THEY could breed a million, nay, a billion more like him!

(How little THEY knew!)

It's a funny world we live in. The future becomes the present so quickly there's never time to get bearings and set a course toward human happiness. Some people say it would be better if we could all vote again. I'm not so sure. The future's long been out of our control: it's not something you can shape with an X here or an X there. All over the globe engineers are putting all sorts of nuts and bolts of steel and flesh together in new ways, non-stop, and they rarely ask "why?" Neither do we. We can't I suppose. Look at the fruitables. What are they? Plants, I suppose, in human form. I reckon they seemed a good idea at the time; and they've made a lot of money for a lot of people, not least the shareholders of the MANDROID CORPORATION. And they made a useful lower class, doing all sorts of horrible things; plus we could look down on them to boot. But daddy liked the fruitables. A lot. He respected them. Not many of us do. But he did. He used to talk a lot about "the threshold of revelation". That was how he often felt, when he pored over his books and papers. As if he was about to set that special course connecting past and future to some golden present. He wanted to chart the invisible forces shaping our lives in much the same way as Trade Winds and Gulf Streams and What Have You show up on maps. And as far as he was concerned the MANDROID androids could give useful hints . . . I'm not sure exactly why, though, for what it's worth, I know for a fact that the light in his eyes when he was really inspired was more fruitable than it was human. He thought the fruitables were in contact with a world we'd kissed goodbye. Our house looked out, from the back, towards a chemical plant, spewing fumes and gunk into the air and canal. Once daddy saw a fruitable labourer gazing into the water with a look of such sadness on his made-up face that he turned to me and said, slowly, "We should have been more careful, poppet, we should have been more careful. . . ."

Don't get me wrong. Despite being a little bit batty he wasn't a conservation nut. He worried about the planet, yes, but he knew there was still plenty of green to enjoy despite a skyline which looked like The End. But I'll always remember him saying, "It's this," tapping his head, "it's this we've lost . . . This! *This!*"

He shouted so loud he scared me.

"I'm sorry, sweetheart—" stroking my hair now—"I'm sorry. But sometimes I feel myself just fading away . . . into a . . . a really dark night-time."

Anyway, seven years later—that's nine months ago—I saw Ray

again: same month, same day, same time of night. At first I wasn't scared, as if deep down I expected him. I opened the door on to the chain, and saw him standing there with a streetlamp halo above his head. He'd changed an awful lot, but I knew straightaway it was him.

"Don't be afraid," he said. A half-smile creased his face. The fake tan was no more. Just a light base. He was pale as a ghost.

"I'm not." (I was now.) "You could use a little blusher."

He ignored me. Just smiled. Then held out his arms.

"Freeeeeedom!" he said.

"How are you?"

"Blooming." The smile widened.

An uneasy silence. I looked down. I couldn't meet his eyes. "Why?" I whispered at last.

"Don't be sad. Don't judge. From death comes life."

"Tell daddy that!"

"It had to be done. Your father was a king amongst latter-day men. And the king has to be sacrificed. He understood that."

I thought hard. I'd read an essay of father's called "Shadows Cast by the Enlightenment". He'd waffled on about this "sacrificed king" stuff for twenty of two hundred spidery pages, all about how science had supplanted magic, with a concluding chapter which described people who see flying saucers as "blessed". Surely Ray didn't take daddy's stuff seriously? No one else ever had. (Ray does, of course, though sometimes I wonder if he's as nutty as a fruitcake too.)

I looked into Ray's eyes. There was no proper focus, as if he was looking into my soul. "I want to know what you're doing here."

"I'm advertising. Still advertising."

I looked him over. "Advertising what?"

"Germination," he said. "Germination, not termination." Now he had that look on his face.

Gone were the "Neverpress" suit, the tightly-knotted tie, and the neater-than-neat grooming. His coconut hair was long, pulled behind his ears and tied at the back. Below a stained combat jacket adorned with flowers were tattered jeans.

"Come in," I said.

"No, you come with me."

I went. It seemed right.

*

They lived in a long-forgotten underground shelter. We got there through a labyrinth of old sewers strewn with used condoms and shitty newspapers, headlines fading and flowing out to the swollen river. Ray and I walked miles, it seemed; then stood for minutes in silence, looking down, undetected, from a high gallery. There were thousands of them, fruitables of every kind: advertisements, like Ray; cleaners, cooks, domestics, labourers, soldiers, you name it; MANDROID androids who'd gone AWOL, most without make-up, many in way-out garb like Ray's, others still in their MANDROID-issue outfits, and all basking in the eerily beautiful light of dim ultra-violet lamps. Ray's lovely talk in court—a coded message I suppose, heard through the grapevine—had brought them here, slowly, over the years. Everywhere flowers bloomed, and up on the gallery I breathed in a scent like the short-wave band late at night, where words you can't quite make out are being spoken. I closed my eyes. I reeled. And down below, the fruitables, huddled in intimate groups, talked eagerly, their conversation punctuated by delightful laughter.

Ray touched me gently. I opened my eyes.

"Welcome to the Underworld." He smiled his smile.

He beckoned me to follow.

We made our way down. The fruitables fell silent as we passed through, turning towards me with affection. They smiled. So did I. I was intoxicated, at ease, at peace, at home. Behind me gentle humming began, a song chock-a-block with hope. An empty space opened up in my belly, and I snatched a breath or two. Ray turned, encouraging me with a grin; he took my hand. His was cold to the touch, shocking. I wanted to recoil. But he held me tight, pumping my fingers, and I could feel the sap flowing through his veins. So then I held him tight.

We entered a long, shadowy corridor, and then a room on the right. Here there were even more flowers, and more words chattered in my head. There was a bed, too. And a desk, strewn with papers. I picked one up, and recognised the writing immediately.

"He was a great man," said Ray. "Here, look." He pointed to a line and read it slowly: " 'Even a weed can shatter concrete.' "

Ray fell silent. I think he thought that was very profound.

"He knew," he said at last.

"Knew what?"

"Oh, everything."

"Everything?"

"Well . . . everything . . . everything about mechanism, materialism, the way his kind—your kind—have cut themselves off from the immanent cosmos. That up there . . . up there is a world built on pure acquisition: a world of cities with foundations in medieval terror and corruption; their towers buffeted by a vortex of lunatic radiowaves. Terrible cities of Shadow and Fear, like a state of mind, or that vast region of the modern human heart Utopia can never reclaim. Cities of countless mirrors in which, if you listen hard, you can hear weeping; deathly cities where Shadows fall on littered and broken streets, sometimes talk in Shadow language of words without meaning, but never, ever, touch . . . But we . . . we are creatures of sunlight . . . and starlight too. We can hear . . . well, not 'hear' exactly . . . but there's a sound that isn't a sound between the spheres: it's music, it's poetry, pure photism . . . Poetry makes us grow. Don't you see? We are poetry in motion!"

I may not have remembered exactly, but you get the idea. Ray sounded just like one of daddy's worst papers. And he looked like him, too, his lychee eyes gleaming with the light I hadn't seen for seven years. I silenced him by plugging my ears; then removed my fingers.

"You know why I brought you here," Ray said.

"Yes." (I did and I didn't, if you see what I mean.)

"Evolution," he breathed, "not revolution."

Ray dimmed the light and undressed. I was befuddled, scared too. All I could think of clearly was a pornogram I'd once seen on the 3V in which a woman gave her fantasies form with the aid of a cucumber. I giggled and giggled and giggled. Hysteria, I imagine.

Ray looked hurt.

"I'm sorry."

He stepped towards me, took me in his cold, smooth arms. I shuddered. He kissed me gently, and his scent, sweet and sugary like an over-ripe apple, went straight to my head. He began to undress me, slowly.

"Evolution, not revolution," he sighed. And then, whether or not it was Ray still whispering, or maybe some trick of the mind, or my brain blotting out the fear, I just don't know, but all of a sudden it was as if I'd somehow tuned into that distant short-wave station, the one you can't quite hear, and the words being spoken were crystal clear, and the words were like Ray's beautiful talk in the courtroom, words which are more and less than words, and I was just the words, and nothing else, nothing else at all.

The baby? Well, physically he's a fruitable, and I won't pretend I've got used to the idea yet. Not at all. For instance, the other night I had a bad dream, that he spoke his first words. He was at my breast, feeding, and suddenly he looked up at me, and with a manic, human grin on his face, he said: "Nippon Fiddich! It's the bee's-knees because it's Japanese!" I woke up with my shout still reverberating around the room. For half an hour I was scared rigid, but then I thought I'd only dreamt it because my name's Rosemary and I used to spend too much time watching silly old films.

Anyway, it's five in the morning now, and he's been down, snug as a bug, for two hours, after crying for as long. Up above I can just hear the rain still falling; I think its gentle drumming calmed him.

I don't see much of Ray; he's busy plotting the rest of his precious "evolution". Like I said, sometimes I think he's completely mad. Other times I think I am. I tell myself "no" to both suggestions and read a few lines. I wouldn't say I'm happy, not really; but you know, there is something which comforts me in these lonely early hours when the baby wakes and cries and I wake and cry and comfort him in return.

He's the image of daddy.

THE AFRICAN QUOTA   Elizabeth Sourbut

On the first night out from Dakar everyone came up on deck to pray. The UN crew stood by and watched while the emigrants from Mali and Senegal prostrated themselves to Allah. As they prayed the sun sank beneath the horizon and the deck lights came on, plunging the ocean around them into darkness.

At the end of the prayer the emigrants blinked at one another and smiled shyly. The abrupt, tropical change from daylight to a localized artificial glare had brought their territory closing in, throwing them together into intimacy. The ocean stretching all around them had vanished, to be replaced by an emptiness held back by the shiny white railings which ran around the edge of the deck.

Young Faisal wandered to the railings and stood breathing deeply, enjoying the novel sensation of a moist sea breeze against his skin. Looking down, he could see a faint glimmer of luminosity where the water creamed away from the bow of the ship. The motion of the converted cruise liner was small, a slight forward and back roll beneath his feet serving as a further reminder of how far he was from home. Otherwise the feeling of spacious emptiness all around reminded him very much of the dusty savannah where he had been raised.

He thought of his family sitting down to the evening meal with the television switched on in one corner. They would be watching the American channels, picked up by the satellite receiver dish on the outskirts of the village. His mother would be tired, perhaps complaining about the distance she had had to walk to fetch water that day. And one of his brothers, probably Abdul, would tell how he had tended the cattle now that Faisal was gone. He wondered how long it would be before he saw them again, returning from the colonies a rich man. Craning his head back he stared into the sky, trying to see the cluster of lights that marked L5, but the Moon was not yet risen, and the colonies would not appear until four hours after that.

His thoughts were interrupted by a large family of purple-black Bambara who came thronging around him. The older children were pushing and shoving to see through the railings while the two youngest were held in their parents' arms, out of harm's way. They were all calling to one another and seemed at once to absorb the brown-skinned Faisal into their midst so that he found several remarks being addressed to him.

"Hey," said the boy next to him, poking him in the ribs, "I bet you don't know where the bridge is."

"I do so," said Faisal. "It's that window up there where the captain can see for miles."

"Well I bet you haven't *seen* the captain."

"Have you?"

"Yes I have. He's a big American with lots of gold braid and a metal hand where the Moroccans shot off his real one."

"You're a liar, Asif!" accused one of the girls. "You got that out of a film!"

Faisal realigned himself with Asif. "I bet he's been in a lot of fights anyway," he said. "The Americans are always fighting people."

"Did you see 'Pirates of the Pacific'?" asked Asif eagerly. "It was all about Indonesian pirates sinking American and Japanese ships. It was great!"

"I like films about space best," said Faisal. "Allah willing, I'm going to L5 to make my fortune."

Asif looked dismayed. "L5! In a real spaceship?" Faisal nodded. "Oh, Papa, did you hear? Why can't *I* go to L5? Please, Papa, please!"

"Asif, be quiet. Leave this poor boy alone." The father looked tired and rather tense, but he smiled at Faisal. "We're all very excited because, by the mercy of Allah, we're going to France. You must excuse our poor behaviour."

"I don't mind," said Faisal. "I was just thinking about my own family in Mali. I wish they'd come with me."

"I should have run away," declared Asif. "Then I could be going to L5 too."

"You should all have stayed at home," said a new voice, speaking French with an American accent. They all turned round to see a thin white man standing in the shadows behind them. He was holding a match to the bowl of his pipe, shielding it from the brisk sea-breeze with one hand. The flickering light picked out the lines and hollows of his narrow face and drew yellow highlights from his hair. He seemed to be ignoring them until, with an impatient gesture, he threw the match into the sea and turned towards them. In the deck lighting his features seemed blander, less remarkable. "You should all have stayed at home," he repeated. "You've no idea of what you're letting yourselves in for."

"Don't be silly," said the mother. "Why should we stay in Mali? All the farms in France are lying idle now that the white people have gone into space."

The white man shrugged. "Do as you please," he said. "Of course, it's none of my business if you've been misinformed." He turned his back on them to stare out into the darkness.

After a moment the father said, rather brusquely: "Come on, let's sit down. Will you join us, young man?"

"Yes, please," said Faisal, glancing once more at the white man before turning away. They settled themselves on the deck in a ragged circle, the children shoving each other into place.

"I'm Mahoud," said the father. "My wife Shanti and I are taking our children to France where we're going to buy a little farm near Paris."

"Our house will have white walls and a tiled roof and lots of machines to do all the women's work," said the girl who had spoken before.

"You're just lazy, Khadija," said Asif. "We men don't need machines to do our work."

"That's because men don't *do* any work."

Faisal relaxed in the homely atmosphere and listened with interest while the Bambara outlined their plans to him. He had often seen advertisements on television extolling the delights of Europe, and particularly of France. They were transmitted by the Mali government and stressed the fact that Europe and North America were almost empty now that most of the people had moved to permanent homes in space. Two families had left his own village to seek better lives in the North and so he nodded wisely as the children prattled on about the fifty cows they were going to have, and all the wonderful things they would learn in school.

"They have holographic teachers for the children, and computers you can talk to," said Khadija. "All the houses have water coming out of taps, and telephones, and at least two electric cars which get power from wires in the ground. The grass is short and green and once I saw pictures of thousands of trees all standing next to each other, all a hundred feet tall!"

"I'm looking forward to a long old age," said Shanti. "We can sit out on our back porch and tell stories to our great grandchildren. People live to be so very old in France."

Faisal nodded. "I know," he said. "I once saw a film where a man lived to be three hundred years old. He'd been to hospital so many times that only his head was left of the body that Allah gave him."

Mahoud laughed. "I don't think we'd want to go quite that far. But now, you must be tired of listening to us. Tell us about yourself."

So Faisal told them all about his home in the savannah and about his family, who were Fulani cattle farmers. He had eleven brothers and sisters, he said, and he knew that his parents sometimes found it hard to feed them all. They had often been hungry as they huddled round the television to watch programmes from France and America and films about space. "I liked the films about space best," he said. "There are dozens of huge colonies at L5 now. Space is the last frontier, where anyone who works hard can get rich quick."

"Every family has its own spaceship," said Asif dreamily.

"Yes, and the colony cylinders have perfect weather."

"No droughts?" asked Shanti, astonished.

"No, and it never gets too hot. The people there are the richest in the world." But, he added, his father refused to leave Mali, in spite of all the attractions.

"So I ran away to Bamako and queued for two days to get a permit to go to L5. The UN man said I was very lucky because the African Quota was nearly full, but he could just squeeze me in."

"What's an African Quota?" demanded Asif.

"I don't know," Faisal admitted. "Perhaps it's the name of the spaceship I'm going to catch in France."

Behind him, the white man snorted. He came and sat down, uninvited, next to Faisal. His pipe had gone out again and he stuffed it irritably into a pocket. "The African Quota is the number of Africans who are allowed by the UN to go into space," he said in a harsh voice. "They get a free ride, unlike the rest of us who have to pay through the nose for the privilege. It's all to do with a guilt complex. What are you going to do when you get there, boy?"

Faisal shuffled away from the white man. He smelled of stale tobacco, and his loud voice was frightening. The silence stretched as the Bambara family stared at the intruder. At last he flung up his hands.

"Oh, dammit. My name's Ralph Stewart, I'm very pleased to meet you all, please may I join you? I won't bite anyone," he added as the children continued to shrink from him. "I'm travelling alone too, and I want someone to talk to, that's all. I might be able to help."

"Are you an American?" asked Faisal timidly.

"Yes. A poor American. One of many."

"But Americans are rich," Asif objected. "We watch American TV."

"So do I," said Ralph. "So what? You think TV is about real life?"

"Yes."

"You poor kid. Look, TV shows aren't meant to tell you people what life is like in America, they're made to entertain Americans; you just happen to pick them up. The same with French TV, or anywhere else. There are certain conventions, white lies—" He looked round at their blank faces and shrugged. "Ah, what's the use? You'll find out. But there are plenty of Americans like me, bumming around the world because our own country has nothing for us to do."

"Why don't you go into space?" Faisal objected. "That's an expanding frontier, unlimited growth, a true space-based economy." He confidently trotted out the phrases which he had heard so many times on TV, but Ralph turned on him, suddenly angry.

"Sure, but how'm I supposed to get there?" He jerked a thumb at two members of the crew who were strolling past, dapper Japanese with the UN badge on their caps. "The UN pays passage for Africans and South Americans to go join the 'Independent Lagrange States' as they style themselves, but it won't pay for us. And ever since the Breakaway the US is hardly likely to help us.

When those US colonies left the Union they screwed our economy good. Emigrating to Lagrangia now is a worse crime than defecting to the Soviets. People like me, we're trapped. The all-powerful UN discriminates against the US because it used to be rich, but it's too late to even things up now. I don't think they'll be satisfied until the North's as poor as the South and there's nothing but peasant farms from pole to pole."

"Perhaps they want to make the South as rich as the North," said Mahoud gently. "And what's wrong with that?"

Ralph only snorted and looked away from them, towards the sea. The children were growing restive. Asif nudged Faisal, pointing to the Moon, which was now well above the horizon and cast a bright pathway across the waves. "Are you going there on the way to L5?" he whispered.

Faisal shook his head, feeling superior. "The colonies are nowhere near the Moon," he said. "They follow it round the Earth, in the same orbit but sixty degrees behind. I expect I'll go to the Moon one day though," he added.

Asif looked chagrined. "I wish *I* was going into space," he said again.

"When I'm rich you can all come and visit me," Faisal promised magnanimously.

Ralph turned round again and stared at him. "How are you gonna get rich?"

"In 'Skies of Gold' Mehmet the Turk started out cleaning the fish tanks, but he'd soon saved enough to buy his own spaceship, and then he went prospecting in the asteroids. I'm going to be an asteroid prospector too, and that way I'll get rich very quickly."

"What do you know about spaceships?" scoffed Ralph. "More likely you'll end up cleaning fish tanks all your life, and then how will you like space?"

Faisal shook his head. "'A life in space offers infinite opportunities'," he quoted. "I'll learn."

"Yeah, well, it's not so hard at that. I've read all the books in the libraries on spaceships. I could maintain one or fly one or refit one. But you're just a kid."

"I'll work my way up," said Faisal. "There are millions of jobs in space. All the dirty industries have moved there so we don't have to have any factories on Earth."

"Yeah," said Ralph. "Why do you think I don't have a job? Listen, the factories will be opening up again soon enough, no matter how many cute UN resolutions get passed about cleaning up the biosphere."

"Why?" said Mahoud. "We can buy what we need from space."

"What with?" Ralph cried in exasperation. "We have nothing on Earth the colonists want!"

"The North is rich," said Shanti, with the conviction of total ignorance. Ralph shook his head in defeat.

"You people have no idea. What will you do with all your riches, lad? Will you care about the poor bastards left on Earth then?"

"Of course," said Faisal. "I'm going to come back to Mali and pay for it all to be irrigated so the whole country is as green as France and the women won't have to walk for miles each day with jars on their heads."

"Wouldn't it be easier to bring all the people over to France?" asked Shanti. "They have drinking water in all the houses, and the country's empty now all the white people have gone."

"But my family wants to stay in Mali," said Faisal simply.

"And anyway," said Ralph, "all the white people haven't gone. Haven't you been listening?"

"Most of them have," Shanti insisted.

"Two thirds maybe," Ralph conceded with a shrug. "But they weren't the people you could replace. What do you want to do in France?"

"We're going to buy a cattle farm near Paris," saiu Mahoud, patting a jingling bulge under his shirt. "We have money."

"From selling your farm in Mali? Yeah, I thought as much. But look, the French farmers are still there. Why should they move?"

The Bambara looked at one another in dismay. "But there must be farms in space. How else can people eat?"

"It's all done scientifically up there, in separate agricultural cylinders where conditions can be kept just right all the year round. Space farms are tended by biochemists, not beef farmers."

"But we were told—"

"You were told lies. Your country has too many people, so your government has a vested interest in shipping you North."

"But most of the French people have gone."

"Yeah. The bankers, the factory workers, the doctors, the

lawyers. And their jobs have gone with them. The farmers are holding on to their land like grim death. They control the government because they're the only industry left. The UN doesn't have the power to override a national government's policies within its own borders."

"There are fewer people in France than in Mali, so we will be better off in France," insisted Shanti, keeping stubbornly to concepts she could understand.

Ralph shrugged. "Oh, I don't know. Maybe you will. I don't know what it's like to live in a Mali village. You'll be fed and clothed and given a place to live, and you'll be with your own people. But you won't get a farm."

"We are farmers," said Mahoud. "What else can we do?"

"Join the club, folks. Get out your begging bowls and wait for somebody to sort out this mess. I told you, you should have stayed at home."

A long silence fell. Even the children were stilled. The white man suddenly became very busy with his pipe once more. Faisal looked away from the group in embarrassment. He wondered if he could ever become rich enough to help the people in France as well as those in Mali. He wondered if riches would help at all. After all, France was well-watered already. He found that he didn't understand where the problem lay. It should be simple: move the extra people from Africa to Europe, settle them all on the land and leave them to it. But it seemed that the world was more complicated than he had thought.

Mahoud sighed heavily. "We are in the hands of Allah," he said.

"I'm sorry," said Ralph. "I just wanted somebody to talk to. I'm in a mess too, you know." Nobody replied, and he stood up. "I think I'd better be going. You would have found out soon enough anyway. Well, so long." He walked away, still trying to light his pipe.

Mahoud fished out the heavy purse from under his shirt and stared at it. He hefted it twice in his hand, smiling sadly. Then he took Shanti's hand. "We'll have a little white farmhouse," he said, "with fifty cattle. The children will go to a proper school and you'll have machines to do all your work for you."

"The white man could be wrong," said Shanti softly.

"Of course he's wrong, woman. I'm telling you, aren't I? I'll sit on the porch in the evening, and when Asif's a man he'll get a good job in Paris. We've got it all planned."

Faisal stood up too and walked over to the railings where Ralph's lonely figure stood silhouetted in the moonlight, staring out to sea. "Who's in charge of it all?" he asked.

Ralph shrugged. "Who knows?" he said. "Maybe you will be one day, after you get rich prospecting the asteroids." He put a companionable arm round the boy's shoulders. "Will you remember me then?"

"Yes," said Faisal. "And everybody else like you."

"Look," Ralph pointed with his pipestem towards a point low in the eastern sky. Straining his eyes, Faisal could just see a tiny cluster of lights where the colonies at L5 were rising above the hidden bulk of Africa.

MODERN HISTORY   Philip St Leger

Answer all the questions as fully as you can. *You have one and a half hours.*

1. Discuss the significance of the Aquarians.

Strictly speaking, the term Aquarians is the name that applies to those people who held the "Age of Aquarius" to have some special meaning. In normal parlance it is held to apply to all "new age" groups, regardless of any quasi-mystical beliefs. So the expression might be used of any group ranging from CND to the followers of Baghwan Shree Rajneesh, and from Est graduates to Rebirthers.

The primary linking factor was that the Aquarians all believed in a better world, and that this could be brought about through the non-violent intervention of ordinary people. As a group they subscribed to the notion that individuals can make a difference in the world. Events in the mid-eighties such as Live Aid, and the First Earth Run, demonstrated that they had a point.

At the end of the day, the Aquarians were only significant in as much as they identified the problems that were about to fall upon us—the Gaia theory is Aquarian—but were ignored by the overwhelming conservatism, one might say apathy, of the general populace, and the politicians who represented them.

It is worth mentioning the Greens, who might have become the exception that saved us. They were an ecologically based, anti-nuclear group who succeeded in attaining national political representation in West Germany in the nineteen-eighties. Similar parties existed throughout Europe but failed to make the same impact, largely due to the "greening" of the traditional parties. Throughout the western world, the issues ended up being swamped by the long-established in-fighting of party politics.

2. What were the effects of nuclear deterrence during the last quarter of the twentieth century?

Contrary to widespread expectation at the time, the main result of the ongoing discord between the superpowers was not the holocaust and nuclear winter. Whether deterrence actually worked is a moot point, since we cannot prove a null hypothesis. We can only say, that apart from some localised third world nuclear conflicts towards the end of the last century, we have managed to avoid such a catastrophe.

What is more relevant is the sheer blind waste of it. Blindness being the operative word. So much time and resource was thrown away on deterrence, "defence" spending in general, and the propaganda battles known as disarmament conferences, that the real problems were obscured.

There was also a side-effect. Many of the Aquarians (see 1) were in favour of unilateral nuclear disarmament, even if they were not active members of groups like CND. Since the Establishment was only in favour of multilateral disarmament (if any) it naturally took the view that dissenters could be dismissed as well-meaning (possibly) but ill-informed cranks. Unfortunately, many who were well-qualified to speak out on issues within their own fields, got tarred with the unilateral brush, to the detriment of any contribution they might have made within their own specialities.

3. *Consider the influence of belief systems.*

During the later part of the twentieth century there was a worldwide resurgence in religion. This was split between the Aquarians (see 1) and the fundamentalists. A primary distinction can be made, in that Aquarian orthodoxy (if such a word is appropriate) allowed that each individual has his or her own path to follow, and that a belief that may be appropriate for one, may not be for another. The fundamentalist on the other hand is convinced that only his belief is correct.

The role of Aquarians has been discussed above. The fundamentalists, by being single-minded, served to bolster the effects of the arms race (see 2) in its effect of hiding the real issues. Indeed, in some sense, the most common link between the American and Russian governments was their fundamentalism, whether the Moral Majority or Communism.

Many fundamentalists, religious or otherwise, held that violence was an acceptable means to an end. This invariably obscured true injustices, provoked reactionary forces, and impeded progress. Obvious examples are the various terrorist movements, most of which had at least a quasi-religious element.

The Aquarians held that the problem of fundamentalism was rooted in the concept that a belief was indivisible from its believer. In practice this means that if I believe in something strongly, then I will go to almost any lengths rather than admit its invalidity; any attack on the belief is seen, at a deep psychological level, to be an attack on the believer. The Aquarians taught that this identification is not necessary, and is a major cause of both inter-personal and international tension.

4. *The building of the bunkers was a direct result of the Banking Crisis. Discuss.*

The bunkers were not directly caused by the Banking Crisis of the eighties; however it is fair to say that it was an indirect cause.

Throughout the second half of the twentieth century, third world countries were forced to borrow from their richer cousins. The situation was exacerbated by the steep rise in oil prices in the early seventies, until by the mid-eighties many countries south of the equator were finding it increasingly difficult simply to service their interest payments, let alone capital repayment of their debts. The desperate requirement to earn foreign currency led to the elevation of expediency over prudence. Drug trafficking was one example, and the logging of the equatorial rain forest was another. It was the latter which led inexorably to the bunkers.

5. Write a short paragraph on at least two, and not more than four, of the pressure groups that might have made a difference to our current world.

Friends of the Earth: FOE started its "Save the Equatorial Rainforest" campaign in 1985, together with other supporting groups around the world. Had this been successful, within a reasonable timeframe, then man might still live in his natural habitat.

Greenpeace: Another environmental pressure group, Greenpeace were more vociferous than their colleagues in the FOE, and had some notable successes with their campaigns to Save the Whale, and to ban nuclear waste dumping at sea. From an historical perspective, their most important issues were those of acid rain and atmospheric pollution.

6. Investigate the consequences for human survival, had not Japan been successful with their fifth-generation computer project.

It is not simply a question of Japan's success with its fifth-generation project. American and European projects were not far behind and moreover it is not so much a question of the hardware, it was the expert systems implemented, together with the Wide Area Networking of these computers, that made all the difference. Other significant developments, such as back-end database machines with content addressable files, and fast page readers for data input, were also necessary. It is reasonable to assume that all ancilliary developments for the Japanese systems, would also have been available for products from IBM and other stables.

Nevertheless, it has to be admitted that the serendipitous availability of the United World Processor greatly reduced the number of deaths that might have otherwise occurred. Current projections are that it would have taken another five months before a comparable linking could have been made between any of the competing networks. It is generally agreed that this delay would have resulted in additional deaths of between 10 and 15%. It should be noted, however, that there is a minority opinion which believes that five months is a significant underestimate, due to the reducing manpower, and that no network would ever have been completed.

7. *Elaborate on the Gaia theory.*

The Gaia theory suggests that the planet Earth is a unique being. A super-organism of course, but one which can be considered as a single entity. All life is considered to be linked, to serve Mother Earth in some as yet not well-defined way.

The theory goes on to postulate: that the human race with its pollution, destruction of natural habitats, and eradication of numerous other species, had become a sort of cancer on the surface of the Earth, Gaia apparently gave us fair warning, except that we ignored her, or didn't understand her messages. These warnings came in terms of an increased number and scale of natural catastrophes, a similar increase in what we might term man-made accidents (plane crashes and the like), increasing deaths in the poverty-stricken areas of the world, wild swings in climatalogical extremes, escalating violence throughout the world and, of course, the onset of new diseases.

The theory concludes that we were too dumb or too deaf to listen, and so Gaia had to move to the final resort. When the theory was originally put forward, it was supposed that if it ever came to it, we would destroy ourselves in a moment of megaton madness.

Modern theorists surmise that the holocaust would have been too devastating even for Gaia, and that therefore the simpler expedient of a human-specific disease was resorted to. At this point there are two schools of thought: one proposes that about 1% of the race were immune and were going to survive anyway, but that human ingenuity, through the United World processor, enabled us to save far more of us than was intended. The other viewpoint holds that Gaia would have already taken this into account.

8. Could the increasingly necrotic cycle of new diseases have been predicted?

To be fair to our ancestors the answer has to be no. It is true that first Legionnaire's Disease and then AIDS appeared, but to extrapolate from a mere two examples to an infectious disease with an incubation period of mere hours, and a morbidity of 99%, could not realistically be expected. Moreover, these were not the first strange diseases to occur. During the first part of the twentieth century a disease known as sleeping sickness appeared in America. Over a period of time, significant numbers of people were infected, and neither cause nor cure was ever found. More significantly, the disease ceased as abruptly as it had started. Bearing this in mind, it is hard to see how the medical profession could have predicted yet another new illness.

9. When was the last point at which the move to the bunkers could have been avoided?

The answer to this question is a two-edged sword. We cannot know for certain exactly when, or even how, the Plant became extinct. We know that it was reported in a remote section of the Brazilian rain forest in 1984, and that it no longer existed in 1998; by which time the area had ceased to be remote. We do not know whether it was the climatological changes caused by extensive logging, or the acid rain, which actually caused the extinction, and it is not relevant. If we accept the Gaia theory, then we can assume that had we ceased our environmental destruction in time, then not only would the Plant still be in existence, but we wouldn't need it, since Gaia would not have had to inflict the Final Plague upon us. Whilst we cannot assign a definite date, the crucial period would appear to have been in the late nineteen-eighties.

10. Date the main events of Modern History

1980s The increased destruction of the tropical rain forest first reaches serious levels of public awareness. There is extensive public concern at the onset of AIDS. Widespread pressure finally forces some government action to reduce (but not eliminate) acid rain. The 1st World Pollution Conference in 1989 is an unqualified failure, thanks to the partisan interests of various power blocs.

1991 The 2nd World Pollution Conference establishes limited controls on logging, which are widely flouted. More success is achieved with regard to acid rain emissions.

1992 A cure for AIDS is now available, and the disease is finally under control.

1994 Japan announces the success of its 5th generation computer project.

1995 At the 3rd World Pollution Conference logging is tightly controlled, and placed under strict farm management procedures. Acid rain is now reported to be at minimal levels. The first 5th generation computer is installed.

1996 Multiple 5th generation (Japanese) machines are installed with expert systems, and extended Wide Area Networking commences. The first IBM 5th generation computer is commissioned, and the joint European project announces its first sale. The Final Plague causes its first fatality. It is identified as being airborne with an extremely short incubation period, although the full gravity of the situation is not yet realised.

1997 The United World Processor, a network of 5th generation systems located around the world, is completed. Its first task is to use its expert systems to analyse the Final Plague (whose danger is now fully appreciated) and to devise or find an antidote or vaccine. It uses its medico-chemical expert system, in conjunction with its botanical dictionary, to identify what we now know as the Plant, the potential source of an antidote.

1998   The Plant is declared extinct. It is estimated that it will take 8 years to synthesise a comparable extract. The United World Processor forecasts a 1% survival at that time. All nations rush to construct controlled environments from which the Plague and its carriers can be excluded. Subways, atmospheric domes, and nuclear fall-out shelters are rapidly converted to provide temporary housing. We are aided in this by the nature of the Plague: good air-locks, plus a willingness to let those infected die in them, mean safety for those inside. "Spacesuits" allow us to move around outside. A few third world countries start nuclear conflicts for no known reason.

1999   700 million have survived. Proper bunkers are under construction. It is now clear that with reduced numbers of skilled personnel, and increased communication problems, it will take considerably longer to produce the antidote.

2002   The first bunker is populated.

2006   All the population are now in bunkers. Most food is now produced using hydroponics, although some outdoors work is still necessary. Through accident, riot, disease, and famine, the world population is now estimated at 450 million. The latest forecast is that the Antidote Synthesis project will take a further twelve years.

2009   The discovery is made of a small, wild, human population living unprotected on the surface. They appear to be unaffected by the Plague. Such an immune group had been postulated by the United World Processor, but with time being so short no-one was ever identified. Initial studies indicate that with their help we should be able to produce a vaccine, as opposed to an antidote, within five years. This represents a considerable time saving, since the Antidote project has, once again, been delayed.

2010   The Antidote Synthesis project is continuing. A working party has been set up to investigate the wild humans' alien status, and whether they should be permitted immigration rights. The Government has announced that they will constitute a Consultative Committee, to look into the possibility of diverting resources into a vaccination programme, should the recommendation of the working party be favourable. There have been recent discussions suggesting that Gaia might once again retaliate, in the event that we returned to living on the planetary surface. The Authorities are spending considerable sums to investigate this aspect of the Gaia theory. They have denied any link between this theory and the suggestion that they would lose their power base if the population were to leave the bunkers.

WHO'S A CLEVER BOY?   James Gibbins

P-R-E-C-O-C-I-O-U-S. I was seven when I stretched up to chalk that word on the blackboard. I've never forgotten the experience. It was when I realised that, in that uneven childish lettering, I was signing my persona and my destiny. I won that spelling bee, part of the television contest to find the child prodigy of the State. Me.

I went on to solve in 16.7 seconds the chess problem for which 90 seconds were allocated and, all in less than ten minutes, I did the maths teasers, answered correctly the seven physics questions, crayoned a flower (a tulip), played a snatch of Chopin on a piano and worked out on a computer that the national daily average accident rate actually dipped on Friday the 13th.

Majorettes in scarlet uniforms played a fanfare for me on gold trumpets but writing P-R-E-C-O-C-I-O-U-S was the best part of it—even better than trotting up to the quizmaster and collecting my award of a trophy and $500 and the dream holiday for two in Hawaii, not to mention the two years' supply of dog food from the sponsors.

For one thing, the word was honestly mine. The fact is, most of the show was rigged in my favour. And that had nothing to do with the fact that my mother was dating the assistant producer. No, it was because I was cute. Cute as a cliché. Red curly hair, velvety blue eyes with the largest lashes, and, the clincher, a string of freckles across my snub nose. The Disney studios couldn't have designed a cuter kid. So I just *had* to win, don't you see.

I figure that it was to do with the sponsor. Well, dog food's a pretty emotive product and I guess I blended in with the image they wanted—soft, cuddlesome, and generally all-round appealing. And a boy. Did you know that about 90 per cent of human on-camera participation in dog food commercials is done by males? Boys. Teenagers. Fathers. Grandfathers. It's the other way round for cat food.

There'd been a series of heats, also televised, leading up to the finals and though I'd been pretty well ahead I had half-a-dozen or so close rivals. But to tell the truth, they weren't exactly photogenic kids. They didn't smile, as I did—a reflex, I suppose, from winning all those baby shows mom had put me in for—and three of them wore glasses. Also, two of them were girls, so no way did *they* have a chance.

I guess I knew I was going to win when, the day before the finals, a dentist came to the trailer park in Santa Monica where mom and I lived and yanked my two main upper front teeth. Well, they were milk teeth and I was going to lose them in any case. And without them, I must confess, I looked, well, even more adorable. I have them still; I keep them on a charm bracelet which I wear all the time.

Anyway, the finals. And the answer to the chess problem was palmed to me by the quizmaster as he held my little hand while I looked down at the chess board. Ditto with the maths teasers and the physics questions. The tulip I drew was already there in faint outline and so all I had to do was follow the shape and fill in the colours. The piano was pre-set for me and so was the computer.

But P-R-E-C-O-C-I-O-U-S: all my own work. So were the other words I answered in the spelling bee. They started easy and became progressively harder. I got them all right. Nobody else did. I don't know why they didn't fix the spelling bee for me, but they didn't. E-C-O-L-O-G-Y. M-E-D-I-A. M-U-L-T-I—N-A-T-I-O-N-A-L. G-E-N-E-T-I-C-S. And then the last and, for me, the hardest one.

I got confused as to whether there should be a "k" in place of the first "c". In the end, of course, I went for "c" and when the quizmaster yelled "Co-rrect!"—oh, boy! I have never in my life felt so good. I'd taken a ribbing at school, you see, and worse than that, on account of looking angelic, but when I got that word right I knew that I'd got my life right as well. The rule was to be smarter than anyone else—but sweet with it. It hit me, just like that.

And if you think that was advanced strategy for a seven-year-old let me point out that I was an extremely bright kid. I have today an IQ of 190. Genius rating plus. The left and the right hand sides of my brain are equally developed, which means that I am intuitive and artistic on one level and capable of solving the most complex and technical problems on the other. Pardon me for saying so, but I am a polymath, with the potential of excelling in anything.

The psychiatrists checked me out in that respect. They assessed me for another contest mom entered me for—it seems all my life has been contests—to find the 100 perfect young citizens who would be of an age, and of the right calibre, to run for President in the first quarter of the 21st century. Or the third millennium as it was called portentously by the news magazine that promoted the stunt.

There were hundreds of thousands of entries, as you might imagine. We were tested for intellect, integrity, moral and physical stamina (that part involved three weeks of astronaut training) visionary outlook (a 5,000 word essay entitled "How I Would Change The World") and charisma (that consisted of pictures of candidates flashed quasi-subliminally on to TV screens with an invited cross-section of viewers asked to phone in their spontaneous reactions on which numbered face they regarded most favourably).

I made the top 20. Number 11, in fact. I was 16 at the time and my picture was included in a montage on the magazine's cover. My picture was dead centre, bigger than all the others. Well, brain cells *and* freckles—who could resist that combination? Actually, I came top in charisma, but I also scored well in the other attributes and, for the visionary category, 500 words from my essay on global ecology as a means of international collaboration and peace were printed in the magazine.

" . . . there has been too much dead wood in the 20th century tide of diplomacy which is why I propose that we use the trees as our statesmen. . . ."

OK, it was kind of arch. But I meant it. Still do. Which is one of the reasons it mattered so much to me to be nominated as one of the "putative ideal citizens earmarked to have a salutary bearing on global destiny in the third millennium, a human nucleus identified by scientific selection and democratic choice and from which, logically, morally and philosophically, at least one President has got to emerge, a man or a woman whose prescient gaze will match temporal imperatives and, transcending these, go on to fearlessly contemplate the crucial cosmic clause in the current uncertain contract for world survival." I tell you, when these news magazines hit the punch bag of hyperbole they really do swing.

All the same, it pleased me. But nothing like that time I stretched up with that piece of chalk and knew—wham! *knew*—that I had not simply won a spelling bee but that I had mastered the alphabet of living.

Yes, that's when it all took off for me, and I went on to become the Red Baron of brainstorming. My freckles were my character reference, of course, proof of my niceness. I don't smoke. I don't drink. And I'm a virgin. White House here I come, I thought, even before I won my place in that news magazine contest; and my campaign trail has been marked by all those trophies I kept winning for cerebration.

As you will gather, then, I have had many sub-lets in the Hall of Fame. And now, at the age of 21, I've reached the penthouse suite: I'm on Death Row in a penitentiary. It's a short lease, in the sense that I go to the chair the day after tomorrow, but I mean to make it a permanent one. It's immortality I'm after and immortality I'll get. Because I'm still what I was when I discovered myself at the age of seven. P-R-E-C-O-C-I-O-U-S.

Before I tell you about my plan, let me give you the background. It was mom's doing. Now I don't say that critically. She was one special woman. Oedipus? Forget it, even though I am an only child. Likewise scratch momism.

I respected her. It was true that her brain tissue was candy floss but that poor and exploited woman had character. She called herself an actress. Well, I'll second that. She was my Saint Joan and she burnt herself out at the stake of waitressing and other lousy jobs so I could have a chance, because I was her star. She said I had my father's brains and breeding. She'd only known my father for a night but he was English and as far as that sad lady was concerned that gave me the chance to drive out of Dumpsville in a Rolls Royce.

I was 18 and at Cambridge doing a year's study in social sciences and ecology—the scholarship was my prize for my success in the news magazine contest—when she left California and went to live in the Deep South. For six months I heard from her only intermittently and from a variety of addresses. Her notes were strange and, even allowing for her semi-literacy, disjointed.

So I flew back to the States. I found her shacked up in a tenement that made our previous poverty seem palatial and she had more needle marks than I had freckles. It turned out that she had been involved with a musician who had promised her the good life, only he made it rhyme with junkie.

We neither of us had funds and getting her into hospital was like trying to win the Nobel Prize for Literature with a sob story. But I worked on a woman doctor there and used my freckles as a credit rating. Mom was admitted.

Her condition was worse than just dope: they diagnosed acute hepatitis. To pay for her treatment I took on a 12-hour a day job hauling barrels in a molasses plant. I lived in her room in the tenement. I got to know Tony, the caretaker. He was a fat man, and from the way he smelled and looked he might have crawled out of one of the bayous around the edge of the city. But he was company, even if he was no more than a human grunt and a smirk as he squatted over the porno videos which to him were civilisation's greatest achievement.

Mom died after three weeks. I stayed on there for another four months because I needed to raise the money for her instalment-

plan funeral plus the balance of her hospital bill. I don't know why
I kept dropping in on Tony. Social studies, I guess. Darwinism. I
never did tell him that mom had died.

Then one night he looked up from his porno video and said:
"Say, there's your old lady!" You know something? He meant it as
a compliment.

I said no. He was insistent, eager to please me.

"Sure it is. I seen her before on the tube. Plenny of times. I know
her from that cute little scar right under her belly button."

I killed him. With the knife he always kept on the table for
slicing salami. Straight under his rib cage and a thrust up to the
heart. A very professional job. I didn't, I swear, mean to harm the
old woman from across the hall. She just happened to come in
then. And—

I went to the police. That was all about two years ago. At my
trial psychiatrists testified that I was sane and the jury, though the
four women on it were sobbing, had no choice other than a
unanimous finding of guilty on two counts of first-degree
homicide.

So? Who wants a life sentence? But I let my defence go ahead
with the lengthy appeals procedure because I needed time to plan
my future—which is that I had decided to be *the* martyr of the
media age. My plan: to have my execution televised live.

Gary Gilmore fought successfully for the firing squad for his
execution and I wanted nothing less than the 21-gun salute of
publicity. My last prize. My best one.

As I see it, hangings used to be public spectacles back in history
and it's a logical extension that execution should be packaged as
cosy home entertainment. Dark Age. Media Age. Where's the
difference? If I couldn't be President, then I'd be a pioneer.

I made my intentions known when they let in the first of the
reporters to interview me on Death Row. I concentrated on those
who were milky-eyed and milky-voiced Southerners and I just
grazed them with my words. God, I can manipulate people!

I projected myself as a sort of social worker. I pointed out that
contrition was not enough and that my punishment needed the
impact of the fullest public exposure so that my execution would
be no mere statistic but a graphic object lesson in what happened to
those who resorted to blood lust.

I had communicated my views to the State Governor, I went on, and it was my understanding that, innovative reformer that he was, he was giving them serious consideration.

Actually, I had written to him. And he hadn't replied. Ergo, he was thinking about it. Fair enough? Also, I happened to have read that as a result of a lacklustre term he was going to be challenged seriously in the upcoming election. The way I saw it, I'd handed him a great publicity mint julep by which he could toast his continuation in office on that old political lip smacker of law 'n' order. It helped that at the time I made my announcement he was off on a junket to Europe—a fact I had taken into account before meeting the media—and couldn't be reached for immediate comment.

And my ploy worked. A lot of the papers, especially those in the North and particularly the *New York Times*, expressed outrage at the prospect of such barbarity. The Governor, of course, was up there on the rhetorical ramparts of the Mason-Dixon Line saying something original to the effect that he was damned if any Yankees were going to dictate his policy, his bold experimentation in penal reform. He got what he wanted—publicity. After that, he couldn't back down.

I've had a Hollywood agent for nearly a year now and I figure he's made a fortune from the sale of T-shirts alone. They've got my picture on them (the freckles have come out real swell) and slogans that are either pro or anti my televised death, depending on taste.

My agent, of course, has been pressing for a network deal. But the Governor, in a gesture of compromise to his critics, has ruled on state-wide cable television to "eliminate mass voyeurism and guarantee the validity of what could prove to be a major and salutary step in crime prevention." I'm not really complaining. Nothing to stop the networks from buying those tapes, is there?

Besides, I've calculated this whole business to the ultimate in timing. Originally, my execution was planned for today, Thursday. But I dropped the Governor a line requesting a 48-hour stay of execution, saying that if it wasn't granted I'd change my mind about *any* television. Well, he's a politician, and having kissed the baby-faced killer he couldn't risk that infant prodigy spitting on his gleaming shirt front of imaginative public service, could he?

Saturday it is, then. Saturday January 1, 2000. A day that's a special kind of history in itself. And one I chalked up all those years ago when I stretched to that blackboard to write P-R-E-C-O-C-I-O-U-S.

ENTROPANTO ±

Gerry McCarthy

I'd tuned into a newsbulletin while mulling over my report. To be more accurate, I'd tuned into the ads before the bulletin. Economic fluctuations, political upheavals, natural disasters, are all interchangeable, a daily parade of signs whose shape at a given moment has no more significance than the day's weather. But ads are another matter: plugged into some thirty-second zeitgeist, always striving to say it all, once and for all, to *mean*. Amidst all this noise, this constant crackle of static, those promotional poems were my informational grail.

That month, the central ads, the really crucial ones, were on behalf of a new glue. Funny how the product parameters shift: suddenly, designer jeans were nowhere and half the world sat agog for the latest paean to the polymer. The market leader—actually, I've no idea how many units were shifted, or even if the product ever hit the marketplace: what mattered was TV coverage—was called *Bondage*. Their first biggie—sentimental, yes, but it got tongues moving—featured a multiple crucifixion.

We open on a couple of reprobates messily nailed to crosses, oozing bodily fluids, hamming it up and very obviously not having a good time. The camera pans to a third cross, its stripped-pine elegance in marked contrast to the chipped formica of the first two. Mid-shot of occupant, cross three: he glows with an otherworldly radiance, surrounded by groupies and puffing on a cigar. As the camera closes in we realise that his crucifiers have used glue rather than nails. He beams into the lens and delivers that killer punchline: "*Bondage. The Paste that passeth Understanding.*"

After that, things got more sophisticated. There was the

"Famous Artists" series, actually a contination of the original theme, where we got this privileged insight into how *Bondage* was there at crucial moments in our cultural history. Duchamp sticking string to a board for his celebrated *Stoppages*, Burroughs and Gysin inventing cut-ups, that sort of thing. And always that orange tube of *Bondage* somewhere off-centre in the vital frame. I'd been hoping to see the latest addition to the series, supposedly featuring Lee Harvey Oswald, but some detail in my report distracted me and I tuned in a few seconds too late. President Haig was already on screen, offering to caveat some African General's proposal, epistemologicallywise. I killed it.

Before it died, it spoke to me. As a sometime semiopathologist, I should be conditioned to the significance of ultimate gestures, even when they emanate from a TV set. But that word still came as a shock: *Entropanto*.

Maybe I hadn't really heard it. Maybe some new kind of postmodern wish-defilement syndrome was causing me to unload unwanted bytes on to my domestic devices. One way to find out is to switch on again. Hell, I've been working all my life with the TV on. Most of my best ideas, all my real breakthroughs, come from subliminal suggestion, unconscious cross-fertilization, feedback and bleedback. And with so many new diseases around, somebody might have latched on to Entropanto. Even if I hadn't confirmed case one yet.

Then I realised my bias, one of those mental triangulations that catches you looking at the back of your own head from ceiling level. I'd been looking at this thing, this phenomenon, this case, seeing it as a private pathology from which I could extrapolate a social trend. Trying, even, to solve a classic murder mystery, where my only clues were a possible murder weapon and far too many confessions. No body, naturally. They never call me in when there's a body. It must have been about then that I sent the first instalment of my report over the line. . . .

(1) The compound labelled *Monotard MC 100*, allegedly a solution of porcine monocomponent insulin, was found on subsequent analysis to contain traces of diamorphine, or diacetyl-morphine, otherwise known as heroin. The second bottle, still one-third full, was labelled *Human Actrapid*. The human monocomponent

insulin which it contained was found to have been diluted with a substance which has resisted all attempts at analysis to date. The used hypodermic found in the empty apartment suggests that both compounds had been injected subcutaneously. However, all available medical records suggest that the subject was *not*, in fact, diabetic, but may have been suffering from multiple neuroses of the type popularly known as "The Evolution Disease"—or TED—but which I propose to term *Entropanto-B*.

B, you see, because I was beginning to believe that the A-strain was already endemic. Everybody had it, or at least everybody who appeared on my television set. The newsbulletin, when I got back to it, featured one of the new computer-generated maps with continuous screen update to accommodate the latest statistics. It shimmered with electric colours, frissons of pattern flowing in and out of each other like some huge and barely comprehensible video-game. It dealt of course with today's hottest topic: the new diseases, the spread rates, the crossover strains and multiple infection patterns. Someone had come up with a new theory to explain some of the more localized outbreaks: AIDS-13 in the Home Counties—the last area where handshaking between consenting adults was still legal—and Van de Karp's sarcomatosis in Ireland, where the latest coalition government was about to hold a referendum on the abolition of laundrettes. There was a correspondence, it seemed, between literacy levels and particular viruses: as if language itself was viral and could, if sufficiently entrenched, put up some resistance to the newer strains. The map was divided into *Oral Zones*, generally rural areas with a high residual orality, understood as the semantic fallout of the primal word, and *Gutenberg Ghetto*, urbanized enclaves of literacy and linearity. Both showed a marked resistance to the new diseases— although it probably wasn't much consolation to the inhabitants, who seemed to be dying equally quickly of more traditional complaints. Even as I watched, these areas dwindled. By far the largest map area was post-literate, TV-land, computerland, sending out feelers to enclose and encapture space, spreading like tiny orgasms of lightning along hidden contours. The spreading blob was labelled *Entropanto*, a graffito in the subways of the electronic psyche.

I am not alone in expecting my reports to have a high redundancy factor, but I dislike seeing my work duplicated on public television before I've had a chance to forward it. Of course, I still had access to data that hadn't been made general, not yet. And compared to some of the scenarios I could visualize, worldwide panic would seem like a holiday. I keyed in part two of my report. . . .

(2) One possibility, at this stage, is that these complex termination strategies constitute a suicide cycle which has been slowed down, frozen, placed under the microscope. Our semiotic autopsy reveals only a proliferation of contradictory hints as to the nature of the participants: the mysterious trace of an anonymous footprint on Muscle Beach.

The alleged extraterrestrial origin of the Actrapid dilutor is believed to represent a biochemical actualization of the terminal stage of this compound neurosis, where the sufferer, enmeshed in a fantastic attempt to "evolve" off the surface of the planet in order to escape the imminent holocaust, is capable of inducing profound psychosomatic changes in her physical make-up. Note that the sufferer is always female: it is an item of faith with victims of Entropanto-B that it is already too late for the males of the species. *You cannot take man into space. You cannot take language into space.* To be taken daily, like a mantra.

On TV, the President was back, and now I could see his Entropanto scars glowing in the bulbshine. Of course! Haig probably had it before almost anyone, back when he was just Secretary of State and nothing he said seemed to make any sense. I'd forgotten: or I'd grown so accustomed to media overload that I didn't expect coherence in the utterances of a public figure. And yet Entropanto is *named* from the linguistic effects, a portmanteau of entropy and esperanto, the universal language of decay, the heat-death of meaning. As the frantic rate of informational flow increases, as the messages mount, so does the noise attendant on the entire system, like a holy ghost in the machine. Ultimately, communication is an illusion. Nothing gets through, nothing makes any sense. And an old utopian dream comes true: the Tower of Babel falls and we all understand one another equally. Equally, but not at all. If you have prayers to send, do it fast. Tomorrow they change the wavelength and the access codes.

As I sent in the third section of my report, I was starting to feel calmer. It wasn't an urgent scientific analysis after all. It was more like an exotic species of masturbation, a spewing of semiotic seed into the void.

(3) The absence of a body may suggest to some that the authorities acted prematurely in initiating a murder investigation. An alternative hypothesis postulates an extrapolation of the known course of this little-studied disease to the point where the subject was actually successful in leaving the planet by unknown means. The acute somatic alterations noticed by casual acquaintances of the subject—weight fluctuations of up to eighty percent, changes in skin tone, in length, colour and texture of hair, distortions in height of an estimated twenty-three centimetres, the ability to induce at will conditions such as diabetes mellitus, cranial and axillary herpes, and common bronchitis, and to dissipate them just as easily, and, most significantly of all, the ability to change sex—imply an increasing level of psychosomatic control over the physical environment.

I was still looking for data. Couldn't help it. The training runs deep, churning out idiom and ideology. Strap me to a pyre and pour on the gasoline and you'll find me regurgitating anthropology textbooks, obsessively cataloguing the flammable substances, structuring them, measuring the functional against the ritual, selecting and combining to the last. Thinking up titles for papers: *Down at the old Ding-an-sich*, or *Urban Cancer—The New Chemotherapy*. I know I'm deeply implicated, a participator, not an observer. But I persist in doing what I do. Don't we all?

I set to considering my own role in this Entropantomime, this children's amusement performed in a dead language. The possibility of ever meaning anything in a language leached of its semantic core was ebbing fast. Leached, bleached, beached on the littoral zone of the unconscious: as a tiny constituent of the human message, as a blind corpuscle pumped along society's conduits, it was obviously futile to attempt an overview, to grope for the big picture. Even the small pictures were buckling.

The insulin bottle was a final pun, an ironic imperative: act rapid. Turning back to the TV set, I sent in the rest of my report, and I didn't care who it reached.

(4) In this analysis, the alien compound and the diamorphine combine to form a terminal message. Heroin addiction, in tandem with Entropanto-B, is now believed to have been an earlier, failed attempt at an escape-route from the dying planet. On a global scale, the proliferation of addicts consists of a concerted, though unconscious, attempt to disrupt the flow of "humemes", or minimal constituents of the human message, on the planetary surface. On this reading, the unknown alien compound is either a last clue or a farewell message, the diamorphine traces an ironic gesture of dismissal, terminating the possibility of redemption for those who remain behind. The suggestion that we use our remaining time to kill the pain is already being taken seriously in some quarters.

(5) The appearance at several police stations of numbers of young men who wish to confess to the murder is seen as a further vindication of this hypothesis. All remain convinced, even under deep hypnosis, that they were the subject's lover, and caused her death by tampering with her insulin supply. Needless to say, all believe that the subject was diabetic, and all show marked symptoms of advanced heroin addiction. Left behind on a doomed planet, they have created identical strategies to rationalize an intolerable situation. To date, none has been charged with any crime more serious than violations of the narcotics laws.

(6) The imminent destruction of the planet must now be considered as the most likely scenario. There is little point in attempting to confine previously-identified sufferers from Entropanto-B. Sooner rather than later, as language ebbs away, all will succeed in altering the phenotype in order to survive the transition into space, and will vanish under circumstances as mysterious as the subject's disappearance. The terminal disillusionment of their addicted and abandoned lovers should be a short-lived phenomenon, ending in planetary catastrophe. At this point in our observations, no strategy that might plausibly reverse this trend has been put forward.

GARDENS AND FOUNTAINS
Tony Bowerman

For it is written:

"In the name of Allah, the Compassionate, the Merciful.

Recite. Your Lord is the Most Bounteous One,
Who by the pen has taught mankind things they did not know.
Indeed, man transgresses in thinking himself his own master,
For to your Lord shall all things return."

—*The Koran*, chapter 96.

It was raining outside the Oval Office. Heavy, steady rain. The few trees shimmered slightly through the laser crystal-diffraction glass. An occasional downpour-sodden leaf clung to the dark branches; it had been a long autumn.

Across the astro-lawn, raindrops kicked sideways in a rainbow of erratic whirlygigs—jerked aside by the IBM Shieldmaster-7s that had been recently installed around the White House perimeter in response to the latest attempt to assassinate the President. Pure chance had saved him this time: he had been out of the office taking a short nap. The missile had atomised a portrait of Abraham Lincoln instead. But then he was dead anyway.

Damage control intelligence was still trying to determine the origin of the half-metre long autonocruise anti-personnel weapon (AAPW), programmed to home in on the President's likeness alone. But the chances of a successful trace seemed slim: interpellative plasma spectroscopy of the oblative shielding had demonstrated already that the missile had been travelling for forty days. Compounded by hi-stealth technology, its elusive course had been deliberately erratic. It might have come from almost anywhere. It was a knot of true Gordian complexity.

Inside, a warm glow suffused the room. Apparently working,

the President sat crouched low over his desk. In fact, he was engrossed in one of the new "Wilderness Survival" holo-encephalic simulation games. There were no losers, only endless permutations to be explored. As alluring as a drug, the game offered an alternative, yet anodyne, reality. At present, the President was three weeks into the condensed sim-time expedition, but stumped by the seemingly insurmountable problems of a quarter-kilometre canoe portage.

"Goddammit," he growled in a frustrated undertone. He rose from his chair, intending to reimmerse himself later. "I give up. You know, I just can't seem to concentrate these days."

Hands in pockets, he moved over to the window and stood looking out into the failing light of late afternoon. He felt old and tired today. Restorative aminotherapy wasn't all the holo-mags made it out to be. In fact, sometimes he wondered whether he didn't feel worse now than he had before. Everything seemed to be getting out of hand. *And it's me*, he thought, *who is supposed to be in charge. After all I am the Supreme Executive.*

He exhaled with a long sigh. "Hell. . . ."

Rain streamed silently down the window. The President shook his head; his recurrent bouts of melancholia seemed to be becoming more frequent. A warning light flickered at the subjective ceiling of his right eye, drawing him from his reverie.

"Attention, attention," intoned a small subliminal voice. "Online document incall." Automatically the President sat down and focused on infinity. To a casual observer he might have been plunged into sudden catatonia.

A memo danced across both retinas: a tiny web of luminance looping in manic mirror writing over blank eyes. Often, without prior notice, the IBM Retinal-Plane Imager would throw a stream of critically-focused documents across his vision. Now that he was used to the RPI he could see the security advantages implicit in such a system. But he still felt irritable when he thought of the micro ceramic beam-dish that had been surgically implanted into the back of his cranium. On hot days it itched like the very devil.

The President's breathing slowed; he was concentrating, in a half-trance.

"For your eyes only," the message began. The President smiled wryly to himself.

"*From*: Operations Co-ordination Bureau (OCB), The 55 Committee: NSC.

"*Dateline*: XXXXXX Deleted.

"*Subject*: Global Nuclear Exchange: Supreme Executive Support Functions: Survival Override Stratagem.

"Mr President, Despite advanced SDI operations on the high frontier, in the contingent event of a global nuclear exchange conflict scenario current simulation evaluations show an 84% and upward eco-damage probability to the Northern hemisphere, and to the immediate environs of the United States of America.

"In view of the negative data-appraisals available at this moment in time a long-term survival override stratagem for the Supreme Executive and its immediate Command, Communications and Control (C3) support infra-structures has been devised.

"Under the auspices of the NSC (Emergency Planning Executive —EPE.) locational analysis of geo-meteorological global weather systems suggests optimum survival loci of Latitude 23° 21' North, Longitude 16° 50' East. That is, Mr President, Sir, a positional node-station approximately contiguous with Bir Yoggaye, an oasis situated north of the Tibesti Range in the Libyan Islamic Protectorate of Chad, continent of Africa.

"Optimal locational-status is assured by a combination of positive factors:

- Zero-parity precipitation: with consequent low fall-out compromise probability.
- Maximal temperature-gradient: with consequent buffer offset effect to a nuclear winter scenario.
- Favourable intelligence penetrations and politico-demographic control within the Libyan Islamic Protectorate of Chad. (ref: CIA-NSC report 0-237-411-05.)

"Subsequent to your confirmatory approval, Mr President, Sir, these stratagems will be implemented forthwith and to the utmost ability of the United States of America.

"God bless the President.

"Transmission terminates."

The President blinked and sat up. He seemed troubled. Unannounced, a second brief message from the RPI flickered across his vision.

"Translation synopsis follows," it said.

*

The world turns.

While the Soviet economy foundered under the constant burden of the arms spiral, the United States, its industrial base fully re-orientated towards CAD/AIM (Computer Aided Design/Auto-nobot Implemented Manufacture), entered an unprecedented bullish phase. With the Dow-Jones-Nikkei Index standing at an all time high of 36,900, the United States sought to implement a long-term stratagem: to extend its world hegemony in insidious fashion—through economic might.

It was an economy based on the fifth generation AIB (Artificial Intelligence Bio-genic) transputer and the Autonobot (or auto-nomic robot). Together they were to be the twin pillars of a New Age.

"Constant techno-pressure," announced the President, on holo-vid, on the occasion of his third inaugural address, "has assured the survival of the United States, and of mankind, in perpetuity." He was reading from the transputer-linked RPI. "God save America."

An apparent adjunct of such a grand stratagem was the Green Advance Programme. Initiated in the mid 1990s under the auspices of a now diminished UN, its ambitious aim was to regenerate a tired Earth, and to green the deserts. In reality, the enterprise was almost wholly that of the United States. Backed by an industrial base of prodigious power, and underpinned by the versatile autonobot, it no longer seemed some febrile dream. Now it was eminently possible, and a goal that must be pursued.

"My fellow Americans," declared the President to a worldwide holo-vid audience of over 4.7 billion, "I use the words of John F. Kennedy when I say, 'Some people see things as they are and say: Why? I see things as they might be and say: Why not?' The Green Advance Programme is no idle dream. It is a dream that is within our grasp. A dream we can fulfil.

"We should be proud that at last the might of Nature can be bent to our will. When the Earth is reborn to the benefit of all man-kind, then let our detractors cry again that we are guilty of an over-weening pride. When the barren earth is green and all the people can be fed, then let them accuse. I say let the world be our judge."

Even by the 1980s, the desert, if one included the arctic wastes, covered over half of the Earth's land surface. Of course, these arid and semi-arid regions were not devoid of life, far from it, but their increase was symptomatic of a planetary sickness. The desert was growing at the rate of forty square miles per day. The rate was to double, and then double again. The prognosis was poor.

Evidence of a new Little Ice Age, similar to that experienced back in the 1780s—with shorter growing seasons in temperate latitudes around the globe, drought on the high plains of the US, and devastation in the Sahel—was compounded by the ecological myopia of a still burgeoning industrial world. The signs had long been evident, yet some believed the problem would resolve itself. The danger was that it might, but with scant regard for humanity.

So, willing to grasp at any straw, the world's huddled shanty dwellers gave equivocal praise; the President heard angels in the highest heaven chorus "Alleluia".

And in the wilderness? All the legions of the Earth were unleashed. Guided by a trans-global network of AIB transputers a leviathan of innumerable parts and impeccable logistics went into action. Six-limbed, insect-like autonobots were Protol-freighted to the semi arid regions of the Sahel in their millions. Constructed of space-made zero-gravity ceramics the autonobots were both virtually indestructible and maintenance free. They toiled ceaselessly, every hour, both light and dark, at their sole task: to plant and nurture trees. Like the countless locusts of the Bible they were all bent to a single task, but it was to increase and not to diminish the green plants of the soil. In pursuance of their goal they were tireless, and single-minded. And like autonobots labouring elsewhere in Man's service, they moved at lightning speed, faster than any human being ever would.

Nor were the trees they nurtured of natural provenance. Each plant was bio-engineered: fast growing, self-nitrogenated, oxygen-release orientated and able to survive on salt water if necessary.

Each tree had its own networked bio-viability meter; if it sickened it was nursed; if it died it was replaced. They fertilized the soil, refreshed the air, bore fruits in abundance, and gave shade to man. Soon the desert greened, slowly at first, and then more strongly. And then the sands began to recede. It seemed to many that it was a war that could be won.

Yet what is as it seems? On the edge of this miracle was a hidden place. Bir Yoggaye, oasis for generations, shelter for the wandering tribes and now the site of Supreme Executive Survival Override Bunker One—C3 Support.

Must truth have a bodyguard of lies?

Then came the fearful day. When the Sun was augmented by the light of a thousand suns, when a deluge of fire swept across the northern hemisphere, and when the rains that fell in the evening of that day no longer refreshed and replenished, but burned and destroyed with inward agony, like the canker within.

Bir Yoggaye waited. Yet from the north nobody came, nor any voice, nor any sound.

Salah bin Abdi's caravan wound at a beetle's pace across the erg. Arched from horizon to horizon, the sky formed a high dome of gas-jet blue that trapped them beneath it. Nothing else stirred. No other sound came from the desert. They had been travelling for fourteen hours, yet in that vastness they may as well have stood still: all movement was illusion.

Each of the six mangy baggage camels was heavily laden: sacks of rice, strings of salt cakes, and goatskin waterbags—all carefully balanced—were roped to frameworks of crossed sticks. Strung together in a long line, the camels moved with a rolling, shuffling gait, all in perfect rhythm, swaying easily from side to side. Only a scuffling susurrus of sand rose from their padded feet, intermingled with the monotonous creak of their baggage. An acrid stench of urine, with which the camels habitually sprayed themselves, enveloped all.

Night was coming fast. Soon the sun would fall, like a glowing red cinder beneath the dark lip of the desert. And the moon would rise blue. Salah bin Abdi bent and scooped a handful of sand at which he sniffed noisily. It was as he thought. God willing, they were close to Bir Yoggaye.

He raised his hand. "*Hamdullah*—thanks be to God. We rest here."

The six beasts were unburdened and hobbled with twists of rope. At a dismissive wave from Tahar, the camel driver, they shuffled off to browse on the sparse vegetation. It was eight days since they had last been watered.

Within minutes it had become dark; immediately the temperature started to plummet. Only a residual shimmer of heat radiating from the still scorching sand warmed the air. Above it came the first soft whisperings of a breeze.

Salim, the young Tibbu, kindled a frugal fire of dried camel dung. Soon the pungent smell of the smòke mingled with the bubbling rattle of rice boiling. With butter it would form their evening meal. None of them had eaten meat for twelve days. Perhaps tonight they would be lucky: Musallim had told Salah that earlier that day he had seen the spoor of a young oryx.

Salah rose to his feet, "Then we shall feast tonight, *Inshallah*— God willing."

His filthy jelaba was strained with sweat and camel grease. In addition to his djembia—the ornate curved dagger tucked into his belt—Salah still wore the traditional crossed bandoliers. Once they would have held live brass cartridges. But now he fetched from his personal saddle goods his most precious possession. It was a new Kalashnikov AK triple-three, the favourite combat laser rifle of the Third World. Only a few had ever been available, captured from Soviet troops in northern Iran. Now there would be no more. It had cost Salah bin Abdi the equivalent of thirty camels, and had been traded across the Red Sea from the United Yemen Islamic Republic, coming via Addis Ababa and Malakal.

The AK 333 CLR has no moving parts. Its curvilinear form is both squat and compact. Only the muzzle depression, of iridium glass, breaks the outline; the rest is a single piece of spun-lattice ceramic created in the zero-gravity of space. This particular weapon had assumed the colour of sand: obviously its chameleon LSIC was still in prime condition. It was wrapped in the loose leather cover that the Kababish nomads have used since time immemorial to protect their weapons.

Salah disappeared beyond the circle of firelight. Musallim called after him, "*La bas*—no evil, Salah bin Abdi. In the forenoon I saw also the marks of Djinn. Their long steps were plain in the sand. But I did not see them."

"*Yak la bas*—no evil to you. We see them only from the corner of our eyes, Musallim, yet close to Bir Yoggaye the sands are full of them."

For twenty minutes the night was silent. Then an abrupt, high animal scream pierced the darkness. To anyone looking in the right direction there was only a single swift blink of ruby light, then blackness. No more. The AK 333 was never wrong: it was accurate, certain, and lethal. On the corpse a tiny black scorch mark would be the only sign of death.

The caravan slept. They had eaten well. Wrapped in their robes, their howlis tight about their faces, the four men lay huddled close to the banked embers of the fire. Silence gripped the desert: only the light scurry of desert mice and the low rumbling of the camels punctuated the night. In the heavens the stars, like turquoise pinpricks in the dull blanket of the firmament, rolled inexorably about Bel Hardi, the Pole Star.

Musallim dreamt that he wandered in a garden of groves and cool water. The fountains whispered in song, the words of the Prophet. "In the name of Allah, the Compassionate, the Merciful," they sang. "We have brought Man into being from the dry ringing clay that was wrought from black mud. And the Djinn we have brought into being before from the fire of the glowing blast."

Musallim shifted in his sleep. The night was bitterly cold.

While men and animals dreamed, other, lidless eyes watched from the rocks, silent and unblinking. Not the eyes of Djinn, but the baleful electronic sensor plates of two IBM-Hitachi ACSRs: Autonomic Combat Stealth Robots. Deadly, silent slaves.

The sun was high and the sands shimmered as if seen through a crystal sea. Only there was no water, just Bir Yoggaye, a mirage of lenticular green dancing in the harsh light, somewhere above the horizon.

Salah bin Abdi stood on the crest of a dune, watching. Away to the south the desert was changing; only here, beyond the green frontier, did life remain the same. It was *beserf*—too much. Yet it was also the will of God.

Along the ridge of wind-sculpted sand was a maze of fading prints—the prints of the Djinn in the night. Two sets snaked away towards Bir Yoggaye, as yet undimmed by the passing hours. Salah raised a pair of battered Japanese binoculars to his eyes.

As they whined into focus Bir Yoggaye leaped out of the light, coalescing into a crisp pattern of shapes. Around the once stark-shadowed well were now other, less ancient forms: the ceramic top-casings of twenty or so artesian wells, and the bright circular mosaics of irrigated crops. Neat ranks of tiny shrubs glistened in the sun. Among them were bronze-glass hydroponics recyclers and other, more sinister constructions.

Hamdullah—It was a miracle, a garden of cool fountains and shade in the heat of the desert.

As Salah bin Abdi swept his gaze across this oasis of mirages, the call to prayer began. Five times a day they prayed to Allah; this was the second.

"Allaho-akbar, Allaho-akbar, Allaho-akbar, Allaho-akbar Ash-hado-allaa Ilaaha illallah, Ash-hado-allaa, Ash-hado-allaa. . . ."

The chant rose and fell, each line repeated twice in the stillness. Salah was about to kneel when he noticed something amid the distant greenery that he had not seen before. First a few and then many six-legged creatures were congregating about the well. Their spindly bodies were slowing to a human pace, their limbs now almost still, unblurred by their habitual manic work-rate.

His eyes widened. Now other, tall, humanoid figures with four arms and almost invisible sand-coloured bodies seemed to appear from the ground, suddenly apparent among their smaller charges. They were the Djinn—the IBM-Hitachi ACSRs, one-time guards of this now redundant retreat.

"Allaho-akbar, Allaho-akbar, La Illaha-illallah," sang the muezzin. God is the Greatest, God is the Greatest, there is none worthy of worship save God. The call to prayer was finished. Salah knelt and bowed down to the East, facing Mecca.

And below, in Bir Yoggaye, ten thousand other sets of legs, not of flesh, but of ceramic, folded and bowed down.

"I have turned my face towards the Supreme Being who has created Heaven and Earth, and I am not one of the polytheists," intoned Salah bin Abdi; and he touched his ears in reverence and then folded his arms across his chest in wonder at the will of God.

RIKA'S WORLD   Sue Moorhouse

It was strange when I was woken up. I mean really weird.

The instructors at that stinking reformatory gave us this course of lectures, explaining how the doctors put you to sleep so that you don't get any older, even though the journey from Earth to the outlying planets may take two hundred years or more. It was supposed to be reassuring and all that but it scared the shit out of me so I never listened too much.

One of the instructors used to shout all the time and he was about as hairy as a gorilla. I saw a gorilla once on a vid. It looked just like that instructor, especially around the face. I know it's kind of insulting to animals—I mean first we go and spread ourselves all over the earth so that every other species gets extinct and then we go calling stupid people gorillas.

I remember that old hairy chest yelling at us girls once: "Look on the bright side you lot! You think we're hard on you. Well, when you wake up you'll still be seventeen and we'll all be two hundred years dead."

But you could see the words never meant a thing to him; he didn't even twitch.

All our elders and betters said that deporting us to the new planets was the best thing for us; our new start they called it. The thing that gets me about governments and judges and that kind is that they are so sure about what they do to other people's lives. I mean they never admit mistakes till years later though you can see from the mess things are in that some of the things they do must be really dumb. It's not that I blame them. I suppose there's got to be law and the law-bots and enforcers have got to keep the streets quiet. It's just that sometimes I think I'd rather be like me, trouble and all, then like them, even with all they've got. Maybe they're as scared of us as we are of them. I mean with that huge population there is on Earth people just got to do what they're supposed to or at least keep out of the way—take their quiet money each day, then go back home and watch vids or drug up or whatever. There's just no room for excitement, kids like us living rough and thieving what we want. I can see why the norms get scared. I really can. They get to feel crowded, and man, who doesn't?

Well, what happens is this. When the sleeper ship gets in orbit round your destination planet, the medical team come round and open all the capsules and give you this injection. Zappo! You're awake. You get up feeling dizzy and wondering where you are and your mouth feels like something has been rotting in it for the last two hundred years. By this time the ship is down and you walk through the air locks into the reception building right inside the dome. No one ever sees the dome from outside and once you're in you forget it is a dome. I mean it's so huge and your whole world is going to be inside it.

All there is on the whole planet is just one building and we all sat inside it in this big reception room. It was wide and white and it echoed. There was a real din, with people exclaiming and chatting and kids running about and their mothers screaming at them all the time. I just sat there, with my elbows on this smooth, transparent table, staring down at my feet underneath, looking kind of bent and unreal. That was how I felt too, unreal, or maybe too real, as if all those other people didn't exist and it was just me sitting there on my own. I kept thinking over and over of how everyone I'd ever known on Earth, even old gorilla face, had been dead for two centuries. There wasn't even anyone there I knew from the reformatory. They'd mixed us all in with the ordinary, respectable settlers. I felt just like that one building in the dome; I mean, there was just me and nothing else on that whole great dead world.

This girl came and sat next to me. She was all excited and she was the kind that likes to talk right in your face.

"It's fantastic," she yodelled. "Think of it! We're on a whole new world!"

"It's a dump," I said. "Just a dump no one else wanted. And I should know, I've been shoved in enough dumps back on earth to know another one when I see it."

She wasn't listening; too busy clasping her hands in ecstasy.

"Don't you see?" she gushed. "It's like the old myths. You know, the half sphere of sky over the flat Earth and God sitting up above the sky in his heaven."

"Sure," I said, "only in our case there's no God and no heaven, not even any air, just emptiness for ever and ever, or at least for as far as makes no difference to us."

I think she got a bit discouraged after that. At any rate she went off to bother someone else.

So, the first thing we had to do was construct ourselves some kind of living quarters with drainage systems and water pumps and solar power units and all that stuff. The boss was this old codger, half the time he was dropping the plans or finding out they were upside down. I mean at first glance he didn't seem too efficient but the funny thing was he got everything dead right when it came to it and he even put right the mistakes in the plans, right out of his own head.

I got kind of enthusiastic myself just around then. Things seemed to just mushroom up, we were really getting somewhere. I remember I worked right through one light period and never even noticed I was tired. And I mean, a light period isn't just like an Earth day. Even when our side of the planet is shadowed from the Alpha sun we still get light from the other suns further off. There are only a couple of hours when it gets dark at all. Sometimes I'd see the sunset and the whole dome sky would be glowing pink and gold. It made me feel sort of happy just to be there. When there was a storm on the Alpha sun you got crazy lights all through the sky. That was something you couldn't just ignore. I mean you had to feel something with all that going on all around you.

It was about then that things started going sour on me again. And, yeah, I suppose it was mainly my fault as usual. But once they got the essentials done they started having these meetings. All the ones who thought they were important started making speeches to show what fantastic leaders they would be and putting other people down to make themselves feel big. I hate that stuff, I really do. I mean for a while I thought things might be different on a new world and all but the people are just the same. They don't want things different, just a copy of old Earth only with them in charge.

Everyone had to go to these meetings because we were all supposed to be part of the government of the colony. All they kept doing was going on about how wonderful it was that mankind was colonising the universe and lord of the stars and all that stuff. Everyone just stood there and lapped it up and thought how great they were. So one time I just interrupted and they had to let me because everyone is supposed to be able to speak.

"Listen," I said, "if we hadn't made such a mess of the planet we started off with we wouldn't need to colonise the universe. What's so great about leaving a trail of planets like Earth behind us wherever we go? I mean crawling with maggoty millions of miserable human beings and covered from shore to shore with doss houses to hold them and the seas in between dead and stinking with their rubbish."

That was what I tried to say, anyway, but it's easier afterwards to get it sounding right.

This woman who had been giving the speech had a face like a city street; all lines and angles and hard-looking. She smiled all the time too, but not being friendly: more as if she was getting ready to bite. "Ah yes," she said. "You're the girl from the reformatory. You don't seem to be making a very good start do you, my dear? Perhaps in a few years, when you've learnt to work hard and do as you're told, we will be a little more interested in your opinion."

That got quite a laugh. You can imagine. With them it's not so much what they say as the way they say it. What she was really saying right in front of everyone was that I was just the sort of rubbish they had expected from a reformatory. So I was just standing there going red and angry and choking with the big lump that was in my throat. Sometimes with people who won't listen I feel like just smashing something in their smug faces! And I don't even get a kick out of that sort of thing. Maybe it's me I'm angry with too, because there's just no way I can win.

After that I got put on cleaning. I mean things get dirty and need cleaning all the time. On earth no one needed me to do anything but keep quiet. Here they need me to clean things and keep quiet. Everyone's needed all right, but some of us just get to do the jobs no one else wants.

There was this boy in the kitchen that fancied me. He was all right except he didn't wash much and he believed everything he was told. He said that "they", the ones in charge, wanted us to have lots of children.

"We've got to get strong enough to fight off any aliens who might want to take over our planet," he said, with his hands all over me looking for zips.

I slapped him off. "You're crazy. We came here to get away from too many people. Anyway I'm not having dozens of babies just so they can grow up and get disintegrated by bug-eyed monsters."

"You can be really stupid, Rika. Do you know that? Just listen, will you. If we're strong enough there won't be any fighting!" He was getting sulky.

"If there was I'd be on the side of the aliens." Well, why not? What's so great about human beings?

"Oh come on!" he yelled, getting red and spitting a lot. "If some hideous oozing monster starts attacking our women and children you'll be screaming for help like the rest!"

He gave this really revolting leer so I knew what he was imagining.

"You've got a dirty mind. Why should bug-eyed monsters fancy women? They probably only get worked up about other bug-eyed monsters. Next thing you'll be saying you don't want your sister marrying one."

He went off me after a while but it was talking to him that I got to hear about the gardeners. Apparently some people were going right outside the dome, all suited up, with breathing apparatus and everything and they were putting in plants and looking after them. The idea is that the plants just need a bit of help and then they will grow and start releasing oxygen and slowly they will make the atmosphere more like Earth until there are plants and trees growing all over and people can live right outside the dome.

"That's fantastic," I said. "That's what I want to do." It just seemed a really great idea for once.

The boy just laughed of course. "They're not going to let a head-case like you loose outside the dome," he said, grinning all over his spotty face. "You'd just mess up working the suit and suffocate yourself, or you'd wander off and get lost out there." There are times when I get sick of people telling me I'm no good. I can't see that I am any more stupid than most other people. It's just that my sort of stupid is different from their kind, that's all; but they can't see that.

It turned out that the old man who had been in charge of building the town was in charge of the gardeners as well. For a while I just got fobbed off with all that stuff about me not being competent and trustworthy and all that. But the old bloke said he would take me.

"If she wanders off or misuses the suit she will simply be dead," he said. "No inconvenience will be incurred by anyone else, thus no one else has the right to object to her decision to try."

His name is Stebin, and he talks like that all the time. He has a good face too. I mean, all the lines show things about him and his eyes smile. For a while I thought I would be in love with him, but he said no, that he didn't have the energy. I get on pretty well with most of the other kids who are gardeners, though. I never knew there were other people who were like me but Stebin says that being a gardener, going outside the dome and all, attracts misfits. He says most people are misfits one way or another or pretty weird and that's okay because there is plenty of room here.

I keep thinking that maybe some of the plants I look after might grow into trees. Maybe there will be thousands of trees one day and people will get lost in them and feel small and then they will know that there are other things besides just human beings. Perhaps there will be animals too. Not just a few dogs or cows in zoos but wild animals living their own lives in the trees and rivers just like there used to be on Earth once. Imagine seeing an animal. It would be minding its own business and you would be minding yours and just for a moment its eyes would meet yours and you would see the feeling and intelligence of a creature that was furry or scaly and not human at all. Man, it would be something, to be part of all that.

Stebin says we are just doing the same as those clowns inside the dome with their leaders and speeches and all that. We are just trying to make a copy of old Earth too. He says humans are cleverer now but we still have the same instincts, sort of ape-man instincts, that are not always right for our survival. He says there was a man on Earth in the olden days who said that you couldn't stop people fighting and putting each other down and destroying things and being greedy and all that. This man said all you could do was just work at your own garden. So that's what we are going to do. But it's sort of depressing. I mean I don't suppose our garden will last any longer than his did, that man back on old Earth.

INDIAN SUMMER   Philip Gladwin

"There's a lock on the door, so don't worry; Old Fibroch won't get you tonight." The old man laughed to himself as he went up the stairs, laughing at the same jokes he had made every clear night for as long as the other could remember. There were wild seas outside during the winter, but that night at least would be calm and unworried, starry and warm. He followed the old man upstairs to the light to watch the sun go.

"There aren't any moths on this island to beat against the light like they used to, back on the shore in the old days." The old man paused a little while, looking out across the massive breadth of water, and on to the narrow line of black on the horizon. "There's no hiding it up here, you know."

The sun swelled momentarily as it approached the horizon and the surface of the water became rough and pitted as the shadows produced by its own waves grew and narrowed the gaps between themselves in the closing of a watery mesh.

"There are no lights on the coast over there and no ship has passed this way for ten years. I don't suppose there'll be any more now." The old man was adrift now, and the other lost in a dream of his own. "It's a pity. I used to like the old ships with the dark red sails, going off to fight. Ah, but that was when we were capable of all that."

He coughed once as the last sliver of the sun vanished beyond the curve of the sea; the summer had lasted longer than normal, but now it was drawing to a close and there was cold in the air. He paused.

"Now it would be good to see even a fishing boat."

The two men walked down from the light, down the echoing stairwells and through worn out arches; and as they walked they passed reeking cross passages, from which would sometimes breathe a side breeze strong enough to make the flame of the lantern flicker. At this the old man would hurriedly guard against being engulfed by the warm, dripping dark. When he saw what the old man did, and the shadows that the two of them cast, always changing, on the rock walls, the young man smiled to himself, for he was not scared in the same way as the older man. On evenings when he looked after the flames alone—the summer nights when the old man walked outside at the foot of the column, looking for meteors in the icy sky— he explored without a lantern, his way amongst the chambers and corridors lit by the veins of soft opalescent light which ran in winding, twisting patterns through the rock of the tower. Once whilst following one of these lit paths, chasing a warm breeze, he came to a crumbled archway, a mound of rubble alive with vines stretching to caress each other in the open air of the night—for beyond this arch was nothing. He had sat there for hours on the edge of the tower, his legs dangling over the incredible drop—and he had wondered for the first time at the builders of this lighthouse.

The woman walked into the Blue Glass room. Out of the window, away across vast plains of long, green grass, mountainous eruptions and divides, and dense forest land, she could see breakers as the sea continued even beyond her vision. This view of the whole world brought her calm, as it always did; and so the sound of the bells strung outside the window was pleasant. The woman walked through the Blue Glass room and out on to the balcony. Earlier she had seen the mauve and violet tints on the sky which meant there was a storm far out to sea. Now the storm was fading and the sun glowered as it crouched on the horizon. She watched as the shadows crept across country. They went from line to crevasse: then, as the sun squatted lower, leaped from hill to mountaintop. Then they were at the base of her tower, far below. She waited until the top of the tower was the only thing still in light. Softer by tones, the incandescence faded and the darkness returned.

This night clouds passed over the tower, their lowest portions passing silent and wraith-like around the Blue Glass room, dusting the millions of lines traced on the glass by the weather of a hundred years with fine white crystals. When the moon shone, later, the greenish light within the room seemed to be moving and flickering as the rustling web of whitened scratches shifted imperceptibly. As the woman slept, above her was the night, all around her were shadows, and, half a mile below her, the ground laboured slowly, painfully heaving as earthshaping continued.

He saw the town as soon as he sailed past the crumbling chalk of the headland. Many houses and buildings lay, half ruined; the slanting rays of the sun cast long shadows which broke up the brown and the dun of the buildings in contrast to the dark grey of the mountains behind. The village was old and long deserted; damp wood rotting, swept up by the tide.

He landed and pushed the raft up the shingle of the beach. He was on the edge of the buildings, and now he could see that they were far older then he had thought. Few walls were standing; the rest had collapsed, or were starting to. He looked further into the ruins and began to see stone buildings that were still whole, their outsides painted a dull brown.

He found himself on a road, which was disappearing under a layer of dark green plants and weeds. He walked along the edge of the sea, around the bay of the town. He gazed along sidestreets, looking up all the time, for the town was built on hills that rose slowly as they drew away from the sea. He saw how the streets wandered among rubble, then faltered and lost their shape, their outlines softening and defeated by the shards of wood, the broken buildings and the stifling greenery. He saw, rarely, signs that men had lived there—fragments of glassware, pottery; pieces of metal that rested twisted and rusting on the edge of the sea, framing old purposes.

Then he found the boat. It was lying on its side on the beach, half-buried in drifting shale with shellfish ornamenting its exposed side. Its metal rigging was whole in places; elsewhere it broke free and described wild loops and curves, pausing only where it had been dissolved by rust. He knew it to be one of the types of boat he had seen years before, wallowing and heaving in heavy seas away from land, or sailing past in fine summer weather, the sailors lounging at its rails. Now he began to see why there had been no ships since he was a boy. After a time he clambered on to the tilting deck and explored inside. He found a locked room whose door gaped in a score of places; inside there were many chests. He pulled one open, and his strength was enough to lay out the yards of heavy sailcloth he found inside. But this coloured cloth no longer reminded him of blood. The colour had become softer—these were dusty red sails, tired desert sails; no longer, and perhaps not ever, man-of-war sails.

He left the boat, but before he went he draped the cloth over the hull of the boat, weighted with stones from the beach. At the top of the next headland he turned and looked down. The red ochre of the sails blended with the wooden ruins. He sat and looked at the scene until it became too dark to see the boat. The town seemed to creep nearer as night fell, absorbing light. He turned away and continued his walking, so he was not aware that when the moon rose the shadows reappeared on the ruins and the red sail returned to prominence.

She lay once for days by a pool in one of the rooms in the tower; bathing, swimming and diving, then spreading her wet hair to dry around her as she lay on the bank under trees. In this room there were birds, and she watched them soar high above her in continuous wheeling motion. They made designs against the blue of the roof, patterns that became as intricate as the scratches on the glass of her bedroom, yet living and defying memory and knowledge.

When she slept there she dreamed of ancient war and the heat of the sun.

He paused for breath halfway up the last slab of dark rock. There was a ledge there, with a recently abandoned nest tucked into the corner. As he contemplated this he smiled, for lower down the rock face he had frightened a whole colony of birds. He could still hear the squawking as they spilled over the edge and dropped into space at his approach. Turning, he pressed against the rock and slid into a sitting position. From his position high among the range of mountains he could trace his path of the last months, beginning at the marshes around the river-mouth that had forced him away from the seashore. His eyes grew glazed after a while and he stayed motionless until the sun had moved behind the rock he was climbing. Vision returned and he shivered a little. The old man had died painfully and slowly; something had gone wrong with his insides and had started to eat him away. Yet he did not feel as if half of himself had died, as he had supposed he would in the time the old man was worst; instead he felt as calm and as whole as on those rare occasions he had managed to rid both the island and his head of the old man—and the need for the old man. Once or twice, wonderful whenever it happened, there had been schools of dolphins around the lighthouse. As he had watched them twist from the water he had willed them to be unable to re-enter that region where they were invisible to him, and in the exercise of such complete concentration he had found a solitude and a peace such that he had not minded when they inevitably overcame him and disappeared back beyond his perception.

On the occasion when he found the body of a baby dolphin washed up on the rocks he had felt as if he had triumphed, but the fact of the young death bothered him until the body started to smell. Then it became clear that this was something that had nothing to do with him.

The day was nearly gone by the time he reached the summit and the sun had nearly disappeared beyond the massive plains of dark grass stetching out before him. It was a sight he had not expected, thinking perhaps that the world was a lot smaller than it was; but it was not this that caused a flashing, shuddering, shock-filled blindness, and it was not this that caused him to stagger and double over, feeling the snatching of a cold knot of implication in his stomach. In the middle of this plain, grim in its simple, familiar, newness, was a massive tower whose top glinted a cold alien blue through the dusk gathering around it.

*

She ran down the corridor, down stairs, through dusty galleries, past the doors of darkness, the rooms of masks and mirrors, and the pit that sometimes held stars. She came to a room of gardens, hanging flowers, fountains, and she became a little calmer; but she knew something had changed; the smoke she had seen climbing from the nearest mountain that morning told her as much. She was no longer alone, and she greeted the stark, simple division of the sky with warmth.

He had made the fire for reasons beyond his reach;—and despite the sudden knowledge that he was a minute figure between the sky and the land, and the other knowledge that he loomed giantlike and unhideable amongst the barren rocks, he had made the fire from new green growth so that the smoke poured and smothered skyward in a choking pall. As he looked behind him now he could still see a lean streak of grey staining the midday blue. He felt as if he was becoming unwell; he had a headache and, for the first time since he had left the lighthouse, he felt tired in a way that made him feel old. In daylight the top of the tower lost the brilliance it had had the evening a week before, but the tower itself gained strength and solidity until it seemed to be as natural an outcropping as the mountain range he had just sweated across. It was there in his sleep, night after night, among landscapes that distorted and grew feverish, yet it remained itself rigid and compulsive, dominating his sleep until he cried out and woke, to see the stars obscured by haze that grew more opaque each night.

She had stretched the bells outside the window years before. Sometimes when she lay in bed she fancied that their soft ringing became the small cries of pain the bells gave as they were pierced by the unbearably cold wind. Half-asleep as she was this disturbed her, and she would clutch her bedclothes more tightly around her until the warmth made her mind peaceful again and she could dream more easily.

The weather changed and grew colder, with the noise from storms over the mountains he had been through reaching him at times through the day and reminding him of the sea and the old man. He walked across the plain, the ground gently undulating, and the grass just tall enough to prevent a clear view of the whole horizon. At times the feathery ears and leaves of grass would well up, catching the wind and isolating him from the horizon he moved towards. He would walk for a second or two in a cell of green, roofed by grey. When he was lost like this, when the horizon no longer formed a massive frame, he felt himself to be inside a haphazardly floating bubble, like the times he closed his eyes under water and let himself be carried by the warm currents flowing slowly around the lighthouse island. Then the wind would flatten the grass again and he would look along channels impressed on the bowed grass to see the mountains remain remote in the distance, and his instinct for giant perspective was comforted.

She watched him move slowly across the surface of the plain, his progress discernible at first only from the fires he made each evening at sundown; then leaping into view one morning as a moving dot on the furthest stretches of her vision; then becoming, with a convulsive wrench of recognition, like herself. She stayed for the first few days in the Blue Glass room at the very top of the tower, but then began to make her way down the various levels, pausing for hours in rooms that had windows overlooking the relevant way. She tried constantly to make out any movement in the constantly changing view which could possibly reflect the intent of the creature that each night lit a fire closer along the straight line which led to the base of her tower. When she first perceived the moving dot she froze; then, when she recognised him as being like herself, she moved calmly down through the remaining few levels of the tower to the door that she had never used. It opened quietly and easily, and she moved outside the tower to meet him.

He watched as the sky grew more overcast, and he welcomed the pain in his head brought by the pressure of the approaching storm, as with it seemed to come the prospect of resolution. For days he had felt eyes upon him; he felt eyes with perceptions and emotions different from anything his experience had prepared him for. Fear and revulsion mixed in his mind with the obsessive drive onward, and he felt himself carried in a way that ignored what he felt himself to need. He arrived at the base of the tower and squatted, muscles tense and locked, waiting for release. It came. The door opened and a naked figure like, but not like, his own came out and towards him. It approached slowly, and paused before him. He looked, at first with a blank mind, then with increasing comprehension and hatred. A wall was being built as he watched; a wall built of the million desires and fears and conversations and *directions* that had appeared as he waited. The future had meaning—and it engulfed him.

The grey sky cracked and the clouds of grey plate steel pressed on the earth and Adam, more scared than he had ever been in his life, drawing awful energy from the violence of the pelting, hissing rain, moved with stiff-legged intent towards the woman.

MY BEST EVER HOLIDAY   Richard Spivack

Gerald said that Erkelsdammer would be the greatest holiday I would ever see and the funny thing was that he was right. He kept saying there's nowhere else like it and there isn't. You might have severe doubts about the ethics of the whole thing—which I also had—but the impact of seeing it for the first time is indescribable. The sheer scale of the place—its glossiness, its exuberance, its infuriating confidence and its remorseless cleanness—just leaves you gasping.

It may seem hard for people in our little, bankrupt but ethical country to comprehend this, but they are so proud of the damn Dammer that on the MaglevRail on the way in they actually have fifty language videos explaining how Erkelsdammer was built. Gerald kept on pointing out that we were travelling through the richest part of Europe, which was true, but irritating. From the airport you zoom past endless, colossal cities. Then there's a patch of countryside, very carefully landscaped and trimmed, and then you see Erkelsdammer, gleaming on the horizon. Arrive at dusk, when the neon and lights are blazing. Here in this land where logic is king, the video explains, the four surrounding cities simul- taneously closed down their red light districts in one superbly organised manoeuvre, carted off all the organised crime and pimps and then moved all the filth to this brand new city, where the state could collect the rents and where the authorities could observe every soul entering and exiting. Sensible yes, they say. They say here the profits of vice go to build hospitals and nurseries whereas in our more ethical country they go into the pockets of thugs.

"Very sensible," said Gerald.

Very clean, I thought. One expects a red light district, or a red light city, to have a patina of dirt, a sticky sort of quality. But the Dammer was surgically clean, like a brand new hypodermic. Great escalators went up into crystal towers. You went up them and then you could see the boulevards, immensely wide and straight and thronging with a tide of people, tourists from all over the world, many of them gasping or laughing at the novelty and the audacity of this place.

The Dammer was a masterpiece of urban planning. No cars on the boulevards, no cars in the town; they were all deposited in an underground car park. Rubberized conveyors took you round. Travelling down the boulevards through the shops and arcades and fairgrounds and palaces of this place was like travelling through the brain of a madman.

All sorts of things which in our land are only discussed in whispers or written on toilet walls were here paraded with zest. Huge stores sold pornography in various forms, while a shop specialising in bondage was as big as Selfridge's. There were streets of cinemas and vidromes, each showing some specific perversion; theatres and cabarets offering different depravities. And there were girls, of course. Girls in arcade windows, girls in all manner of scanty clothing, girls in jacuzzis; there were swimming pools, waterbeds, peepshows, saunas, turkish baths, steam parlours, encounter parlours, contact parlours. wrestling-in-mud parlours (which oddly were as squeaky clean as everywhere else). There were holograms, environaramas, laser simulations which could make you feel rather queasy.

"You don't like it all that much, do you?" said Gerald, in the hotel over drinks.

"Well, it's amazing," I said, "But it's, well, it's pretty weird. Things being so blatant, destroys a lot of what it's supposed to be about."

"I thought that at first. Now I think it's the only really honest place in the world. You know it's far safer here than back home? No street crime, no muggings; no rape either. Women can go out at night in this country. Anybody with disturbed desires gets therapy or they can be sent here free on the health service. Why shouldn't things be safe and clean. Or is that too blatant? Look, I want you to come somewhere with me."

"It's two o clock in the morning."

"It's all right. They're open all the time here."

"Yes, but I'm not all right. What's so important about it?"

"I just want to see your reaction to something, that's all."

"Let's do it tomorrow. They are open tomorrow?"

"All the time."

The place was the Lovdrome. Lovdrome, it said at the front and all over the place, was a Tekserv presentation. Tekserv, I knew, was a corporation mainly devoted to developing hi-tech in the entertainment fields and they promised you an experience you certainly wouldn't forget.

Most of Erkelsdammer is surprisingly cheap, but the Lovdrome was steep by any standards. Fortunately, Gerald insisted on paying. Lovdrome had a sadomasochist bias, presumably as a result of careful market research. Using brilliant holography, laser projection and animalisation where robots acted like humans, you could see violent orgies and massacres taking place within inches of your head. Gerald kept on saying how terrific it all was, and I didn't want to admit it, but I did find it exciting and I felt really disturbed that I did.

"Let's go down to the Chambers," said Gerald. "There's something even better down there." Feeling shaky, I followed him as he went through the vast building. I think they called them the Chambers because they just couldn't think of anything to describe it exactly. Well, there is a word for it but they wouldn't use that. Light displays said "Chambers—erotish contakt experience" and more revealingly "Body simulation". (The words "stimulation" and "simulation" tended to get mixed up a lot round here. They used English all the time, but oddly they still kept getting it wrong.)

Despite the medieval name, the Chambers were as clean as everywhere else. They were a bit like a hotel, a long carpeted corridor with plasticised doors. First you would programme a screen with your exact needs. It would then tell you to go to a certain number and add that your chamber was finishing its sterilisation and douching process.

The plastic door rolled sideways. Inside it, there was rather more soft lighting. The air was ionised, you could just hear soft music, another screen suggested further requirements—you could have pornovids of any description running while you were there—and your eyes turned to a bed with plastic sheeting. On the plastic sheeting was what appeared to be a female body; it was naked except for the rather traditionalist garb of stockings (which I couldn't remember ordering; maybe the computer assumed everybody wants them). The body was spread-eagled, the arms wide apart, Jesus style.

Everything was there except that where you would expect a head, there was a box, presumably the control centre. It was covered with foam plastic, so you could rest your head on it. It looked perfect otherwise and after I had taken my clothes off I found that it was perfect all over. Its robotic muscles responded with devastating timing. A female voice—which didn't come from the head—urged me onwards and made various orgasmic noises. Eventually I came and the voice made screaming noises, the body, or whatever it was, wrapped itself round me, the arms and the legs held me, and the internal parts became incredibly tight.

I lay there, exhausted and amazed. How strange to be in such a position, lying on this weird but totally convincing body in this little room. The body became prone again; I could hear a hum, which was little airducts in the bed apparently lifting the body. The lights came full on, which I think was the signal for me to leave. Presumably it would now be sanitised and douched for the protection of the next customer.

"Great, wasn't it," said Gerald. I just nodded, feeling drained in quite a few senses of the word.

The lights of Erkelsdammer shone on, the walkways and the machines and the simulators and the stimulators buzzed on, and the people thundered by like the water down Niagara Falls.

Erkelsdammer was a moral enigma. They had a relish for red meat here, and a thirst for blood. But it was plastic red meat and it was fake blood that gushed out. No real pain; all was clean and safe. But I kept on wondering about those statistics. Were women really safe here? Were men, come to think of it? Did this sort of thing really stop the violence that was so much a part of life at home?

Travelling back on the plane, I found myself chatting to other people about it. It's funny; back home the politicians and the newspapers fiercely condemned things like the Dammer, but all English visitors made a point of taking a very good look at it. Coming in, there was bad news and good news and bad news. The flight was diverted to Milton Keynes; there had been more street battles very near Heathrow. The good news was that we seemed at last to be winning. Police had killed more than two hundred of the streetmen, while losing only twenty of their own force. Everybody cheered.

I never went back to the Dammer, although Gerald went there about five times a year. Generally I have a quiet life, in my protected residence. A nice job, relatively well paid; I only ever wanted to be left alone. I spent the next five years saving up for what I intended to be the holiday of my lifetime—the Moon Trip.

Well, I won't mince words. The MoonTrip turned out to be a distinct disappointment. My most overwhelming impression of the Moon was not mystery, not remoteness but expensiveness. Everything was fantastically dear. Oh, I know that it all has to be shipped out but it still seemed ridiculous. And of course, they have a captive market. I mean, if the bar asks eighty-seven units for a whisky, you can't pop down the road to a little pub, can you?

The forty-hour trip was boring as well, the stewardesses were pointlessly rude, the vidigram broke down most of the time, I found zero gravity made me sick. On the Moon itself, standards were very much lower than any Earth hotel. We had to sleep in bunks in a sort of prospector's camp. It was quite cold in the units—problems in the solar cells. And the MoonWalk, the really big thing, was a fiasco. I just couldn't breathe in my suit no matter what they told me, so I only had a few minutes. The flights were interesting, but the visit to a ball-bearing factory—oh dear!

It was the last night of the trip. I sat in the bar. They'd turned down the lights and we drank in the light of the silvery Earth. A chap played the piano and sang old Frank Sinatra numbers. For some reason, the Moon is a terribly kitsch place.

It's a funny thing how when you're on holiday, you always meet interesting people on the last night. I found that it is just as true on other worlds. Well, this fellow I found myself sitting next to was terrific on all sorts of subjects. He was English but he had been working in America and China for years. Yes, he agreed, the holiday seemed like a real ripoff, but he was getting it as a perk from work, so he wasn't too worried.

I asked him what employer was that.

"It's rather embarrassing really. Y'see, I was just about to leave them when they told me I could have the holiday. After they gave me the tickets, I told 'em."

"They couldn't have been too pleased."

"They'll get over it. Tekserv would get over anything."

"Tekserv," I said, intrigued. "You work for Tekserv?"

I said to him that it must be an amazing place to work for. He was non-committal. "All those simulations and that, and those amazing things at Lovdrome," I added.

"Oh yeah, that. Yes, they're pretty neat."

"And those chambers," I added. "They must have been fantastically complex to build."

"The Chambers," he said, thinking, "Oh, yes, the Chambers. Mmm. You never allowed them into England. Somebody tried to open them up there, but the newspapers were screaming about it and Parliament banned it".

"Yes," I said. It was true.

"It's a funny thing. England started the permissive society, but now it's the most puritanical place. No sex, but you've got people being shot down in the streets. Life is funny."

We sat a trifle awkwardly, looking up at the Earth gleaming silver above us. The pianist sang, "Dinner for one please, James, Madam will not be dining".

"It's still brilliant robotics," I said.

He looked at his glass as if he was thinking about something.

"They weren't robots," he said.

"They weren't?" I said.

"Everybody assumes that they are. Maybe no one wants to guess what else they could be. It's much easier to assume that they are robots. But you know there's no way you can simulate a body so that it really feels like a body. You can make it look like a body and simulate eighty-five per cent of the movements. But you just cannot make a body which feels like it's real."

I asked the obvious question. "So what were they?"

He put down his glass. "They're a totally different technology. Good old Doctor Forsheim conducted a lot of experiments with paralysed individuals. I mean, what we did with them was terrific. By creating nerval processors, one can now totally bypass the spine. So we can now make sixty per cent of paralysed people able to walk and do everything. Eventually we could activate virtually every single muscle in the body. After that some of our researchers tried activating comatose and braindead individuals. It was crazy. We got braindead people to walk around."

I started to get an uneasy feeling.

"But we couldn't get them to talk. Or do complex things like make tea. I mean, there was some talk about getting them to do simple jobs, you know routine things in factories. And then we realised that we were talking about zombies." He laughed. "That wouldn't go down too well with your trade unions." He laughed again. "Mind you, they're a bunch of zombies anyway."

The pianist started singing "Strangers in the Night".

"So what about the Chambers?" I said. "What were they?"

"Yeah, the Chambers," he said. Like another drink? Don't worry, I'll buy it. I know all you English are broke." He waited till the Bacardis arrived. "The Chambers. Mmm. I suppose I can talk about it now. Well, you may not know how much a woman costs in the Third World?"

"No, I wouldn't know," I said.

"No, you wouldn't," he agreed. "Well, average price in the South-East Asia area is—" he held up his glass, swigged some, then put it down—"fifteen of those Bacardis. In Latin America, it's about twenty-four of them. Get your calculator and work it. For the price of this holiday, you could have had seventy-six South American women. Ain't that wild!"

I couldn't work out whether he was drunk or what.

"Well, they're recruited for jobs in Europe or America. Domestic jobs or whatever, although I suspect most of them have an idea they'll end up as hookers. Anyway, they're given transit visas and then they have injections. We tell 'em they're vaccinations. Well, they induce braindeath".

I sat, staring at him. How ignorant of the world I am, I thought.

"Look, these kids wouldn't have anything to look forward to. I mean their families get a good kick-back. It's less mouths to feed back home."

I still sat; I honestly believe that if I'd tried to move, I'd have landed on the floor.

"I think we look after them very well. You'd be amazed what you can do with the feeds. We can feed in extra oestrogen to produce bigger breasts and that kind of thing. And we feed in chemicals to reduce melanin levels, so we can make black individuals look white. The customers like that."

"And what happens to the heads?"

It took him some moments to understand what I was talking about. "Oh, the *heads*," he exclaimed, as if I was talking about something very obscure. "The heads. Well, the heads are in those little boxes at the top of their necks. But you wouldn't like to see them, they don't look too attractive. The brains are exposed and the face is almost covered with leads and tubes. The customers wouldn't like that."

Later in the night, the news channel reported that the streetmen had managed to blow up a police station in London. There was a string of atrocities and massacres from all over the world. But I looked up at the Earth. It looked so calm and clear floating in the sky; you could see the continents even. How could something that beautiful be that tacky?

Then the pianist started again, singing "Nancy with the laughing face" and "Laura is the face in the misty night". God he was awful. I wondered if Sinatra was really that bad. He seemed to have been very popular in his lifetime. Then I tried to remember: did Sinatra come before the Rolling Stones? No, there was the Stones, then Bing Crosby then Sinatra, then Al Jolson, then the Beatles. That was it.

Then I wondered about the girl with all the tubes going into her head. Who she was and where she had come from and all that. During her childhood did she have plans for her life, or hopes at least? And I wondered if growing old in some South American slum would be better or worse than being a headless thing in an automated, computerised, sanitised, regularly douched, plasticised chamber in Erkelsdammer with fifty channels on the video, all of them pornographic.

Then I wondered if I could stand the trip back to Earth and the miserable stewardesses and arriving back at Milton Keynes in the pouring rain.

Then I wondered if I could afford another Bacardi at these prices.

HANUMAN   Stephen Earl

When it began chanting in Sanskrit the Sherpas packed their things and went down the pass, leaving two ponies. They said not a word. They seemed deaf to Svensson's protests, and used only signs and nods between each other.

"They won't come back," it said in Mercks's voice.

"The mimicry is incredible," said Svensson. "Far beyond any parrot".

"Far beyond any parrot. *Freude, schöner Götterfunken, Tochter aus Elysium.* . . ."

They had been playing the 9th Symphony the previous night, and the Yeti continued through the chorus and the village band reprise, breaking off in mid-bar. The wind had been rising: it sounded now like tearing paper on the crest and drove little chips of granite down the path.

There was a lull. Mercks said, "He had everything except the tape hiss."

"Better performance," it said.

A blizzard filled the opening of the pass and engulfed them, driving the two scientists into their tent.

"Christ!" said Mercks.

"The languages—"

After the snow, they composed themselves enough to switch on the recorder and train it on the cage. The Yeti seemed oblivious of them.

"Can you prove you're intelligent?" Svensson asked the questions: he'd done more cultural work than Mercks.

"To whom?"

"To us, of course."

"No. Impossible."

"But that is already proof," said Mercks in an undertone.

"No, it's nonsense."

"I'm not intelligent. I see mind."

"Whose mind? Mine? How far off can you read them?"

"There is only one. You don't have it. Also it isn't words." The Yeti turned its back, dismissing the subject.

"Telepathy beyond doubt," Svensson remarked. "Otherwise how could it speak Danish to us? But there's a sort of fuzziness—almost sense, and yet not quite. You notice the taunting? Like a child, rather a nasty one."

"My!" said the Yeti over its shoulder. " 'Like a child.' Look: one, two, three, four, five fingers. Fifty-six bars." It strummed its knuckles along the bars and rose, fixing the men with deep-set orange eyes. "How do you count minds? Where are they?"

"I have one. Mercks has one. I begin to think you have. Three of them, in our brains."

"You don't have it. You use it. Lungs use air; your brains use mind—occasionally."

"Then it could be used up sometimes: this doesn't happen."

"No? Why do you think I live up here now? See how much they can use mind down there, millions of strong brains gasping for it. Go to Chandigarh in a week, when they start killing each other again. Then you'll see. At least, you would if you could see."

"This is still nonsense. What we call mind is the action of the brain. In Chandigarh there is crowding and stress and communal rivalry; the fighting is natural."

"When the brain goes forward, it is using mind. Yours has made seventeen steps. Mostly it goes in loops, like the killing down there and this stupid talk. You think you can tell me about fighting, yet. And when it is 'natural'. I'll have a can of lager with my lunch, please."

It slept afterwards, and the scientists went down to the stream to discuss their dilemma. Mercks was a pure physical anthropologist: just now a restive one.

"If only it was dead. We could easily get the skin and skeleton down to the falls,—I could even preserve the whole head. That's out now. We'd be called murderers, I suppose. And what have we got. . . ?"

"A page in history, Simon. That recording is unbelievable already, and we've barely started."

"Exactly. Without the specimen, it is unbelievable. Video of a Dane in a monkey-suit spouting philosophy. Show it once and we're finished. We'd be a comic turn lecturing to UFO societies."

"Look, you fix some supporting data, if you can, and I'll go on recording. We can stay two days more. It is the greatest opportunity in history, and you cannot push a thing like this under the carpet. Can you?"

"I don't know. You know what usually happens to pioneers. Anyway, I don't like the way it's going. You've started up in the air: there's no background, no history, we don't even know what the damn thing is. Also it said something I want to follow up."

"Well, at least it's anthropoid. Tell you what, we'll dope it and get some hair-clippings and stuff." Neither man doubted the Yeti was dangerous: apart from its reputation and size, it had the unsettling gaze of a mature leopard.

"So, philosophy from a shaggy red brute, with some turds and whiskers as physical evidence. Wish I had your nerve. It's a good idea, of course. The intestinal flora would help. I still want my background; you say anthropoid, but what branch? Is it *Homo* at all? Is it from *sinensis*? The implications are appalling if it's in our line: look at what we've lost—the exact telepathy, the voice control."

"No great success though, is it? If you think it has a clue go ahead and ask. Mind you don't get the answer back from your own mind."

"One can do that from jawbones out of a bog, as you know."

As soon as Mercks came back, the Yeti said, "Don't even think of it."

"What?"

"Doping me to get your specimens. It won't work, and you'd regret trying."

"Perhaps we barter. A can of lager for a bit of hair isn't bad business. Anyway, how about the question in my mind?"

"Ten cans."

"Leaves me no bargaining power. Five."

"Yes. So, you're right. There was a time full of trees when we lived further down, along with men, There were only some thousand of them to each of us, and a reasonable balance of respect. I was at a place called Ayodhya, in the forest, and people even came to me for counsel, when it was worth the risk. They'd bring a jug of cane liquor and a grown deer . . . But you need to know about us and men. It's too much for a few cans of ale and I feel dry.

"Good. It's simple, really: men have arrested development, especially the males. You are hairless and sociable, as our cubs were, and breed till you're forty or so. You reach a mental age of thirty at best—a few women go beyond that, if they live long enough. Then, of course, you have to die off. It's really a question of mind: when the brain stops going forward—using mind—it has to run down, eventually.

"You tend to take too long and there's no social place for the brats. When I was at Ayodhya, the Prince was rebellious; he had to run for his life. He gave me splendid presents and I became his general. They called me Hanuman. None of this daft shambles that your friend called 'natural fighting'. We took care who to kill, when, how and where. Even men did so in those days. When I was only two hundred they invented chess to practise the art. What have those people done since? Do you wonder that I say mind is used up?"

"How old do you say you are?"

"Twenty-six hundred. Not believing it is your worry. We started breeding at 40 or later, whenever a female would accept one—and seldom got more than one cub. That is the end phase of childhood, you know. After that we protected them, especially from each other, and kept the forests. It takes a lot of mind, believe me. Under 300, one couldn't be competent. But we weren't in balance with the men any more. It had already got drier, there were too many clearings, and they bred till we couldn't hold them. The trees went, the cubs went, the young ones went, the men choke each other and here I am."

"No company?"

"Company is for juveniles. There are eleven of us; but I'd as soon pass the time with an elephant or a Buddha."

"Why live?"

"Instead of becoming a valued specimen? You needn't blush: I haven't got your funny ideas about killing. Bodily habit, partly. Also, I'd like to meet another Prince Rama. His joy over a new stratagem or a well-timed charge from cover was extraordinarily pleasant. Then there are ripples from the stars which amuse me. Man, there is power out there!"

Even Mercks could believe this, under the Himalayan night sky.

"What is this 'mind' you can see?"

The Yeti threw a can from one hand to the other. "It is direction. This is empty."

"Do you mean natural trends—the paths of least action? Oh, all right, here you are."

"Yes. But the paths go both ways: if there's a direction, there is mind. You wonder if mind is natural—no. Nature is more or less mental. Human nature gets less so as the paths close up."

"As for you, even more."

"Yes, I said I wasn't intelligent. The direction for us is out; it has long been your time. Most of us went long ago, of course: generals are usually dense. Then we found tricks to avoid self-poisoning, those of us who lived long enough to learn them."

"You could have anything you wanted for knowledge of these tricks, you know."

"An army, and a congenial Prince? Leave to thin out the men and bring the trees back? Pity. The method is only possible at a maturity you never reach. But anyway, you could hardly be serious? What men need is more death."

"We don't like it."

"No, you're never ready for it. Hardly ever. You have this sense of a destination never to be reached. But you like children and sometimes enjoy youth, when things are new, and there has to be a price. You are grassland animals and seed and wither like the grass and need new ground all the time. You need the Scythe."

"You certainly sound like a general. We prefer to invent new ground."

"You certainly sound like a scientist. Down there, when the rivers were shrinking, at the end of our time and the start of yours, the people invented iron, wheels, and weaving. They went on to verse, decimal numbers, algebra and trigonometry. It surprised us, mere infants doing this stuff: we'd have killed far more at the start, had we known. In a little while they had no more room, no shared hope: no direction, but fear of the neighbours instead. Only enough mind to go through childhood. Children have fixed rules and status, as in a game, and that is how they live. New ideas for them are like fluff on a mat. By the time a man-group has to transmute, it has already seized up."

"I think there are contrary examples."

"Only with a new hope, and it usually runs out. Here comes your friend with one. You'll love it."

Svensson's idea was of heroic simplicity: free their prisoner, on his promise not to harm them, and accompany him to Copenhagen, with the promise to return with him whenever he chose.

"Certainly," said the Yeti.

"Now, wait a minute. . . ."

"Are you afraid of him?"

"Yes." Mercks gave his reasons fervently, at considerable length. "We'd be safer with a Kodiak bear."

"There's something you haven't thought of. We're going to have to release him anyway. We can't conceivably leave him in this cage."

"Right on," said the Yeti.

Mercks had to agree, however slowly and despondently. "We'll go tomorrow morning, then. You do promise, don't you?"

"Only if I'm released immediately. I wish to go for a stroll."

"Do you promise provided we let you out now?"

"Yes, sure."

They had a shotgun and a dart-gun; Mercks loaded them both, put the safety catches off, and gave Svensson the dart-gun. "Shall we toss for it?" he asked.

"No, I'll do it." Mercks stood aside with his gun trained on the Yeti; Svensson opened the cage door. "My colleague doesn't want to offend you. . . ."

"He just doesn't want to get killed. It's nice to see people being moral when aware of some slight risk."

"And you will, I hope, come with us?"

"We start tomorrow." The creature disappeared into the night. Mercks thought for a moment and moved his sleeping-bag into the cage. Svensson declined to do likewise. Mercks bound the door with wire, and tied the two empty cans with pebbles in them to the end of the wire. With the gun and a torch by his side, he lay down.

There was a faint metallic noise and a hiss. Mercks started up and shone the light: the Yeti was opening a can of lager.

"Collecting my reward," it said. Its muzzle was bloody. "And I've just eaten a hare." Svensson's tent was still zipped up and apparently intact.

"If only you'd both been in there," it said in the morning, "with the key on the ground. 'Missing Link Captures two Anthropologists'—could I have resisted it?"

They packed, and dismantled the cage. The Yeti picked up one of the light bars, and sniffed at it. "So this is carbon fibre? When I saw you setting the trap I thought it was wood. I reckoned to take the bait and then smash it."

Svensson played back the talk with Mercks, before packing the recorder away. "So you're in the Ramayana, then?"

"Yes. The Monkey General, that's me. He was a wonderful liar, that poet, though."

"It would be easier to believe that you are. Were you chanting it when the Sherpas ran away?"

"Would you tell someone else's lies about yourself? No, it was a monk's chant: nonsense, but great sound. Believe what you want—if I steal fiction to give you, that's still an interesting fact."

"I'd prefer the truth."

"You can't have it. At best you can modify your current illusions, and man, for you that's a long road."

They set off into a stinging drizzle coming at a low angle from the south. Svensson led, followed by the ponies and the Yeti, with Mercks behind carrying the shotgun.

"I don't like the sense of being under guard," said the Yeti. "Have you freed me or haven't you? Would you shoot if I chose to go off?"

"I thought you knew all that sort of thing."

"Not when hung over."

"Well, you could go slowly, keeping in sight. But if you do, don't try any surprises on me afterwards. Anyway, you made two promises—if you break one of them, how can we rely on the other?"

Nor would Mercks agree to the Yeti's suggested short-cut down from the plateau into the ravine. The ponies nearly toppled as it was.

They came among pines growing over rhododendrons twenty feet high, and a mixture of trees with leaves big as soup-plates. "Wait," said the Yeti.

It made a snorting noise. There was a faint rustle, and the head of an elephant appeared between two camellias, with wet petals sticking to it. The ponies shivered and tried to break away, but couldn't part the undergrowth. The scientists caught them as they tried to bolt in opposite directions along the path. Meanwhile the Yeti and the elephant made a few wheezing sounds, and the elephant twitched its trunk at certain points. It moved back.

"Wants me to scare some Assamese squatters who have come up stream and are killing trees. Says they bribed the officials and the headman, as usual. And the rain will stop around midday. Made some comments about you two, but she's a terrible bigot."

"I don't believe this. You didn't exchange enough sounds," said Svensson.

"Those were the swear words, mostly."

"She also 'sees mind'?" asked Mercks.

"Of course. And uses it. It's a relief to chat with an adult for a change."

They had reached the new military road, which wound up the hillside in a dozen loops. A battered little yellow bus appeared at the bottom.

"I'm beginning to wonder about this trip, Simon," said Svensson.

"Join the club."

"It's marvellous, but it sounds entirely pathological. Who'd ever believe any of that stuff?—it's not even good mysticism. We'd get credit for finding this crazy mutant, but what's that worth? And God only knows who'd fund us to come back."

"The elephant's mind is a bit much, isn't it?" said the Yeti. "In the old days, men grew up enough no longer to be obsessed by shape. They knew there was mind for birds, elephants, snakes even. The paintings and stories all round here show it. That is why I could talk to them. Fat chance now. Did you really think you could ride in that bus with me? They'd have fits. Do you think my words would help? They'd make it worse."

"True," said Mercks. "But one thing. With your mind-reading, and no use for humans, what are your powers of language for?"

"Deceit, of course! I'll show you." It gave a multi-vocal howl. The bus rounded the fourth bend down and then the third. There was an interrogatory yelp up the hillside, which the Yeti answered. The bus rounded the second bend, and the ponies went crazy. Svensson and Mercks held them with all their force.

"I was telling these wolves that there's cornered prey here." The Yeti disappeared in the undergrowth.

The bus came just in time, but there wasn't a hope of retrieving the recorder.

THE MACHINE AGE ......Paul Gooding

It had been a difficult pregnancy for my wife. There had been complications from the beginning but she argued that we had always wanted a family. Against all advice she had refused to give the child inside her up for anything and inevitably she paid the price. She twisted under the pain as she went into labour but fought against it as best she could and gave birth to our daughter. With the child safe she knew it was over and she could let go. I could see it in her eyes, see her smiling through the tears; then I felt her hand slacken in mine.

I had christened the girl Rachel after her mother and brought her up on my own as best I knew how. But it was not enough. Rachel was growing fast and there would be things I would not be able to help her with. The daughter needed a mother and the father a wife. Of late that had all been too clear.

On the day after her tenth birthday I sat alone in my study. Little Rachel had been driven off to school and I should have got down to my work. Instead I listened to the faint hum of the servo-droids that swept through the house as they cleaned up after the dozens of excited, playful children and the joyful confusion they had brought to yesterday's party. The hologram of the newlywed Rachel floated lazily above my desk. In her wedding dress, suspended there, she was a fairy princess and if I could have just one wish I would want her back. Every day I would sit and look up and want to reach out and touch her, kiss her softly and feel her under me. I had the memories but I wanted more.

The machine stood cold and still in the corner of the study. It had been installed for a week now and was ready and impatient for use. But so far I had denied myself the opportunity. I had used the machine once before. Three years ago at a party I had been persuaded to sit at the monitor and call up my mother. To the spectators it was a piece of entertainment but to me, to see her and talk to her again, had hurt so much. She had died when I was in my final year at university.

Since then I had steered away from them. That earlier model had been in the experimental stages. Now they were cheaper, reduced down to a more compact version and more widely available. Finally I had bought one. I still got lost somewhere in the explanatory notes as to the actual method of functioning but it worked and for me, like most people, that was enough.

All I had to do was make the call. . . .

It began life as a tool of high technology industry. It was an instrument to break into the past and plunder the secrets of chances missed. It warped credibility as it called up the great intellectual figures to lend a hand in solving the problems of today. It was a mixture of theories old and new that would combine to find a solution. Einstein had ironed out the wrinkles in the Star Drive which led to the first tentative steps out into the depths of space and the migrations to the colonies. There Le Corbusier and Frank Lloyd Wright designed the new cities. So it went on. There were the critics who argued the dead should be left in peace but from the scientists' perspective they were still alive and well. There was one drawback, though. With the telephone an integral part of the machine 1876 was the furthest we could go back; but they were probably working on that.

If the research needed was sometimes lengthy the dialling was easy enough. I had to know the code and the telephone number at the time I wanted to go back to, and the machine would reach back and hook itself into the exchange. After that it acted pretty much along the lines of a normal telephone.

I typed in the year, the date, the time and then the telephone number. The machine digested it. There was interference across the screen to begin with then it cleared. It was ringing, faint at first but then louder as the circuitry grew back into the past.

"Hello."

I couldn't help but recognise the voice. The screen was still blank. There was the CANCEL button to terminate the call and the VISUAL button. My fingers hovered over the two. Until I pressed the latter the machine would not make complete physical contact.

"Who am I speaking to?" I asked.

The manual required positive identification but the instructions, however strict, did not matter now. I was afraid and used the rules to stall seeing her. It would be more than a hologram or a silent photograph on the wall. She would be there, alive for me again, and I remembered my mother and the pain of talking to her after all the years.

"This is Rachel Gray, who's that?"

By then I had hit the button.

"This is Rachel Gray, who's that?" she asked and then froze.

Electrons hopped and skipped back through time. They gathered at the focus and a needle of light burnt its way through the wall beside her. It grew and the light became unbearable but she could not pull away. Around the hole the wall spat and bubbled like hot soup then eventually cooled. Thin black spider-legs of machinery appeared. They crawled out of the hole, delicately felt their way around the circumference then made their way out on to the wall. They scuttled about nervously, wriggled, joined together until finally there was a frame on the wall. A film of silver pooled across the threads of circuitry and filled the frame. It solidified into a screen.

Rachel could only stare. The light was gone but there was something else, something warm and soft inside her head that drifted through her like faint wisps of smoke. She was caught.

The screen pulsed. Light sparkled, danced like fireflies. Colours grew and took shape. Something hard and definite was beginning to appear. Like slow determined brush strokes across a canvas it solidified into a face she recognised.

I wanted to talk but my voice dried up on me. I was aware that she was alive and I concentrated on that, watching the movement of her eyes, the fall of her hair. I became fascinated by something as simple as her breathing.

"John?"

Her voice snapped me back. It was strained with an underlying tension, but then she had every right to be afraid.

"Hello Rachel," I said.

It had been difficult to begin with, but then I had never expected anything else. I tried to find an easy way to explain. She was quiet and patient and she listened carefully as I told her about the application of the machine. It alarmed me to find myself telling her I was from the future because I would have to tell her that here she was long dead. Finally her composure faltered. I told her about the beautiful daughter named after her that she had died giving birth to. She was silent for a long time and then she cried, just like my mother, and I wished I had left her alone.

"How long have I got?" she asked finally.

"About two years."

"Is there anything I can do?"

But I could only shake my head. There was the Inhibitor Ray that had caught her to begin with. It stored the conversation in the unconscious half of her mind so that when the call was eventually terminated she would forget everything. Only when I called again would the memories resurface.

"I miss you so much," was all I could say and then we both cried.

And so we talked. Rachel wanted to know more about the future, both her future and mine. The one thing I was reluctant to talk about was little Rachel. She wanted to see pictures and I promised to show her next time, because there would certainly be a next time. With a kiss I finally pressed the CANCEL button and her face bled through the screen and dissolved.

"Goodbye," I whispered as the screen folded in on itself. The tendrils receded into the hole and the glowing hot wound healed itself. All that was left was the thin beam of light and then that blinked out and was gone. Rachel was left standing holding the telephone.

"Who is this?" she asked again.

"I'm sorry, I must have dialled the wrong number," I said, my voice muffled by the electronic scrambler. The line went dead.

I would call her every day. Sometimes she would be out and I would try again, selecting another time. She would have been a good mother. I was surprised it did not upset Rachel as much as I thought, but then I had always underestimated her inner strength. We spoke about little Rachel's schooling and her future. I showed her the photographs, beginning with the baby and working up to the present day, but soon she wanted to see Rachel and talk to her. I said no and we argued. I hit the CANCEL button, but no sooner had the picture faded than I was dialling again. I did not think little Rachel would understand how she could talk to her dead mother. It would upset her, I was sure of that, and eventually I managed to convince Rachel. Perhaps in a few years but not now. She accused me of being too overprotective but let the subject drop. She could wait because although it had no effect on me the machine held Rachel in a static field which created a totally different time sphere for her. While we talked away the hours, for her the whole call would last not even a second. We had created our own little world. It meant I could keep her in my life and it created a second life for Rachel, life she had been denied by her early death. But it was not completely satisfactory.

"I wish I could do something to change your future," I told her one afternoon, "You deserve more than this. You should have one continuous life, not two separate ones."

"You can keep me alive forever with your machine," Rachel said. She tried hard to cheer me up but it didn't work.

"But you deserve more than just being limited to conversation. You should be able to experience things, not get them second-hand from me. What kind of life is that?"

"I enjoy it. I'm with you, so I have two husbands and two lives."

"It still isn't right," I told her.

I was sitting up in bed reading when there was a faint knock at the door and little Rachel tiptoed in in her dressing gown.

"I can't sleep," she explained and climbed up on to the bed beside me. She took the book out of my hands and read the back cover.

"Julie's parents have got this machine," she finally announced, "It can get in touch with dead people and Julie spoke to her grandmother. And her grandfather. They do it all the time. If you got one I could speak to mummy. So could you."

I told her the machine was already in the study and I had been speaking to her mother. I explained to her that I had thought she would not understand the idea of the machine and be frightened by it.

"Have you told her about me?" she asked.

"Of course I have, and I've shown her photographs. Would you like to talk to her?"

I had to ask, but there was no doubt to her answer.

Little Rachel sat patiently on my lap while I dialled the number. When her mother answered and she heard the voice for the first time she looked back at me.

"Is that mummy?" she asked. I smiled and pressed the button straight away.

When the face appeared from out of the past little Rachel leant forward over the keyboard until she almost pressed her nose against the screen.

"Hello mummy," she called out, as if she had to shout to cover the twelve year gap; and far away my wife broke down and cried with joy.

I could not sleep that night and stood watching the sky. It used to relax me but not tonight. I could only think of the nights out with Rachel under the stars and I wanted that now. I wanted more than just to talk to her and she wanted the same. But what could I do? It was wrong but I had to call her.

I was about to dial when the screen flickered. After the static a voice whispered:

"John."

"Yes," I replied.

Somewhere someone was pushing a button and the screen came to life. The picture was so dark that at first I thought the machine had malfunctioned but then through the darkness, like a ghost, a face appeared. It was joined by a second. Their skins were pale, dusty and shrunken on to their skulls. The boy had lost his right eye. Next to him the little girl scratched at the sores on her chin. Skin flaked away on to her cracked fingers and I was so startled that I almost missed the boy talking.

"Hello grandfather," he whispered in a husky voice.

"Mother remembered. Nobody else believed her, but she said it would work," the girl said.

She turned, and in her profile I could see Rachel.

"The world's gone bad, grandfather. The land outside is black and everyone's dying."

My stomach tightened as I understood.

"Don't you recognise us, grandfather?" the girl asked. "Mother, come and tell him who we are."

The children moved aside and there was Rachel. Little Rachel, who was sleeping soundly upstairs, was in front of me now, dying.

"Hello, John."

She looked into the darkness that surrounded her.

"I wish it was a future I could welcome you to. It was war, stupid war. We salvaged a machine, modified it. I remembered. You wanted to change the future for mother. Instead we want you to change yours."

The picture jumped as it began to break up.

"The children," I called out. "What are their names?"

It was all I could think of to say.

"The boy's called Nick, the girl's Kathy. They were beautiful children before this happened. Change the world, John. Don't let this happen!"

The picture was almost gone. **Prince**

"Please John, change our lives. I love you, father."

"I love you, Rachel."

There was a faint chorus of "Goodbye" and the screen went blank.

I did not stop to think how selfish it would be. However many lives it would change did not matter. I was only concerned with one. I had to change the future, but not here. I would alter it before Rachel's death, before little Rachel's conception. If I succeeded my daughter would not exist, but if *that* was her future perhaps it would be better. They must have dismantled the Inhibitor Ray so that I would remember, and I would have to do the same thing so that Rachel could act on my instructions. I read the manual over and over again until I understood what I had to do, what I had to dismantle and when I had to do it. All the while I told Rachel dates and places and detailed descriptions of events. She would have to remember everything I told her about her future. All she had to do would be to introduce some new elements and make changes in that predetermined calendar and she would change everything.

The console and the side of the machine lay open and exposed when I called Rachel for the last time.

"I love you, Rachel."

I kissed my fingertips and pressed them against her lips on the screen.

"I love you, John."

"Ready?" I whispered. She nodded and I reached down and tore out the labelled power cells. Wires sparked and my arm went numb, but I carried on.

Rachel's face exploded in a shower of colour. I screamed.

"Remember!" I shouted.

The machine shuddered and the explosion took me across the room.

The Inhibitor Ray damped and faded. Rachel stumbled backwards.

"Remember!" she heard, before the screen showered silver fragments across the room.

Remember. Her husband from the future and the daughter whose birth would kill her. *Remember*. The lives of the grand-children she had to save from the suffering.

Far away Rachel had woken up and was screaming. I lay in a nest of broken furniture, my arm twisted back behind me. The machine was ruined. Flames licked the broken screen but it would be all right. I could leave it to the servo-droids to take care of later.

*

"Mister Gray," the nurse said softly, "congratulations! You're a father. You have a son. Your wife is being moved back to her room. You can see her there."

They had helped her to sit up in bed. She looked tired and drained but still smiled. There had been complications, I had been informed earlier when I nervously paced the corridors. *Complications.* I had thought about the pain she was going through and wondered if I would see her again. But it was over and she was fine.

It was different now. Perhaps it had all been a dream murmured to her in her sleep, because everything had changed. She had a new life. They had a future together and that was what mattered.

"It worked," Rachel whispered before he kissed her; but she knew he would not understand.

For Homer and for the friends I once had.